KT-221-716

www.booksattransworld.co.uk

Also by Johanna Lindsey

THE PRESENT
JOINING
THE HEIR
HEART OF A WARRIOR

and published by Corgi Books

THE PURSUIT

Johanna Lindsey

CORGI BOOKS

THE PURSUIT
A CORGI BOOK : 0 552 15048 7

First publication in Great Britain

PRINTING HISTORY
Corgi edition published 2002

1 3 5 7 9 10 8 6 4 2

Set in 11/13pt Plantin by
Phoenix Typesetting, Burley-in-Wharfedale, West Yorkshire.

Corgi Books are published by Transworld Publishers
61–63 Uxbridge Road, London W5 5SA,
a division of The Random House Group Ltd,
in Australia by Random House Australia (Pty) Ltd,
20 Alfred Street, Milsons Point, Sydney, NSW 2061, Australia,
in New Zealand by Random House New Zealand Ltd,
18 Poland Road, Glenfield, Auckland 10, New Zealand
and in South Africa by Random House (Pty) Ltd,
Endulini, 5a Jubilee Road, Parktown 2193, South Africa.

Printed and bound in Great Britain by
Cox & Wyman Ltd, Reading, Berkshire.

THE PURSUIT

I

"You don't like your mother very much, d'you, m'boy?"

Lincoln Ross Burnett, seventeenth viscount Cambury, glanced curiously at his aunt sitting across from him in the plush coach that was climbing ever higher into the Highlands of Scotland. The question wasn't surprising, at least to him. Yet it was one that would simply be ignored – if asked by anyone else.

His Aunt Henry – only her husband and Lincoln had ever been permitted to call her Henry – was a sweet, cherubic woman in her forty-fifth year. A bit scatterbrained, but that merely made her more adorable. She was short, pudgy, and had a round face surrounded by an arch of frizzy gold curls. Her daughter, Edith, was identical, just a younger version. Neither was classically pretty, but they grew on you; each had her own endearing qualities.

Lincoln loved them both. *They* were his family now, not the woman who had remained in the Highlands after she'd sent him off to live with his uncle in England nineteen years ago. He'd been only ten at the time, and had been devastated to have been ripped from the only home he'd known and sent to live among strangers.

But the Burnetts didn't remain strangers. From the beginning they treated him like a son, even though they had no children yet. Edith was born the year after his arrival, and they were told, unfortunately, that she would be their one and only. So it wasn't surprising that his Uncle Richard decided to make him his heir, even changing his name so that the Burnett name would be preserved along with the title.

It shouldn't bother him any longer. He'd lived more years in England now than he had at his home in Scotland. He'd lost the Scottish burr years ago, and he fit so well into English society that most people he was acquainted with had no idea he'd been born in Scotland. They thought Ross was merely his middle name, rather than his original surname.

No, none of this should bother him a bit after all these years, but it bloody well did. He kept his bitterness firmly in hand, though – at least he'd thought no one had detected it. Yet his aunt's question suggested she knew the truth.

Oddly, one of the things that Lincoln admired greatly in his aunt was that although she could bully with the best of them if it was a matter of health or welfare – and he'd spent many an unnecessary extra day in his bed getting over a cold to prove it – she didn't assert herself otherwise. If a matter was considered none of her business, she wouldn't try to make it her business. And how he felt about his mother was his business alone.

Nor was he inclined to own up to those feelings, and so he asked Henriette evasively, "What gives you that idea?"

"This brooding you've been doing since we left home isn't like you, and you've never been so tense – nor so silent, I might add. You haven't said a word since Edith dozed off."

Thankfully, he had the perfect excuse. "I've had a lot on my mind since you announced Edith was going to have her come-out in the grand old style this season and volunteered me as her chaperone. I don't know the first bloody thing about chaperoning a young miss who's shopping for a husband."

"Nonsense, there's nothing complicated about it. And you did agree it's past time for you to do that shopping for yourself, since you've no one in particular in mind yet either. You should have already got your own family started. You've been tardy, which is fine for a man, but Edith can't afford to be. So you accomplish the same goal together. It's a brilliant plan, and you know it. You haven't changed your mind, have you?"

"No, but—"

"Well, then, we are back to my question, aren't we?" Henriette persisted.

"No, actually, I've answered that, and if not to your satisfaction, at least be assured there is nothing for you to be concerned about."

"Nonsense," she disagreed again. "Just because

I haven't nagged you about the direction you choose for your life, doesn't mean I haven't been immeasurably concerned when you've trod down the wrong paths."

"*Im*measurably?" He raised a brow, accompanied with a grin he couldn't hold back.

She humphed over his amusement. "You will not dillydally around the subject thinking you can avoid it this time."

He sighed. "Very well, what else has led to this amazing assumption that I don't like my mother?"

"Possibly because you haven't visited her in nineteen years?"

It had been ripping him up, the stark beauty of the view out the coach window. His mind hadn't been playing reminiscent tricks on him all these years. The Highlands of Scotland were as wild and magnificent as he remembered – and he'd missed his homeland more than even he had realized, to go by the effect that seeing it again was having on him. But even that hadn't been enough to draw him back here sooner.

"There's been no need to visit her here, since she's visited England numerous times," he pointed out.

"And you managed to be busy elsewhere most of those times," she countered.

"Unavoidable circumstance," he maintained, though her expression said she wasn't buying that either.

"I'd say pulling teeth would be easier."

"The timing was never convenient."

"Faugh, none of your reasons ever washed. Excuses all. Goodness, don't think I've ever seen you blush, m'boy. Hit the mark, did I?"

His blush, of course, just deepened, now that it had been pointed out. The increased embarrassment turned his voice quite stiff. "This conversation is not productive, Aunt Henry. Do leave it go, before we wake Edith."

She was hurt that he refused to share his feelings with her. He saw it briefly before she masked it with a tsk, a twist of her lips, then a shrug. Henriette didn't pout. She probably didn't know how. But she wasn't usually so persistent either, and he was afraid the subject wasn't over, that it would be brought up again at another time.

His Uncle Richard had known what the problem was, but he'd had no answers for Lincoln. Richard Burnett had never been close with his only sister, so he couldn't explain her reasoning with any degree of certainty, but neither did he take her side in the matter. The best he'd been able to offer was that she was raising Lincoln alone, without a father to guide him – then the trouble began and she didn't know how to handle the situation. Besides, Richard had been in the middle, very grateful that she'd sent Lincoln to him, thus providing him with an heir, so he preferred to ignore the reasons for it.

Lincoln wasn't quite sure why he'd finally agreed to revisit his old home. Most likely because he *had* made the decision to find himself a wife and get his own family started – a new life, a new start – and he wished to put his old grievances to rest first. It was a major undertaking, starting a new family. He planned to do it right and to have no brooding influence from the past mucking it up. But what had him so worried were the strong doubts that he could put those resentments to rest. He was afraid that seeing his mother in the home she had denied him was just going to fan it all to the point of rage again. The previous rage had lasted two years after he'd arrived in England, two long years before it tamped down to mere resentment.

He did want it all gone, though, all behind him. There was even the remote hope that he could forgive his mother. He was almost thirty, too old to be holding childhood grudges. And the blame wasn't even all hers. She'd merely been too much the coward to confront their neighbor and insist he put a leash on his sons, who were determined to kill Lincoln every chance they got. Numerous things could have been done to end the savage onslaught. But she chose not to face it, chose instead to uproot Lincoln, sending him away from his home, his country – and her.

2

Kimberly MacGregor waved the letter in her hand to gain her husband's attention as he entered her sitting room. "Megan has written again," she told him. "She has invitations piling up, too many as usual, but in this case that's ideal. Lets her pick and choose which will be more pertinent to the task at hand. She's sounding really excited. 'Course, she did own up to how bored she was when she made the suggestion, what with Devlin away on business and expected to be gone the whole summer. Want to read it?"

"Nay."

That answer was too abrupt and a bit disgruntled-sounding for a man of Lachlan MacGregor's easy temperament. "You aren't having second thoughts about letting Melissa go to London, are you?"

"Aye."

"Lachlan!"

His disgruntled tone now had a matching look to it when he said, "I dinna like asking the Duke and Duchess o' Wrothston for favors."

Kimberly relaxed. She should have known.

Lachlan might get along famously these days with Devlin St James when he and his wife, Megan, came to visit them at Kregora Castle, or vice versa, but it wasn't always that way. They had in fact met under bizarre circumstances . . . well, not so much bizarre as well planned and executed.

Lachlan had been reaving in those days – the polite term for robbing – reaving the English along the border, to support kith and kin after his step-mother ran off with his inheritance. And Megan and Devlin happened to pick Scotland to elope to, which was how they crossed paths with him.

That might have been well and fine and the end of it, except that Lachlan fancied himself smitten by the lovely Megan and elected to steal her away as well as Devlin's purse that day. Even that had ended well enough, since Devlin gave hot pursuit to retrieve his duchess-to-be and thrashed Lachlan soundly for his audacity.

Oddly, that still wasn't the end of it, however, because unbeknownst to them both, the two men were related by marriage, sharing the same aunt, and when Lachlan decided to put reaving behind him – it had never really worked to support his clan – and marry a wealthy heiress instead to solve the problem of his lack of funds, he turned to that aunt to help him find a likely bride. And his Aunt Margaret just happened to be visiting her grand-nephew Devlin in England at the time.

Kimberly had met Lachlan there at Wrothston – was there for the same reason as he, actually, to find a spouse. He was distracted from that purpose briefly, not having known that the lady he'd tried to abduct with matrimony in mind the previous year was now happily wed to his host. That Megan was now the Duchess of Wrothston didn't deter him from trying to lure her away from her duke.

Kimberly had been aware of his fancy for the lovely Megan, so she had immediately scratched him off her possible-husband-for-herself list, despite her strong attraction to him. But they ended up crossing paths much too often, having been put in the same wing of the huge mansion, and although on the surface they rubbed each other wrong – causing many a harsh word – as fate would have it, the attraction was actually mutual, and Lachlan ended up seducing Kimberly instead.

Devlin, of course, hadn't been too happy about letting the Scottish reaver who'd tried to steal his bride abide under his roof, even if they were somewhat related by marriage through their mutual aunt. Not surprisingly, he'd jumped on the first excuse to give Lachlan a more thorough beating than the previous one he'd administered. To grant Lachlan his due, that was accomplished only because he'd made himself sick unto death with drink – because of Kimberly. He *was* a bit over six and a half feet tall, after all, and had a strapping, muscular body to go with that height, so he was easily able to come out the winner in most fights.

Devlin might have had to apologize for accusing Lachlan of stealing some of his prime horseflesh, which he was innocent of, and the beating he gave him because of it, but they'd become friends in the end – well, a few years down the road anyway – and were still good friends. Which didn't account for Lachlan's remark about favors, which Kimberly addressed now.

"This was Megan's idea, so there's no favor involved," she reminded him. "As soon as she heard that all of Melissa's beaus were being frightened off by my overprotective brothers, she suggested Meli come to England, where the MacFearsons are unknown. You agreed it was a good idea. I agreed it was an excellent idea. And Meli is looking forward to it. So don't be having second thoughts now."

"I assumed she'd be staying at Wrothston as we do when we visit them in England, no' in London town," he grumbled. "The lass has been tae Wrothston enough tae be comfortable and feel right at home. London's no' the same, and she'll be nervous enough—"

"Nervous?" Kimberly interrupted. "Our daughter is *excited* about this trip. She's not the least bit nervous. If anyone's nervous, it's you, and you and I aren't even going until later in the summer. Is that it, then? You're letting your worry for her override your better judgment?"

"Nae, I just dinna want her feeling she has tae find a husband afore she comes home. That's too much pressure tae be putting on her at her young age. You have assured her . . . ?"

"Yes, yes, I've assured her she can be an old maid if she'd like."

"Och, this isna funny, Kimber."

She tsked at him. "You're the one making too much out of it. Most young girls her age go through this – I did myself. Now, *I* might have been nervous about it, but Meli really isn't. She plans to have fun, to make some new friends, to be awed by such a big town as London is, *and* she even figures she'll probably find a husband while she's at it. But that's not at the top of her list by any means. She thought *we* wanted her to make a concerted effort to get affianced, but I've assured her if she does, that's fine, and if she doesn't, that's fine, too. Maybe you should tell her the same before she leaves, so she can just relax and let happen what happens. Now, have we covered all your last-minute doubts?"

"Nae, 'tis still a huge undertaking tae be putting on the duchess on our behalf."

"Would you like us to go as well for the whole summer, instead of just a few weeks as we planned?"

He looked appalled as she expected. "You said that wouldna be necessary."

"Nor is it, so don't backtrack. We covered Megan's willingness already. And furthermore, she isn't planning any events herself, she merely has invitations lined up that she was no doubt going to accept anyway. Besides, she adores Meli and is an old hand at this sort of thing. She sponsored me, didn't she? And had a hand in matching you and me to wedded bliss."

That distracted a grin out of him. "Is that what we've been having, darlin'? Wedded bliss?"

She quirked a golden brow at him, asked, "You don't think so?"

He pulled her to her feet, then meshed her hips to his. "I'd be calling it heaven m'self."

"Would you, now?" She grinned back at him, then made a face, "Bah, you're not going to get out of this subject that easily. Why are you *really* having doubts now? And no more of these lame reasons that don't wash."

He sighed. "I had the hope remaining that our lass would end up wi' a fine Scot brave enough tae ignore the legend and trounce any o' your brothers that think tae bully him."

"What an unkind thought," she said, and smacked his shoulder before she moved away from him. "I love my brothers—"

"I know you do, Kimber, and I even tolerate them m'self, but you canna deny they deserve a trouncing or two for scaring off *all* o' Meli's suitors. If we didna have friends in England willing tae sponsor her for a season there, the poor lass could end up permanently unwed, and I want m'daughter tae be as happy in wedlock as I've made you."

She chuckled. "Listen to that bragging."

"True nonetheless," he said with complete confidence.

"Perhaps," she allowed with a teasing grin, but then she got serious again. "As for Meli and her future happiness, is the nationality of the man she loses her heart to really of importance to you? And before you answer, keep in mind that if you say yes, your English wife will be insulted."

He laughed at the warning. "Half-English wife, though one could wish your Scottish half didna come from the MacFearson himself."

She ignored the reference to her father this time. "Answer me."

"Nay, darlin', the hope was no' that her husband be Scottish exactly. It was more that he just hail from closer tae home than England is. I'm no' looking forward tae our lass moving far away, is all," he ended with another sigh.

She moved closer again to cup his cheeks in her hands. "You *knew* that would be a distinct possibility"

"Aye.

"You knew also that her prospects in our neighborhood were very slim. We don't exactly live near any towns up here, and the other clans nearby don't have any sons of an age appropriate for our lass. And being the MacGregor's daughter limits her choices even further."

"Aye, I ken that as well."

"So this is all just a father bemoaning the loss of his only daughter in marriage, even before she's married?" she asked in exasperation.

He nodded with a sheepish look. She decided not to scold him for such silliness, said instead, "Lach, I'll be just as unhappy to see her go, but we knew from the day she was born that she would be leaving us one day to start her own family, and even then we didn't expect her to start that family near to Kregora Castle. Granted, we weren't thinking as far as England, but still—"

Kimberly amazed even herself when she suddenly burst into tears. Lachlan gathered her close, made all the soothing sounds appropriate to comforting. She finally pushed away from him, annoyed with herself.

"Don't ask where that came from," she mumbled.

He grinned at her, though it was obvious he was still remorseful. "I'm sorry, Kimber. I didna mean tae refresh all your own misgivings."

"You didn't. Unlike you, I'm delighted Meli has this opportunity for a season in London. I just . . ." She paused for a sigh of her own. "Just had the same hope as you still lurking, though I *thought* I had given up on that long ago. And it is pointless. Even those few young lads who did come to call on her live miles away, which is probably why you weren't all that displeased when they got run off."

"Miles away is no distance a'tall up here. They just didna impress me too much is all, and rightly so as it turned out. Look how quickly they turned tail when your brothers started in on them. That last one made his excuses after one wee warning from Ian Two that he'd be displeased if his niece was e'er made unhappy."

"I think it was Ian Two's tone, and possibly because he had a fistful of the poor boy's shirt when he said it."

They both laughed for a moment, remembering how quickly the suitor had departed for home. He'd practically run for the door the moment after he'd made his excuses. The laughter eased their misgivings, or at least put them back in perspective.

"Och, well, this trip canna be avoided, I suppose," Lachlan conceded.

"No, it can't."

"Speaking o' which, is Meli done wi' her packing?"

"She's not leaving for three more days, so there's plenty time to finish that up. She's gone to see my father, probably will be spending the night. Actually, I think her intent was to assure my brothers that she forgave them for ruining her prospects here at home – a few of them have been quite guilty over that, if you didn't know, even though the lads who came to call this last year she wasn't much interested in – so no harm was done as she sees it. She was also going to assure them that when the right man for her comes along, she'll know it herself, so they needn't worry on that account."

"She actually thinks saying so will assure them of anything?"

"Well, she's hoping." Kimberly grinned. "My brothers *can* be reasoned with – some of the time."

Lachlan snorted. Kimberly had met her brothers late in her life, had grown up thinking she was an only child and didn't learn about them until Lachlan brought her to Scotland as his bride. They'd shown up on his doorstep – or, to be more exact, crossed his drawbridge en masse, all sixteen of them. But they'd merely been the vanguard for her real father, whom she'd never met before either, a legend in the Highlands, and not a favorable one.

Ian MacFearson. It was a name mothers used to

admonish their children into behaving. He was reputed to be a blackhearted rogue of the worst sort, so mean he'd sit back and laugh while his sons tried to kill each other – which he encouraged. Others insisted he was just an old recluse who hadn't left his home for over forty years – but why do so, when he had his own harem there? Still others maintained he'd been dead for years and his ghost now haunted the old ruined fortress he'd secluded himself in all those years ago. None of which was true, but then not many people had ever met Ian MacFearson to find out otherwise.

He *had* been a recluse, and he left his home these days only to visit Kimberly and her family at Kregora Castle, though, as was more often the case, she had to do the visiting instead. She never minded. She rather liked the fancy surrounding his home, the gloomy atmosphere, the barren trees, the hovering dark clouds usually present, reminding her of a witch's castle high up on a cloud-covered mountain, rather than the old fortress-converted-to-manor set on a rocky promontory that it was. And there was nothing gloomy on the inside, with her boisterous brothers in residence.

Nor was there any truth to the legend that her brothers were always trying to kill each other, though some of their fights might make it seem otherwise. They merely fought as brothers will, not with any deadly intent. If anything, they were fanatically loyal – insult one and you'd have the whole pack to deal with.

The harem tale was also silly, though understandable considering the number of sons Ian had sired. Although they all shared the same father, only a few of them shared the same mother, and all of them *were* bastards. Ian had never married. He'd wanted to, had loved Kimberly's mother most of his life, but her parents had forced her to wed the Earl of Amburough instead, the man Kimberly had *thought* was her father until he drunkenly confessed that Ian had that distinction.

Ian might not have married, but he never denied any of his children either. He brought them all into his home, even those sired as far away as Aberdeen – at least, all that he knew of. The harem aspect of the tale might have arisen because he'd allowed a few of their mothers to abide in his home as well, even after he had no further interest in them personally. Whichever woman he favored at the time, he was usually faithful to her. Or so he assured anyone who bothered to ask him about it.

It made for a very . . . odd family relationship, to be sure, and Kimberly might have been glad that she'd grown up elsewhere – if the man who'd raised her hadn't been such a tyrant and unloving parent. A few of her brothers had other sisters, but she was the only sister they *all* could claim as theirs, so she was included in their sphere of loyalty. If anything, being the only female among them, and despite her being the oldest of them, she was more protected than the rest. That protection had extended to Melissa when she was born. Since they'd all been there for her birth, they considered her *theirs*.

Lachlan had had a bit of trouble with that over

the years. If he and Kimberly had a spat or if he simply frowned at her wrong, he was likely to get trounced by the lot of them, if even one was around to see it. And heaven forbid if he ever attempted to scold Meli when they were visiting. It was a wonder he did tolerate them, as many times as they'd attacked him first, without asking what the trouble might be. Must be a Scottish thing, that he found their attitude acceptable and as it should be, and never held it against them.

But Kimberly loved her brothers dearly, all sixteen of them, and she was quick to make excuses for their shortcomings, which they did happen to have in abundance. They were an argumentative, hot-tempered bunch. It was surprising, really, since Ian had raised them, and he had a more mellow temperament. At least, he had prior to returning to Scotland to nurse his broken heart. And he'd been nothing but mellow since Kimberly had joined the family.

3

It was an old home, maintained extremely well. Donald Ross had borne no title – wasn't even considered gentry by English standards – but he was rich due to a hefty inheritance that, like the house, had been passed down through numerous generations and was still intact. He had surprised one and all by winning for himself the daughter of an English viscount, but it was reputed to be a love match, so those of a romantic nature were charmed by the tale.

Lincoln's memory of his father was of a tall, strapping man, robust, hearty, good-natured, always with a smile on his lips, always there when Lincoln needed his attention. He had died when inspecting one of his mines in the lowlands. A tunnel had collapsed, crushing him so severely that he lived just a few days after being dug out of it. Lincoln had no memory of that, hadn't been allowed to see his father after the accident, which he'd resented at the time but over the years became grateful for, since it left him with only the good memories.

Lincoln had often wondered why his mother, Eleanor, had stayed in Scotland after her husband died. It certainly wasn't so Lincoln could remain in the only home he'd known, because she'd sent him away quickly enough when the trouble began. He'd never understood why she hadn't gone with him, though. A caretaker could have been left with the house if she hadn't wanted to sell it. With Donald's death and Lincoln sent away, she had no family left there, but she did have family in England. Richard had said they'd never been close, but still . . .

Lincoln's only conclusion, when he was older and could think of more possibilities, was that she had stayed behind to look after the inheritance. It was supposedly vast, including many properties and businesses that required close attention. One of her letters had dealt with the subject, said that when he'd come of age he should take over the management of it.

That was another letter he'd never answered. The inheritance was his now, but he'd wanted nothing to do with it if it meant dealing with her, an easy enough choice to make, since he didn't need the money. His Uncle Richard's entailed estate, which had been left to him the year before he'd come of age, was quite lucrative as well.

Lincoln was home now – the home he'd been born in, the home he'd spent his first ten years in – and his fears had been realized. The rage was back, came the moment he laid eyes on her, standing there alone in the doorway as they piled out of the carriage. Many another time Eleanor had stood there just so, waiting anxiously for him to come home. The sight and memories it brought back should have given him a smile, rather than the bitter taste of bile he was feeling.

It had been ten years since he'd last seen her, on one of her many visits to England. He'd been unable to avoid her that time. As he got older, more excuses occurred to him, excuses that had worked well enough – until now.

She looked old, and not just her age accounted for it. She was almost fifty, true, but she looked much older than that. Her hair was completely gray now, though it had shown signs of turning the last time he'd seen her, when she was only thirty-nine. She looked tired. She looked as if life was a burden to her, rather than a joy to be savored.

She wore black, as though she were in mourning. She was rich, could have traveled while she was still young, could have remarried, could have done anything she liked. Instead she had elected to stay here and live her life alone, and perhaps she was now regretting it.

Lincoln felt no sympathy for her. No kinder emotion would get through his rage, and, in fact, it took all the willpower he could muster not to get back into the coach and drive away. He knew he wouldn't be able to contain his rage for very long. They had planned to stay at least a week here before the start of the London season. He'd be lucky if he could last a few days in her company without the bile's spilling forth.

Henriette had had to prod him into the house.

He'd merely nodded at Eleanor in passing, spoken the single word "Mother," and moved on into the parlor without glancing her way again. He was amazed he'd been able to do even that. His aunt, with her usual prattle, had filled in the awful silence that had followed his cold greeting.

And he couldn't get his anger to calm down. He stood now at the window in the parlor that faced north, the direction where *they* lived, and his rage just got worse, thinking of the savages as well. Thirty minutes passed with him standing there alone, while his aunt and cousin were being settled in upstairs. He honestly didn't know what he was going to do if Eleanor joined him in the parlor without either his aunt or his cousin present as a buffer between them.

It wasn't *her* voice, though, that disturbed him finally. " 'Tis grand indeed, tae be seeing ye again after all these years, young master. D'ye remember me, then?"

Lincoln glanced around. It was Mr Morrison, offering him a cup of tea. Out of all the servants in the house, only Eleanor's maid was English, brought with her when she married Donald. She'd brought with her also her English habits, and having tea served every afternoon was one of them. Morrison had been the butler there even before she arrived, and apparently he still was.

Lincoln didn't recall the man as being so little, though. Of course, Lincoln hadn't reached his full height of six feet four before he'd been sent off to England, had been missing a good seven of those inches at ten, so Morrison had seemed much taller then.

"Indeed, Mr Morrison. You haven't changed all that much."

The little old Scot laughed – actually, it was more like a cackle. "Och, but ye hae, and aplenty. I wouldna be recognizing ye if I didna ken ye were expected."

Lincoln didn't think he'd changed all that much in appearance, other than adding the extra height. Of course, living with his face every day of those years made a difference, he supposed, different than not seeing someone for nineteen years. His hair had been just as black when he was younger, his eyes just as common a brown. His face had filled out some, was more defined. Women found him handsome, though he imagined his title was just as attractive to them as his looks.

Lincoln took the cup, but he didn't drink from it, set it on the window ledge. He would have much preferred something more mindnumbing than tea at the moment.

He nodded out the window. "Do the savages still live there?"

" 'Tis doubtful, since they're all as grown as ye are. But they dinna exactly socialize, so nae gossip comes oot o' there tae say one way or t'other."

Lincoln hadn't had to explain whom he was referring to. He wasn't the only one who called those particular Scots "savages." They'd made that distinction for themselves on a grand scale, even when they were children. They lived nearly four miles north, far enough away that he might never have met them, if he hadn't wandered far and wide as a child.

He decided to find out for himself. In truth, he just needed an excuse to get out of there before his mother showed up again. He'd had no intention of crossing paths with the savages again, ever. Although he was much better prepared for them now than he'd been at ten, he was mature enough not to desire that kind of confrontation. It was simply an excuse to ride off for a few hours. He wouldn't really ride north.

He found himself headed north anyway.

4

Lincoln could blame his curiosity. He'd heard of the legend called Ian MacFearson – who hadn't? But he'd never seen the man himself. He'd seen the man's home before; he just didn't remember it being quite so gloomy-looking. Of course, a child saw things through different eyes, he supposed. What an adult would find dismal, a child might find scary and, thus, exciting.

The place sat on a rocky promontory with barren trees before it and the cold sea at its back. The trees must have thrived once, before the soil had eroded away, their roots now embedded in the rock serving as testimony that the area wasn't always so dismal of growth.

Spring was nearly over, but nothing had bloomed around Ian MacFearson's home – nor ever would, unless fresh soil was transported in. Why anyone would want to live in such barren surroundings was beyond Lincoln, yet the area had grown, with other buildings nearby – none so large as this old manor, but houses that hadn't been there when Lincoln had last come this way. There had been other houses, though. MacFearson had relatives other than his overlarge brood of sons.

There was no activity about the place, but then, as Lincoln recalled, there usually wasn't. If you didn't catch the brood coming or going, you might think the place was abandoned. That is, if you came by in other than the cold months, when chimney smoke would give sign of occupation. There was no sign of that now.

Lincoln had never been inside, had never been invited. No one ever was, as far as he knew. Yet he'd knocked on the door many a time to draw out his friends to chum about with him. They didn't talk about their father. Only people who didn't know them did.

Memories of those happier times were jarring. Common sense prevailed, however, and Lincoln left before anyone noticed him in the area. Those memories still persisted though, of things he hadn't thought about in years. Distracted, he wandered off the southern path home in an easterly direction, to a place he'd gone many times as a child.

The pond was still there, a crumbled ruin of a barn in the distance the only evidence that anyone had ever lived near it. It wasn't even a pond, just a deep hole that collected rainwater, and there was usually plenty enough of that to keep it filled. A few moss-covered bricks along one edge suggested that the hole might have been someone's cellar a century or two ago.

Another memory stirred as he approached the pond. It had been one of the hotter days of a brief summer when he was a lad of eight. Most days here weren't warm enough for anyone to need cooling off, but that day was, and Lincoln had remembered the little pool he'd come across in his wanderings and had gone there for a cool dunking. He hadn't known how to swim yet, but only one side of the pond was deep enough to require swimming, and he stayed well clear of it.

He hadn't been the only one to have discovered the pond, though, for several of the MacFearson brothers showed up that day, with the same intent of cooling off. Starved for the companionship of someone near his own age, Lincoln had been delighted by their arrival and offered them his friendship. Three of them were leery of getting better acquainted with him, but the fourth boy, Dougall, who was also eight, took to Lincoln immediately, and they soon became fast friends.

He eventually met the rest of the brothers. Like those who had been with Dougall at the pond, the others weren't as open as he was and were hesitant at first to accept Lincoln into their group, but it wasn't long before he called them all his friends. And how quickly they all became his enemies.

Lost in memories, Lincoln had nearly reached the pond before he realized that it was occupied. A family of four, apparently, the woman sitting near the edge watching two young girls splashing about in the water, the man lying in the tall grass some distance away, napping – or trying to. The wife was attempting to keep the girls' giggling down to a quiet level that wouldn't disturb her husband.

Lincoln had never known adults to make use of the pond, but of course there must have been many changes to the area in the nineteen years he'd been gone, with more people living there these days. It would be rude simply to ride off now, even though he was in no mood for conversation with strangers – unless he could leave without their being aware of him.

He stopped his horse about fifteen feet away. The woman's back was to him, the children low enough in the water that only the tops of their heads were seen. They hadn't heard him yet, over the noise they were making. Well enough, he could at least try to keep it that way and leave quietly. Then his horse neighed.

"Hello."

He sighed and started to dismount. The woman had turned just her head to see him before offering the greeting. Then she stood up, bonnet in hand, giving him a full view of her now, as well as a friendly smile, and he was quite frankly stunned. His hand stuck to the pommel of his saddle. One foot still in a stirrup, he literally froze there in motion. And the thought crossed his mind that the man lying there taking a nap had to be the luckiest bastard alive.

She was very tall for a woman, only three or four inches under six feet was his guess. She was dressed in plain country garb: a brown skirt with no hint of a train, a long-sleeved white blouse without pleats or other frills, sturdy walking boots – they'd brought no horses with them – and a plaid shawl currently tied about her hips that would come in handy if it rained.

The clothes said she was just a country lass, and probably a poor one at that. The husband and children with her said that Lincoln should think of something other than how her soft lips would taste.

It wasn't just the height he found very intriguing – he'd never held a woman that tall in his arms – but with everything combined, he was quite sure he'd never been so instantly nor so strongly attracted before to any other woman. She was very pretty, true, but he'd seen prettier. Her figure wasn't lush – she was on the thin side – but her height accounted for most of that. Her hips were still gently curved, her breasts at least a handful.

Her face was striking, though, the bones not too prominent, the cheeks graced with dimples while her smile lasted. Her brows were arched delicately, but they appeared natural. Her lips were narrow, but they would probably swell lusciously with the right kissing. Her eyes were light green, like twin sparkling gems, and they drew attention immediately, being so pale in contrast with such dark hair.

Perhaps it was that her long hair was loose, wind-blown, in wild disarray, which gave her a sensuous, earthy look, as if she'd just risen from a wild night of sex. Exquisite hair, an auburn so dark it was nearly black, yet with the faintest hints of red. This could account for the wave of lust cresting so swiftly and shocking the hell out of him.

He'd stood there too long, still not fully

dismounted, just staring at her, which probably prompted her laugh. "I'll be thinking I've grown an extra ear if you dinna say something. New tae the area, are you? Or just visiting?"

"No – I mean, yes."

He managed to get his other foot onto the ground while his face flushed with color. Her soft burr was enchanting. He'd grown up hearing it from other women, shouldn't be the least affected by it, but from her it was the sweetest music to his ears.

He walked slowly toward her, aware that his pulse was racing. "Actually, I'm visiting, though I did used to live a few miles southeast of here."

"Did you, now?" She appeared thoughtful for a moment. "And here I was thinking I knew everyone from a good twenty miles 'round."

"It was a long time ago. You might not even have been born yet before I moved away . . . well, you were surely too young to know all your neighbors back then."

She did look no more than seventeen or eighteen, yet she had to be older than that to have two children already, and older than tykes to go by the sound of their giggling coming from the pond. He'd yet to see the children clearly, just their heads bobbing in the water.

"That's surely possible, I suppose. Your 'long time ago' could be twice m'age, e'en thrice."

Lincoln stared incredulously. She glanced to the side and down, her thick hair falling over her cheek so he couldn't see her face for a moment. But she couldn't hold back the laugh for long.

He blinked. Good God, she didn't even know him, and she'd just teased him. How charming – and refreshing – to meet a woman who wasn't primly demure or excessively stiff upon first acquaintance. He could so easily have taken offense, but she didn't seem to take that into account. Or if she did, she didn't care.

She flipped her hair back, not trying to be enticing or seductive, yet she was nonetheless. She was still wearing an impish grin, one dimple present and so tempting. He had the strongest urge to delve into it with his tongue, to make her laugh while making love to her so he could . . . Bloody hell, had he lost his mind?

He looked away himself, before he did something really beyond the pale, like kiss her in plain sight of her family. He didn't dally with married women. Never had, never would. Well, he'd been absolutely firm in that resolve – until now. He stared at her daughters, could see their faces now as they glanced up at him curiously.

They were both blond, very pretty, possibly seven or eight in age. They didn't take after their mother, but then they didn't take after the father either – at least by what could be seen of his coal black hair under the hat he had tipped over his face. Seven or eight? That was starting a family a bit young by any standards.

Staring at the children for a few seconds did help to get his mind off of seducing their mother – for the moment. "Very well," he said as he glanced back at the woman. "It was nineteen years ago, and

37

I was just ten, which makes me not quite . . . thrice your age."

Another laugh, filled with delight that he'd joined in the teasing. "You're sure, then? Adding up tallies was ne'er m'strong suit, ye ken."

"Quite sure – that is, supposing you're a bit more than nine years old."

"Och, a wee bit more at least."

He smiled. "By the by, I'm Lincoln Burnett."

"Melissa MacGregor."

She thrust out her hand to shake his in a manly manner, rather than offering it for a brief touch as a lady would. He took it, regardless, and didn't want to let it go, wanted to kiss it instead. But hand kissing was old-fashioned, done more as an overture these days, a not-so-subtle statement of obvious attraction. He bloody well hoped he wasn't so obvious in his own attraction to her.

He let go of her hand. He should leave now that he'd done the common-courtesy brief chat, but found himself asking instead, "You live nearby, then, do you?"

He shouldn't have asked, didn't really want to know, didn't want to be tempted to seek her out once he did. It'd be infinitely better if he never saw her again.

"Nae, Kregora is much farther south. I'm visiting m'grandda for a day or so. 'Tis him who lives up here."

He didn't recognize the name Kregora, but he did vaguely recall that a small branch of the MacGregor clan lived in an old ruined castle some nine or ten miles southeast of the Ross manor. He'd never wandered quite that far as a child to see for himself, though.

"I learned to swim in this pond," he volunteered, still reluctant to leave just yet. "A friend I used to meet here taught me, after teasing me mercilessly that I'd been coming here without knowing how."

She looked surprised. "How ironic. M'Uncle Johnny brought me here when I was six tae teach me as well. Much easier tae learn in placid water than in the ocean. I've been bringing m'cousins here for the same thing e'er since."

That was quite a distance to travel just to teach children to swim, especially when most people considered it an unnecessary skill to have, unless they planned to earn their living from the ocean . . . Cousins? He peered at the two girls in the water again. They really looked nothing like Melissa. And for her to have borne them, she'd have to be much older than she appeared to be.

He said as much. "They're not your daughters?"

She followed his gaze. She didn't laugh, but he could see in her light green eyes, when she looked at him again, that she wanted to.

"And here I was thinking we'd established that I'm only nine m'self." She grinned. "I'm also thinking m'da would be going on a rampage, were I tac start having bairns afore I get m'self wed."

It was the oddest sensation for him, to be so thoroughly embarrassed, fighting another blush, yet at the same moment be so utterly thrilled. She wasn't married. She was available for a . . . closer acquaintance.

"My apologies," he offered. "You just seemed like a family enjoying an outing."

"Aye, and we are, just no' that closely related. This is actually only the second time I've met these cousins o' mine, the first time their mother has allowed them tae come up the Highlands for a visit. O' course, I've so many cousins, 'tis doubtful I'll e'er be meeting them all."

Which was the case with many large families, and some not so large. He had cousins of the third and fourth generation as well on the Ross side that he'd never met, since they'd moved to other countries.

Lincoln nodded. It was time to go. In fact, he'd prefer to be gone before the man woke up and possibly ruined this first meeting of theirs. But he didn't mind leaving now that he was sure he would see her again. And he would.

"I've intruded long enough," he said, turning toward his horse. "It was a pleasure meeting you, Miss MacGregor. Until the next time, I bid you good day."

5

Melissa stared dreamily out at the countryside rolling past the open carriage, without really seeing any of it. The trip would take twice as long in a carriage, which was why she usually rode her own mount when she visited her grandfather. But she was too distracted today to care, which was also why she'd asked the uncle who was escorting her home to fetch a carriage for it, since distraction and riding a frisky horse didn't mix well.

Who would have thought that a childhood fear, which she *knew* was silly but still harbored nonetheless, would be responsible for such an exciting outcome to an otherwise uneventful day? It began with meeting her Uncle Johnny's two daughters for the second time – the first time had been on a trip to the Lowlands with several of her uncles three years ago. Johnny had been trying to get the care of them since they were born, but their mother refused to give them up to him. She would only allow him to visit them in the Lowlands where she lived, and had never let them come to him until now.

But Johnny wasn't the only one of her uncles to have such difficulties. Many of them had children spread out all over Scotland. They'd taken after her grandfather in that respect. But unlike their father, who had gathered all his sons to him for raising, not all of those sons were that lucky with their own bairns. Some of the women they'd dallied with were insisting on marriage before they'd give up their children. Others simply didn't care that they would bear the stigma of bearing a child out of wedlock.

The mother of these two daughters was different still – she simply didn't like Johnny any more than he did her. That they had produced a daughter between them was a matter of their both being too intoxicated at the time to remember that they couldn't stand each other. That the same thing had happened again when he'd gone to visit the first daughter – and ended up producing another – was more of a surprise to them than to anyone else.

But apparently the woman was getting more lenient with the passing of years. Allowing her girls to come to the Highlands for the first time was proof of that, even if she had stipulated it would be for only a week. And Johnny, upon finding out that his girls didn't yet know how to swim, had suggested that he escort Melissa home so he could make use of the fine lake Kregora overlooked to rectify that fact.

Melissa had already offered to help with the swimming lesson, but she was appalled that it be done at Kregora. Most of her uncles didn't know of her fear of that lake. It really was a silly fear, but it was one she couldn't seem to shake. She'd got it into her head when she was a child that something big and nasty made its home down there, and the lake was so deep that no one had ever been able to swim to the bottom of it to say otherwise.

So she'd suggested they not wait and instead go to the little pond where she'd been taught to swim and had taken other of her cousins each summer. It might be a bit deep on the one end, but at least you could look down and *see* that there was only dirt and a few weeds on the bottom.

But to meet a man like Lincoln Burnett on such a simple outing – it still amazed her, and her reaction to him amazed her even more.

Johnny's daughters had been quick to tell him about the stranger who'd stopped by while he was sleeping. He hadn't been concerned.

All he'd had to say was "No harm done, or ye'd hae waken me, aye?"

Which was true enough. As for harm, Melissa couldn't stop thinking about him. There was no harm in that, as long as she'd be seeing him again, but what if she never did? What if that one simple meeting was going to affect her husband shopping? Now she'd be comparing every man she met to him. She knew she would. And they'd all be coming up short: not as handsome, not as tall, not as easy to talk to . . .

But she'd spent only a moment on those worries, because she *was* sure she'd be seeing him again. He'd said as much. And he'd seemed as taken with her as she was with him, so she didn't doubt it.

In fact, she'd been wearing a silly grin ever since she met him. She was still wearing it as her oldest uncle, Ian One, drove her home the next morning.

She had six uncles with the name of Ian. Some people might find that strange, but her family didn't. Considering they all had different mothers, and with the mothers doing the naming, the man these six had been named after hadn't had much say in it. The numbers had been added to the names by the brothers themselves, to lessen confusion when they were all together. Most of the family used just the name alone – no number – if only one of the Ians was present.

"You're verra quiet today," Ian remarked halfway through the journey. "Worried aboot London?"

"Nae, no' a'tall," she assured him.

This Ian, being only one year younger than Melissa's mother, was more like a father to her than an uncle. She wasn't in the habit of confiding in him any more than she would her father, whereas her youngest uncle, Ian Six, who was only eight years older than her, was more like a brother to her than an uncle, and in him she did confide quite frequently. She would have told him all about her meeting with Lincoln – everything that had been said, everything she'd felt – if he'd been home last night to hear about it.

But it occurred to her that this uncle, being the oldest of his brothers, might remember Lincoln from when he lived in the Highlands, whereas the others might not. And she had so many questions about the man, thought of only after Lincoln had ridden away yesterday, so many things she should have asked him but didn't.

She didn't know how long he was going to be visiting, didn't know where he lived in England – even *if* he lived in England, though everything about him, including his accent, said he did. It would be the worst luck if he was there in the Highlands for a long visit with her leaving for London in a few days, and she could be gone for the whole of his visit and, even worse, come home just when Lincoln would be returning to England himself.

She couldn't cancel her trip, however, even though she was now of a mind to. Too much planning for it had been done, and the expense of a suitable wardrobe. Besides, Lincoln's visit might be a short one, and she could as likely further their acquaintance in London. He *might* live there. Och, why hadn't she asked?

Ian couldn't answer most of her questions, but he might at least know something of the man. She'd settle for anything at the moment, so she asked him directly, "Did you know Lincoln Burnett when he lived a few miles from you?"

"Burnett? Sounds American, or English."

"Aye, he's all o'er an Englishmon."

"Ye've met him, then?"

"Yesterday I did," she said. "He's verra nice – and verra handsome."

Ian chuckled. "And ye were obviously taken wi'

him. Are ye off tae London for nae good purpose now?"

Ian hadn't been one of the uncles who'd scared off her recent callers. He was much more reserved as he approached forty, and he tended now to let a man prove his worth before he passed judgment on him. Or at least he withheld warnings and threats until he saw a real need for them. He could still be just as hot-tempered as his brothers, but he usually wasn't first into the fray anymore.

"I only just met him, and we didna talk enough tae find out how long he'll be visiting here. He could visit here often for all I'm knowing. I was hoping ye might remember him, is all, and could tell me a wee bit more about him."

"Remember him from when? There's ne'er been a Burnett living in our area that I can recall. There was a Linc, which could hae been short for Lincoln, I suppose, but that fool lad was as Scottish as you and me."

"I'm only three-quarters," she corrected him with a grin.

"Och, and he was only half, come tae think on it, which is neither here nor there, since he was a Ross, no' a Burnett. A lassie might be coming home wi' a new surname, but a mon tends tae be keeping the one he's born wi'."

"He claimed it was nineteen years ago that he lived here, though he didna say if he'd been back tae visit in all that time or no'. I was assuming he had relatives still living here, and that's who he's come tae see, but maybe his whole family moved

46

away all those years ago and he's only returned to look up old friends."

"Hinny, I would hae been around twenty m'self nineteen years ago, auld enough tae know if any English lived nearby – unless he was an adopted son and still a bairn."

"Nay, ten he said he was when he left here. Could he hae been the Lincoln Ross ye know, adopted and maybe returned to his real parents, which would account for a different surname now?"

"The age is aboot right, but if ye've a true interest in the mon, Meli, then pray 'tis no' the Linc Ross m'brothers and I came tae know."

She frowned. "Why?"

"Because that lad was as stupid as they come, stubborn beyond comprehension, and, tae boot, vengeful, all o' which would be hard tae outgrow, I'm thinking. He wouldna take the beating he deserved and let it go at that. Had tae keep coming back for more."

"What'd he do tae deserve a beating?"

Ian sighed. "'Twas as much Dougi's fault, I suppose, for wanting tae be friends wi' Linc. He took tae him right off, ye ken. They were the same age. And we all o' us liked him well enough eventually, though he was still closest tae Dougi."

"But what'd he do tae change that?"

"He picked a fight wi' Dougi that Dougi couldna hope tae win. He'd grown much bigger than Dougi in the two years they were close friends, ye see. One punch and he broke Dougi's nose. There was nae contest. He knew there wouldna be. He shouldna hae started that, but doing so, he shouldna hae been surprised when several o' m'brothers who were present stepped in tae finish it for him. He'd known us all long enough tae ken that we dinna let one o' ours get hurt wi'out the hurter paying a goodly price for it."

"And he came back for more?"

"Aye, he was feeling wronged by then and wanting revenge. He was bloody well determined tae take us all on, everyone o' us, and he didna care if 'twas all at the same time. You canna get much more stupid than that – or crazy."

"They're no' the same person, Uncle," Melissa said now, emphatically. "Lincoln Burnett is no' like that a'tall. Really he isna."

Ian chuckled at her. "Ye dinna hae tae convince me o' that, hinny. I didna think it was him. If I ne'er heard o' your Mr Burnett when he lived here, there can be any number o' reasons why, the simplest being he mun no' hae lived here for verra long. Come and gone, as it were, afore anyone knew he was here. It wouldna be the first time the queen's English subjects hae come tae Scotland tae find oot for themselves why she likes it so well here."

Yes, a perfectly logical reason and most likely exactly why Ian had never heard of Lincoln Burnett. Besides, that foolish young Lincoln had been Scottish. *Her* Lincoln most assuredly was not. She didn't give it another thought and went back to dreamily counting the minutes until she would again meet Mr Burnett.

6

Lincoln knew that it wouldn't be easy, sitting down to eat with his mother. He had avoided dinner last night with the flimsy excuse of exhaustion, and he rarely sat down to breakfast, since he wasn't an early riser. But luncheon couldn't be avoided and was as uncomfortable as he'd known it would be. Even with his aunt and cousin there to keep the conversation flowing, his own lack of participation in it was glaringly noticeable. Though he hadn't counted on being so distracted that he wasn't even listening to them.

That was brought to his attention when his cousin Edith, who rarely raised her voice, practically shouted at him, "Lincoln! Whatever has gotten into you?"

"Beg pardon?"

"You've only been asked *three* times," she stressed, "if you'd take me for a ride this afternoon. This is my first time to Scotland, after all. I'd like to see a bit more of it than what the road up here offered in view."

"I'm sorry, Edi. I just met someone yesterday that has been occupying my mind ever since."

"A girl, I hope," Henriette put in.

"Actually, yes."

His aunt smiled brilliantly, drawing her own conclusions. "Wonderful! It's perfectly all right if you find your bride before the season starts. Yes indeed, no reason to wait, and easy enough for us to plan a wedding while you're escorting Edith about to all the parties."

He nearly rolled his eyes. "I know absolutely nothing about her yet, other than her name. I only just made her acquaintance, Aunt."

"When a man gets so distracted that his hearing becomes as impaired as *yours* just was, he's already thinking of marriage," Henriette insisted.

Lincoln blushed, not because marriage was mentioned and that hadn't been on his mind, but because he hadn't thought of it to begin with. He knew he wanted Melissa MacGregor in his life and not for only a brief time. Every time he considered a short affair while he was here, his instincts balked. "Short" just wasn't going to do it for as much as he wanted her. Only a permanent relationship would satisfy the feelings she stirred in him.

Thoughts of her had kept him up half the night, and before he finally fell asleep, he'd been thinking along the lines of buying her a cottage in England and keeping her as his mistress. But he'd been at a loss for how to broach the subject with her. It wasn't as if he were in the habit of setting up mistresses. He'd yet to meet a woman whom he wanted to keep that exclusively to himself – until now.

But why the bloody hell couldn't he marry her instead? Just because he bore a title and she didn't? That was assuming she would marry him. He supposed he ought to be asking before he took it for granted that she would.

"So who is she, and when do *we* get to meet her?" Edith wanted to know.

"She's a MacGregor from Kregora. I'm not quite sure where that is, though I believe some MacGregors live in an old castle a few hours from here."

"Kregora is the name of that castle," Eleanor explained, her tone hesitant, as if she weren't quite sure whether to volunteer the information or not.

It was on the tip of his tongue to ask her if she knew Melissa, but he refrained. As eager as he was to learn anything and everything about the girl, he'd rather hear it from anyone other than his mother.

"I'll be riding over that way this afternoon if you want to join me, Edi."

"Two hours just to get there, another two back? That's much longer than I had in mind when I'm still a bit sore from four days riding in the coach. Tomorrow perhaps – if you can wait that long," she added with a grin.

He couldn't, and his expression must have said as much, because Edith laughed and added, "Very well, I didn't *really* want to sit on a mount for that long no matter how rested I get for it. A simple tour about the surrounding areas tomorrow will suffice nicely.'

"If it's tomorrow for the tour, I might join you m'self," Henriette said. "Have you enough mounts for the lot of us, Eleanor?"

"No, we keep only a few carriage horses in the stable since I don't ride anymore, but I'll arrange to have a few more suitable mounts available before tomorrow."

"Splendid. Looking forward to it now."

The conversation took another turn after that, allowing Lincoln to bow out of it once more. He was grateful that his mother had yet to speak to him directly – on any subject. She'd seemed about to do so several times, but she must have changed her mind.

Was she waiting for *him* to make an overture? Possibly, and very likely that would have him leaving here with nothing changed. He might have come hoping to put the bitterness behind him, but he hadn't counted on how much added resentment would surface upon his seeing her here in the home she'd denied him.

It wasn't lost on him, however, that the mount he'd ridden yesterday, a fine stallion suited for a man who enjoyed a good ride, she must have bought, rented, or borrowed just for his use. She'd thought of that even before he arrived. She'd also sent a servant to him before he left the house after lunch, to give him directions to Castle Kregora. He hadn't had to ask.

She could merely have given the directions

herself. But after his unappreciative response to her one disclosure there in the dining room, given hesitantly as it was, she was probably reluctant to face being ignored again. Yet she knew he needed those directions, and she saw to it that he got them.

Acting like a mother, seeing to his needs without being asked – God, he wished she wouldn't do that. It was too late. She'd had nineteen years to supply what he really needed from her, but she'd never come close to doing that. Yes, he'd gone out of his way to avoid her, hadn't answered her letters, but she could have found him if it had really mattered to her. She could have pushed her way past his defenses, could have brought him home . . .

7

Lincoln found the lake easily enough. He'd been told to follow it as it wound through the country-side like a river. It was huge. And Castle Kregora sat on a high bluff that overlooked it and the mountains beyond.

He thought it odd indeed that Melissa would travel so far from home to swim in a tiny water hole, when she had such a magnificent lake in her own backyard, as it were. He could be glad that she'd done so yesterday, though, for whatever reason. He'd never have met her otherwise.

Just the mere prospect of seeing her again stirred up more excitement than Lincoln had felt in a very long time. One of the things he hadn't been looking forward to this season was the fact that his aunt and cousin would find out that he'd become rather jaded. The endless rounds of socializing, gambling, and other entertainments the ton immersed them-selves in had never held much interest for him to begin with, and after ten years of partaking from that cup he had finally concluded he must be a country boy at heart. Which was yet another reason he'd agreed it was time he marry.

Kregora certainly wasn't what one would expect of a centuries-old castle. It was in excellent repair for one thing, including all the outer defense walls. The inner courtyard they surrounded likely bore no resemblance to what it once was, today filled with numerous workshops – carpenter shop, smithy, bakery, and the like – but also stone cottages, very much a little village.

Melissa probably lived in one of those cottages, or at least nearby. He asked at the stable where he might find her. He was directed inside the main keep to do his asking of the laird, who was home. And there was his next surprise. You simply couldn't tell from outside that going inside the castle would be like walking into a country manor, replete with all the many rooms one would expect to find in a manor house.

He was asked to wait in an empty parlor. It didn't take long for Lachlan MacGregor himself to show up, owner of Kregora and current head of this small branch of the MacGregors.

Lincoln was tall, but the MacGregor was taller. Somewhere in his mid-forties, barrel-chested, thick-legged, he might be likened to a giant by most people. He was handsome for all of that, and he wore a very friendly look as he held out his hand and introduced himself. Lincoln did likewise, though he didn't include his title, viewing it more as armor, which he didn't need to don here.

"What brings ye tae Kregora, Mr Burnett?"

"I'm looking for Melissa MacGregor. I was told you could direct me to her," Lincoln replied.

"And why would ye be looking for her?"

"I've come to ask her to marry me."

He shouldn't have chosen that reason, when any number of other reasons would have done, for why he was there. And he'd managed to surprise the MacGregor, though the older man masked it quickly enough. They were no one's business, after all, his intentions, with the exception of Melissa and perhaps her parents. And stating them didn't even get him pointed in the right direction sooner, as he'd hoped.

"Let's go tae m'office, where we'll no' be interrupted," Lachlan suggested.

"There's no need for me to intrude on your time, sir. If you could just direct me to Melissa—"

"In good time, lad. Ye'll be telling me first why ye've decided ye want tae marry m'daughter."

"*Your* daughter?"

"Aye, and, if ye werena aware o' that, then ye dinna know enough about m'daughter tae be asking for her – yet. But be at ease, mon, I'm no' denying yer suit. We've a need tae talk about it though, ye'll agree."

Lincoln nodded with a good deal of embarrassment and followed Lachlan to his office. Of all the rotten luck. He'd thought the mention of marriage would cut short any delays, or at least point out the seriousness of his visit, which should have got him into Melissa's presence more quickly, without any more detours along the way. But considering whom he'd mentioned it *to*, it merely made him look foolish.

Like the parlor they'd just left, as well as the entry hall, Lachlan MacGregor's office was paneled in thick wood, with no trace of the outer stone walls visible to remind that they *were* in a castle. The single window in the room had been enlarged from the original, and framed in wood to boot. It was a comfortable room, the furniture thickly-padded, the dark tones of brown, green, and black well suited for a man's domain. Yet Lincoln was anything but comfortable.

For someone who had only recently decided it was time to marry and only just decided on *whom* to marry, he hadn't exactly given much thought to what to say to a prospective bride's father. But having put his foot in his mouth already, he was certainly off to a great start. Bloody hell. He wasn't used to being at such a loss on how to proceed.

The older man helped immensely, though, as soon as they were seated, by simply asking, "So when did ye meet our Meli?"

"Yesterday."

Lachlan's new look of surprise turned rather quickly into a round of laughter. When he wound down, he said, "Ye'll have tae be forgiving me. 'Tis no' often I meet a mon who knows what he wants quite that quickly."

"I trust my instincts, sir," Lincoln said in his defense. "But perhaps I should explain. I had decided to take a wife, was going to actively search for one this social season in London. So the thought of marriage was not really on the spur of the moment, as it has been much on my mind recently. And having met Melissa, I concluded that I really don't need to look any further – that is, if she'll have me. However, I didn't mean to imply that I want to marry her immediately. Actually, that *would* suit me well enough, but I realize that a period of courtship is in order first. I merely intended to state my goals today and to assure her that my suit is honorable."

"Well said, lad. I wasna that sure aboot m'own wife when I met her. Growling at each other was all we managed tae do for a time, though love snuck up on the both o' us, I'm thinking. And perhaps ye'll be telling me what sort o' life ye'd be offering our lass?"

"Certainly. I have inherited two fairly large estates, one in England from my uncle on my mother's side and one here in Scotland that comprises quite a few properties both up north and in the Lowlands."

Lachlan raised a brow. "Scotland, eh? And who would that be from?"

"My father was Donald Ross."

Lachlan sat forward. "I'll be damned! I knew him. I was sorry tae hear about his accident. Yer mother still lives nearby, doesna she?"

"Yes, though I don't. I was sent to live with my uncle after my father died. I've made my home in England with his family."

"And why is it ye've forsaken your da's name?" Lachlan asked.

"That I would never do. My full name is Lincoln Ross Burnett. There was an English title involved, however, and no other close male heirs on that side of the family, which is why my uncle petitioned to have his surname given to me. I am the seventeenth Viscount Cambury."

"I'll own tae a bit o' surprise. Ye dinna look or sound like a Scotsman, ye ken."

Lincoln smiled wryly. "I've spent the last nineteen years in England, which included most of my schooling. My teachers were somewhat determined to pound the Scottish burr out of me."

"Amazing, but I suppose if ye live among the English long enough, 'tis easy enough tae become one o' them."

"You don't bear ill will toward the English in general, do you?" Lincoln asked hesitantly.

Lachlan laughed in good humor, explaining, "M'wife is English, lad. My aunt was English. I've good friends that live there as well. Nae, the only thing I dinna like about England is 'tis so bloody crowded, a mon o' m'size tends tae draw far too much notice. M'height has always made me somewhat uncomfortable, ye ken."

Lincoln nodded in perfect understanding. At six foot four, he'd found himself the tallest in the crowd more than once and was never quite comfortable with it either. Which was one reason he hadn't minded losing his burr. Since he was taller than most his age even as a child, the height and accent together had accounted for quite a few embarrassing moments after he'd first moved to

England. Children, after all, were quick to make fun of "outsiders," which he'd been deemed for many a year – until he stopped sounding like one.

He jumped in now with both feet, heart in hand. "May I have your permission, then, to court Melissa?"

"I have no objections tae ye courting m'lass, nor tae her marrying ye, for that matter, if she finds ye as much tae her liking as ye've found her. Her happiness is all her mother and I are concerned wi'. Though we hoped she'd marry closer tae home, there've been no offers forthcoming so far."

Lincoln smiled hearing that. "May I see her? I won't mention marriage to her – yet."

Lachlan sighed. "I'm afraid ye've missed her this visit. She returned home this morn, but as quickly was dragged off by her mother for some last-minute shopping afore she leaves for London tomorrow."

"She's going to London?"

"Aye, she's tae have a season there. We fully expect her tae be coming home affianced. So any courting ye mean tae do will need tae be done there. Will that pose any problem for ye?"

"On the contrary, that actually will be much more convenient, since I've been elected to chaperon my cousin this season in London as well.

"Excellent. I wish ye luck then, lad, no' that I think ye'll be needing it."

8

Melissa was disappointed that she'd missed seeing Lincoln Burnett when he stopped by Kregora the day before she departed for London, but she didn't really have time to let it bother her too long, especially after her father assured her that she'd be seeing the *Viscount* Cambury – he'd stressed the title with a wink – in London soon enough.

She had meant to grill her father about his conversation with Lincoln, but with all the last preparations before the trip, she never got around to it. Not that it mattered that much after his assurance that Lincoln would be partaking of the season as well, and she'd much prefer to be asking him directly, everything she'd like to know about him.

It was an uneventful trip to England – not her first, but it was her youngest uncle's first, so he was actually more interested in the getting-there part of it than she was. She loved her uncles, all of them, but Ian Six, the youngest of the sixteen brothers and last to be named Ian, was a good friend as well, so she'd been delighted when it was decided that he'd be her escort there.

Having turned twenty-six only a few months ago, Ian was as tall as his brothers, all of whom ranged in height from six to six and a half feet. He was one of the few who didn't have the dark gold hair and light green eyes that most of them sported, same as their father. His hair was a brownish red, more on the red side but not so bright as some, and his eyes were a soft azure blue. He also had a wealth of freckles – inherited, like his hair and eyes, from his mother – which gave him a boyish look that made him seem even younger than he was. He was also one of the more playful of his brothers, and teasing, though he took his duty as her escort and confidant most seriously.

She'd talked Ian's ear off about Lincoln for nearly the entire trip, so even he was looking forward to meeting the chap who'd snagged her interest so thoroughly. Of course, he also cautioned a few times that she not ignore the other gentlemen she'd be meeting, wanting her to have as wide a selection as possible to choose from in the end. But then Ian was one of her uncles who was feeling a bit guilty that he'd been partly to blame for ruining her prospects at home, so he intended to withhold his own opinions – if that were possible for him – and just let nature take its course.

Melissa was all for that. Or at least she had been. Now, however, she was pretty sure nature had already taken its course. Still, she was going to be in London for several months. She meant to take Ian's advice and make an effort to be open-minded and not dismiss other eligible men out of hand, just because she was sure Lincoln was the only one she'd be wanting. Something *could* go wrong with that, after all. Lincoln's interest *could* drift elsewhere. So she'd be foolish not to cultivate as many acquaintances as possible, to keep her own options flexible.

Her second disappointment was that it didn't appear as if she'd be seeing Lincoln again as soon as she'd hoped to. She'd looked for him throughout the entire evening at her debut. It was a dinner party, a rather large one with thirty guests, yet what the duchess considered small and ideal for "getting her feet wet." But Lincoln wasn't one of the guests.

Ian didn't go, but then he didn't plan on going to most of the social engagements, considering the Duchess of Wrothston to be all the chaperon Melissa needed. Which was true enough. Who, after all, would dare to step out of bounds with a lady of such high esteem? To get on Megan St James's bad side was to court complete social ruin.

But the next day when four gentlemen showed up to call on Melissa at different hours, Ian was right there at her side for each visit. A few of those gentlemen realized that, as Ian was her male relative in attendance, it could only be to their benefit to make friends with him, and they went out of their way to do that. Ian even liked one of the men, as they both shared a love of golf, and they spent a good thirty minutes discussing the sport.

Melissa was amused. She enjoyed golf as well

and could have participated in the conversation, but the two men were so enthused over the subject, she decided not to try. It gave her an opportunity to sneak away for a nap instead.

Usually she was a bundle of energy, but even she had to admit that doing a social season in London was going to be exhausting work. Some events would last into the wee hours of the morning, a few until dawn as the duchess had warned. The older folk could sleep late or nap before the next evening's agenda, but the young men and women who were there for the express hope of finding spouses would spend their days either calling on or being called on by all their new acquaintances. None of which allowed much time for sleeping.

Melissa's second night out was to the opera, and she found herself disappointed once again after watching the audience more than the entertainment. Megan noticed this time, however, and remarked, "Are you looking for someone in particular or just admiring the fashions?"

There was no reason to deny it. "Lincoln Burnett. D'you know him?"

"Can't say that I do."

"Perhaps by his title, Viscount Cambury?"

"No, that doesn't sound familiar either. This isn't someone you met last night at dinner, is it? I was sure I knew everyone there."

"Nay, I met him in Scotland only a few days afore we left. He was just there for a visit, though, and Da seemed tae think he'd be here for the season."

"Well, then, he likely will be. I take it you're fond of the chap?"

"Indeed." Melissa grinned. "'Twas amazing how quickly I took tae him, as if we'd known each other forever. Was it like that wi' you and the duke, when you first met?"

"No indeed." Megan snorted, but as quickly she chuckled. "I tried to get him dismissed, thinking he worked for my father, and he termed me a brat right from the start. We were extremely attracted to each other, though, can't deny that – which was probably why we tried to cover up the fact with more animosity than was called for."

Melissa knew some of the story. She thought it was rather romantic herself. To want to marry a duke – and a particular one at that – but fall in love with and marry a horse trainer instead, only to find out afterward that you'd married the very duke you'd set your cap for after all. She hadn't known about Lincoln's title either, when she was so taken with him. Not that it mattered to her whether he had one or not, but at least it wasn't something he was hiding, as Devlin St James had done when he first met Megan.

"It's going to be a long season, m'dear," Megan added now. "Your young lord will make an appearance eventually. He probably just hasn't returned to England yet. In the meantime simply enjoy yourself. That's what you're here to do. Getting married will take care of itself, I've no doubt a'tall."

Melissa took those words to heart and even started enjoying herself for the rest of that week and most of the next. But when her third week in London rolled around and she'd still neither seen nor heard from Lincoln Burnett, the viscount Cambury, she finally had to conclude that she wasn't going to.

9

Lincoln might not have gotten to see Melissa that day at Kregora, but he got instead the excuse he needed to cut short his stay in Scotland, which he was eager to do, since it hadn't turned out as he'd hoped it would. Putting all that old bitterness behind him just wasn't possible, when it was instead refreshed every time he looked at his mother. And short of confronting her and spilling his guts, as it were, which he suspected would be more painful than he could bear, he was resolved to try burying those emotions again, rather than putting them fully to rest.

Melissa would be able to help him with that, he was sure. She was a bright flower in an otherwise dead garden, which was how he'd recently come to view his life – devoid of amusement, devoid of any real interest, devoid of purpose, and filled with bitter memories from his youth. His aunt and cousin were all that had sustained him prior to meeting the MacGregors' daughter. Melissa was going to give his life new purpose. He merely had to make her his first.

He wasn't counting, though, on Henriette's inviting Eleanor to return to England with them, nor on his mother accepting that invitation. He spent an extra day trying to come up with a reason she shouldn't come to England at this time. But considering his duty for the summer – and that both his aunt and his cousin were going to be in London for the duration with him – there really was no reason Eleanor couldn't join them there as well.

To simply state the truth – that he didn't want her anywhere near him – was out of the question. He wasn't quite jaded enough to be that rude and offensive. And besides, to do so would open the very can of worms he was trying to avoid.

But where he had hoped, briefly, to closely follow Melissa to London, even to stay at the same inns, in effect to get a head start on beginning the courtship, his mother's deciding to come along put an end to that idea. But it wouldn't be too much of a delay, his arriving the day after Melissa did. And he knew where to find her, having been told in parting from her father that she'd be staying with the St Jameses, who were sponsoring her. Not that he knew any St Jameses, but it couldn't be too hard to find their address.

Unfortunately, there were four St Jameses with residences in London. The most prominent was a duke, whom Lincoln discounted immediately. It took four days to track down the other three. The first was a struggling actor who wasn't really a St James. The young man had just borrowed the name because he liked the sound of it. The second address Lincoln found was a captain's widow who didn't know anyone from Scotland. The third address was in a poor neighborhood, occupied by a family of ten who barely had room for themselves, much less visitors from Scotland.

Lincoln was left with no choice but to try the ducal town house of Ambrose Devlin St James, though he was sure he'd be wasting his time. He didn't really think his bride-to-be could be acquainted with the Duke and Duchess of Wrothston – certainly not closely enough to be sponsored by them – but worse, if she was, he was going to be flat out of luck in getting in to see her. You simply didn't call on people like Their Graces without either a personal invitation or their calling card as proof that you knew them – or without having legitimate business with them.

Melissa was there. The butler unbent enough to tell Lincoln so – just before he closed the door in his face. Lincoln didn't knock again. He knew how pointless it would be. He hadn't had a card in hand, and had had to ask if she *was* there, both of which told the guardian-of-the-door that Lincoln had no business being there himself.

Moroseness set in long before he got back to the Burnett town house. He hadn't expected to find Melissa at every one of the gatherings his aunt had lined up for Edith, but he *had* expected to see her at some of them. He'd also expected to be able to call on her in a normal fashion. Neither of these was a likelihood now. The St Jameses were simply out of his league, their acquaintances the elite of the realm, the parties they would attend the most premier events of the season.

He knew no one in that crowd, as he had run with a racier set, comprised mostly of bachelors like himself. And the invitations that Henriette had arranged to be waiting on them when they got to town were from her own personal acquaintances, mostly other mamas with hopeful young daughters who had their eye on *him*.

That he would actually be considered a prime catch himself, due to his being titled *and* wealthy, would get them many more invitations as the season progressed. Those invitations just wouldn't necessarily be the right ones. You had to get your foot in the door of those upper circles first, before you had a chance of being included again. He didn't foresee that happening, when he knew no one who could get the door cracked for him to begin with.

How the bloody hell could his courtship of Melissa suddenly turn out to be so complicated?

Henriette, as astute as ever, noticed his new mood that evening. She also knew him well enough not to attribute it, at least completely, to the fact that Eleanor had joined them for the theater that night.

"You look like you've lost your best friend, m'boy. Did something unpleasant happen today that you haven't mentioned yet?"

"Other than finding out that Melissa MacGregor is being sponsored this season by none other than the Duke and Duchess of Wrothston? No, nothing of paramount importance," he replied dryly.

"Their Graces, eh? My, that's quite a coup for the girl. But why are you seeing it as a problem?"

"We don't know anyone in that crowd."

"*We* don't," she agreed. "But *you* do. You know the girl herself."

"Aunt Henry, that is not going to get me past *that* door," Lincoln said.

"Barricaded, is it?"

"It might as well be."

"Well, that's a fine pickle," Henriette huffed. Then she suggested, "Let me call on a few friends tomorrow afternoon and see what's what. I haven't kept up much with the who-knows-who-knows-who sort of thing, but it shouldn't be too hard to find someone who has."

Lincoln nodded. His own instinct was just to barge in and insist on seeing Melissa. But that would cause a scandal that would hurt more than help his cause, not to mention get him in the duke's bad graces, a place no one in his right mind would want to be. And short of appearing the beggar with hat in hand just camping outside the Wrothston mansion hoping to catch her coming or going, which he really couldn't see himself doing, he was left with few other choices.

One of those few options was to find out where she was going and sneak his way into the gathering, at least long enough to see her. Not unheard of, and something those in his crowd had been known to do on a lark, though Lincoln had outgrown that sort of thing himself. It was, after all, highly embarrassing to get caught in such a situation.

His aunt had no luck with her acquaintances, however, and said so the next evening at the recital they all attended. Which was disappointing in the extreme and started Lincoln thinking of desperate measures after all.

Yet the next afternoon The Invitation arrived. Lincoln – and the rest of the household – heard about it soon after, because Edith shrieked so loudly in her excitement she brought even the cook running from the kitchen to find out why.

Henriette was saying as Lincoln arrived on the scene there in the entry hall, "I don't believe it!" Not once, but four times. Edith was still making sounds of excitement, just not as earsplitting as the original one. And two of the downstairs maids were trying their best to look over Henriette's shoulder – the invitation was still held in her hand – to read what had caused such a commotion.

Lincoln suspected he wouldn't get any immediate answers if he asked, so he took the paper from Henriette and read it himself, then raised a brow at her. "A ball? Am I to understand that you weren't expecting this?"

"Not *a* ball, dear boy. *The* ball. The Moore annual ball is only one of the most exclusive balls of the season each year. I heard a number of ladies sighing over it the last few days, bemoaning the fact that they didn't get invited."

"So one of those visits you made yesterday paid off after all?"

Henriette shook her head. "This isn't my doing." And then she looked behind him to Eleanor, who had stopped midway down the stairs. "You arranged this, didn't you? However did you manage it, m'dear?"

Eleanor might have tried to deny it, but her blush was a dead giveaway. She still tried to make light of it, saying, "Elizabeth Moore is an old school friend. As it happens, she invites me to her ball each year, but each year I decline, since I'm never in England when it's given. I merely sent her off a note yesterday to let her know I was currently in London with my family."

"It's an open invitation," Henriette said. "It includes your entire family."

"Yes, she's very conscientious that way, never misses little details that might cause her embarrassment later," Eleanor explained.

"You've actually kept in touch with Lady Moore all these years?"

Eleanor nodded. "When you have a smoothly run household that doesn't require much of your time, letter writing becomes a very pleasant pastime. I had a wide range of close acquaintances in England before I married, and I've kept in touch with many of them through the years. I'm sure you can say the same."

"Certainly." Henriette chuckled. "Though none of my friends hand out such coveted invitations."

Eleanor blushed again, probably because of how hard Lincoln was staring at her. Once again she'd seen his need and taken it upon herself, without being asked, to fulfill it. Melissa would very likely be at that ball, and if she wasn't, it was going to open the necessary doors for him to all the events she *would* be attending for the rest of the season.

He wasn't going to thank his mother, though. Despite how this particular effort was going to help him, he would prefer she stop doing things expressly designed to gain his gratitude. Motherly assistance from her now only pointed out the absence of same for far too long. She could not make up for nineteen years of abandonment with a few paltry gestures. She was a fool to think that anything could make up for the brutal way she'd kicked him out of her life.

"This calls for a new gown, Edi, m'love – no expense spared!" Henriette exclaimed in her own excitement. "Actually, new gowns for all of us are in order for this, and luckily we've a week and a half to see to them. I hadn't planned on attending any of the balls, when Linc is the only chaperon you need, but this one I wouldn't dream of missing. Goodness, I almost feel eighteen again m'self!"

IO

Melissa's disappointment was so strong after the second week rolled by and she'd still had no sight or word from Lincoln Burnett that she'd been ready to go home to nurse it. She couldn't do that to Megan, however, who was going to so much trouble to make sure she had a good time. And, fortunately, Justin came home about then, and Justin had always been able to take her mind off any current distractions, good or bad.

She'd known the St James heir all her life and became really close friends with him the year he spent the entire summer in the Highlands. He'd been eight, she seven, and they found they had *everything* in common – had been inseparable. He'd ended up with three younger sisters and a brother, but he was the closest thing Melissa had to a brother of her own, other than her youngest uncle.

She was surprised, actually, that they'd maintained that closeness, when they didn't live near each other and didn't even see each other every year. But maintain it they did, keeping in touch with letters – anywhere from a few to ten a month

– conversations really, like whispering secrets through a fence, where you couldn't actually see the person you were talking to but knew he or she was listening.

A few times there had been talk – albeit casually – from their parents that they made a splendid pair and might get married someday to each other. Both Melissa and Justin thought that was one of the funnier things they'd ever heard. It might be fine and dandy to marry your best friend, but not when you thought of that friend as a brother or sister as well.

She usually told Justin everything. Oddly, she didn't tell him about Lincoln Burnett, probably because too much time had passed and she was sure now that she'd never see him again, so there was no point. Justin would have been sympathetic, but sympathy was one thing she didn't need or want. Besides, she was afraid she'd start to cry if she mentioned how acute her disappointment was. She didn't want to be that silly. She'd already been silly enough, to base all kinds of hopes and expectations on just one meeting with the man.

She resolved to put it behind her and keep more firmly in mind why she was there: to have some fun and maybe find a husband as well – in that order. Justin was going to help in that, the fun anyway, since he'd agreed to join the women on a few of the upcoming events.

She was grateful for that, knowing that he'd experienced the formal social whirl last year for the first time himself and didn't really like it. He'd bemoaned that fact to her in his letters, since he *had* been looking forward to being included in the realm of adults, only to find that he much preferred just to chum about with his friends as he used to do when he was home from school.

Justin also had two men in mind for her to meet, whom he was certain she would like. Not that he was playing matchmaker. He simply didn't think that these particular fellows much cared for the social scene either, so she wasn't likely to meet them unless he arranged it.

He was mistaken about one of the men, however. Richard Sisley was the older brother of one of Justin's school friends, and as the heir to the family title, he was being prodded by his family into finding a wife this season as well, so he was forced to make the rounds with all the other young hopefuls.

Richard explained this to her as they twirled about the dance floor that evening. It was the second ball she'd attended, more impressive than the first, with half again as many people present. And it turned out she'd already met Richard at a previous gathering, but just hadn't remembered his name that night. She did remember that he'd made her laugh on their first meeting, which was a plus for him, considering that her dejection had been at its worst that week.

He was a very likable fellow, very good-looking as well. Not as handsome as Justin, but then it would be hard for any man to hold a candle to Justin St James, whose parents were both exceptionally stunning in looks. Even Lincoln wasn't *that* handsome . . .

She'd known that it was going to happen, the comparisons to Lincoln. She should have felt some attraction to Richard, if only a little, but no, nothing. Because of *him*.

Justin was going to be annoyed with her, she was sure, for not even giving Richard a chance. He really admired the man, had had nothing but wonderful things to say about him. And Richard liked her. He'd let her know in subtle ways even at their first meeting. But he'd have to be dense not to notice that she just wasn't interested, and without any encouragement at all from her, he was already starting to look elsewhere before their dance even ended.

She was burning her own bridges and couldn't seem to help it. Very well, so she wouldn't find a husband here in London. Her parents had said that would be all right. Why were women expected to marry right out of the schoolroom anyway? Men weren't and didn't. They got to do as they liked for as long as they liked. Well, most of them did.

She could put her energies into something else besides a family, maybe draining the lake when she got home, to prove there was something unnatural on the bottom of it. She would become famous: Melissa MacGregor, discoverer of the first dragon known to mankind . . .

She saw him in passing. She'd been watching for black hair. She'd been watching for tall men. The combination of both drew her eyes like a magnet. She stumbled, trying to keep her eyes on him as she was twirled about in the waltz – impossible. And she was now on the other side of the floor.

She apologized to Richard, who'd managed to keep her from falling when she tripped over her own feet. They were coming around again to the point where she'd seen Lincoln on the edge of the crowd. He wasn't there now. Had she imagined seeing him, just wishfulness on her part?

"Are you all right?" Richard inquired.

Did she look as dejected as she felt? "Aye – nae, actually. Would you mind taking me back tae the duchess? These new shoes have given me blisters, I'm thinking."

That wasn't the least bit true, but Richard nodded and escorted her to Justin – Megan was dancing at the moment with an old friend of the family. After politely mentioning her excuse for leaving the floor, he left them alone.

Justin, watching his friend go straight to another female for conversation, accused, "You don't like him?"

"Dinna fash yourself. I canna concentrate on liking him or no' when I've got another mon on m'mind."

"What man?"

"That . . . one."

He was there again, not ten feet away and staring at her as if he'd found something he'd lost. She probably looked the same to him, or worse. She knew she was blushing profusely, her pulse racing, her breath held in anticipation. If she fainted, she'd never forgive herself.

She couldn't imagine why it had taken him so long to show up, but she was sure he'd tell her if he'd just come over to her. But he didn't, and after a few more minutes passed, she began to think he wasn't going to.

II

This was not the country waif in frill-less garb
Lincoln had carried in his memory since meeting
her. He almost hadn't recognized her, the difference was so dramatic. Her evening gown was
stunning, pale blue satin with white beaded em-
broidery in floral designs trailing up the long skirt
and across the pointed waist and square-cut
bodice, and dotting the short puffed satin sleeves.
The long evening gloves and shoes were in the same
pale blue, her coiffure simple but elegant, without
a single hair out of place.

The gown was stunning – *she* was stunning – and
what had he expected, when she hobnobbed with
dukes and duchesses? The wind-blown country
lass he'd impulsively decided to marry was definitely not this young lady. And she was already
attached. The man she was with was exceptionally
handsome and held himself with a regal air. The
way they addressed each other, though he couldn't
hear the actual words, suggested an intimacy
beyond their just having met. She'd also been left
with the fellow by her dancing partner, which

implied she'd been collected from him, so he was her escort.

Well, her father had said she'd be coming home affianced, and apparently, she'd wasted no time at all in accomplishing that. Of course, the chap was too young for her. No, he wasn't too young, he was probably *her* age, making Lincoln suddenly feel old.

Lincoln turned to leave. He missed seeing her stricken look as he did so.

But he got no more than a few feet when an arm came about his shoulders to detain him and an angry male voice whispered at his side, "I don't know you and you don't know me, but what you just did to Meli makes me want to rip your head off."

"Excuse me?" Lincoln said coldly as he shrugged off the arm.

"The hell I will. Why'd you just cut her to the quick, eh? And if you tell me you've no interest in her, I'll call you a bloody liar and blind to boot."

Lincoln frowned. "You haven't already staked a claim on her?"

"Gad, that's rich." The young man snorted. "And what if I had? That means you must bow out of the running? Damned if *I'd* give up so easily."

"I wasn't giving up, I was merely licking present wounds," Lincoln said stiffly.

Justin grinned at that point. "Were you, now? Well, that's different and acceptable, I suppose. Shall we start anew? I'm Justin St James, quite possibly Meli's best friend. That, by the by, is the only claim I have on the dear girl. I love her, true, but just like I do my own pesky sisters. Now, perhaps you'd like to meet her?"

"We've met," Lincoln mumbled, rather embarrassed now over his mistaken conclusions.

"Then perhaps you'd like to dance with her where you can discuss . . . wounds in semiprivacy," Justin said with a teasing glint in his eyes. "Though you'd best be quick about asking, before my mother returns and puts you to the grill – credentials and all that. Could take hours before she's satisfied you'll do."

"And what makes *you* think I'll . . . do?" Lincoln asked sardonically.

"You could be a beggar for all I care. Meli likes you – that's the only thing I see that matters."

Meli likes you. Such simple words to cause such a stir of emotions. She was standing there watching them. She'd schooled her features, was giving away no clue to what she was thinking. He wasn't so adept at the moment, was flushed, even nervous, which was really very odd, since he was usually quite assured where women were concerned. Perhaps the difference was that none of the others had mattered the least bit to him. But this one did.

She'd caused him a great many unpleasant emotions the last couple weeks. But only because he'd had no access to her. He had access now – *if* she'd talk to him after he'd "cut her to the quick." He hadn't meant to do that, hadn't thought his departure would affect her, had mistakenly thought she'd already committed herself to someone else.

He nodded to the young man beside him and approached her. She didn't turn away as he'd done. She waited for him to reach her. She even offered a tentative smile, more encouragement than he deserved at the moment.

"We meet again, Melissa MacGregor."

Her smile got several degrees brighter, though all she said was "Aye."

"Is your next dance taken?"

"It was reserved for Justin, no' tae dance, but tae give me a chance tae catch m'breath. But I've done that, mind you, and would be happy tae take tae the floor wi' you – that is, if you're asking."

"I'm asking."

The last song had ended, and a new waltz was just beginning. Lincoln wasted no time in leading her onto the dance floor, before her chaperon showed up to "grill" him, as the young Justin had put it. He hadn't counted on the pleasure just being in her presence again would cause him, though, as well as touching her, albeit impersonally. He nearly forgot to begin the dance, merely stood there in the middle of the floor staring at her and causing curious looks from those couples twirling past them.

She remarked, "I was beginning tae think – well, no' beginning, I was definitely thinking it – that I'd ne'er be seeing you again."

Her voice broke the trance and got his feet moving. "I was having the same fear, if you must know. When I found out where you were staying, I—"

"You knew and didna pay me a visit?"

"Perhaps you aren't aware of the consequence of the people you're staying with? Without a calling card for entry, or an actual invitation from one of them, I couldn't get through the front door."

"Och, is that why? I didna know. We're no' so formal in the Highlands."

Most people weren't so formal, but then most people didn't carry the title of a duke either. "I suppose I'll need to meet your sponsor tonight, to ensure that I can call on you in a proper manner hereafter."

"Dinna sound so aggrieved." She grinned. "Megan St James is a verra nice lady, and verra understanding. And she already knows about you."

"Does she, now?"

"I recall asking her if she knew you," she said with a slight blush.

"To which she replied in the negative, of course," he returned dryly.

"Och, dinna take that personally. She's no' a social butterfly herself. The St Jameses dinna come tae London often. They prefer tae live quietly in the country."

"Then why is she sponsoring you here this season?" he asked.

"Their Graces have been friends o' m'parents e'en afore I was born. They had a hand in getting them married actually. And I had few prospects at home, of a matrimonial sort, so Megan suggested I come here tae rectify that."

"I find it hard to believe you had no prospects at home," he said.

She blushed again as she attempted to explain. "My family can be a wee bit intimidating."

Lincoln supposed that was true enough. He might have thought twice about approaching the laird of Clan MacGregor for permission to court his daughter if he'd known ahead of time that she was his daughter. On second thought, it wouldn't have made the least bit of difference to him, but he had to allow that it might to others.

"How much competition am I up against?"

He asked it lightly, but he was dreading the answer. She'd had nearly three weeks to meet the cream of London society. He'd tortured himself a few times to stand outside the duke's residence and watch the stream of men arriving and granted entrance. There to visit young Justin – or Melissa's suitors? He had naturally assumed the latter, unaware that Their Graces had a son nearing twenty.

She answered in a light tone as well. "I've found no one worth encouraging."

"Will you encourage me?"

There was no teasing in that question. He held her eyes with his. His fingers tightened on her waist and hand. Their movements slowed, didn't keep up with the music, almost stopped. It was one of the hardest things he'd ever done, not to kiss her right there.

Would he ever find her alone where he could give in to that urge? Would he ever be in her presence and not have that urge? Probably not, in either case. She was just too sumptuous, too desirable in every way, and he'd never been so strongly attracted before.

Yet another blush, much more prominent this time, broke the spell. That was answer enough. To ask for more would be improper, so he changed the subject instead.

"I haven't noticed your father here. Your parents haven't come to London with you?"

"They'll be coming next month," she told him. "M'da doesna like London. Tae get him tae stay here e'en a week was asking much."

"Yes, I recall his mentioning a dislike for crowded places during our brief talk," Lincoln replied, then added, "My own family is here for the duration. Actually, I have been asked to chaperon my young cousin this season. She's reached the age to marry as well."

"This does seem tae be the preferred place for getting that accomplished."

He grinned down at her. "Hasn't it always been? For my cousin Edith, though, it won't be an easy task. She just doesn't fit the standard mold. But she's a sweetheart, has a heart of gold. Any man would be blessed if she favors him with her devotion."

"You sound verra fond of her."

"I am."

But he didn't let his prejudice in Edith's favor cloud his view. She was still a wallflower and hadn't been drawing the least bit of notice if she wasn't thrust forward. One had to get to know her well to appreciate her sterling qualities. And she hadn't had a single prospect in the couple weeks they'd now been actively making the rounds.

"Is your family here tonight?"

"Yes."

"I'd like to meet them."

"Certainly, though I suppose I should meet your Megan first, before I go dragging you about the room to find my relatives."

Melissa chuckled. "You sound as if you're expecting the duchess tae be a veritable dragon. You'll be pleasantly surprised, I'm thinking."

It was time to find that out as the music ended. Lincoln would much prefer to keep Melissa to himself for the rest of the evening – and longer, for that matter – but etiquette wouldn't allow that. Melissa, though, must not be acquainted with the strict rules of conduct by which the upper crust lived. She thought nothing of pulling him back across the room to her chaperon and holding his hand to do it.

Relatives could do that. Affianced couples could even do that. But those in the early stages of courtship most certainly could not.

A pleasant surprise didn't come close to describing Megan St James, Duchess of Wrothston. For one thing, Lincoln hadn't expected her to be so young, likely not even ten years older than himself, or so incredibly beautiful. But she'd had only to hear his name mentioned to give him a magnificent smile and an open invitation to her home.

"Finally found her, did you?" was the lady's first response. "I'll inform my butler to expect you henceforth. And shall we start with tea tomorrow?"

There was no "grilling" as he'd been warned, just a few of the simple details one usually inquired about on first meeting. And he didn't have to take Melissa to his family to meet them; they found him before Melissa's next dance partner whisked her away.

He introduced his aunt and cousin first and then, almost as an afterthought, his mother, Eleanor. He didn't notice the curious look Melissa gave him over the latter, though he was aware of his stiffness, was unable to help it whenever he was in Eleanor's presence. She might have solved his dilemma completely in giving him access to Melissa again, but that changed none of his personal feelings about her.

His Aunt Henriette was, of course, delighted to meet Melissa at last and would have talked her ear off if the girl's next partner weren't standing there waiting impatiently to get her out onto the floor before his promised dance ended. Edith was too busy blushing profusely over being in close proximity to the realm's most eligible – and undoubtedly most handsome – young bachelor, Justin St James, so for once she was too tongue-tied to say a word.

Lincoln sighed as the young man finally was able to lead Melissa onto the floor. Megan, hearing him, chuckled at his side.

"I've a feeling you'll be doing a lot more of that sighing in the coming weeks," she said softly, so only he would hear. "Needn't, though. She's made her preference rather clear, I'd say. Yours, Lord

Cambury, will probably be one of the easiest courtships of the decade."

He certainly hoped so. And with Melissa's chaperon apparently on his side, he was able to relax somewhat, was even amused when Justin bowed before his cousin and asked, "May I have the next dance, Miss Burnett?"

Poor Edith nearly fainted.

12

It was impossible to wait until teatime that next afternoon. Lincoln would have arrived at the St Jameses' at the crack of dawn if he hadn't been positive he'd be turned away at that hour. He managed to wait until the household would be finished with luncheon, but he was knocking on their door shortly thereafter.

This time he had only to say his name to be invited in and shown to the parlor. And he barely had time to be impressed by the elegance there before Melissa arrived, a bit breathless, as if she'd run all the way, and treated him to her dimples with a brilliant smile.

She gave him pause once again. To him she was so incredibly lovely, not dazzling like last night in her ball finery, but not the waif again either. She actually looked quite English today, in a fancy day dress of cream organza, though her coiffure wasn't as tight, with a few loose tendrils reminding him of the waif.

He was staring, so hard he didn't realize immediately that no one had followed her into the room.

When he did notice it, he even turned around once full circle to make sure her presence hadn't distracted him to the point of seeing nothing else, before he said, "I don't believe I really have you alone."

"My uncle will be coming along any moment. He always gets summoned down afore I do when I have a caller – made some extreme threats tae the poor butler tae make sure o' it," she said in only a halfteasing tone. "Takes his chaperoning o' me most seriously."

"Then I would be ten times the fool to not take advantage of the moment."

Her eyes flared slightly in surprise as he took her hand in his, pulled her off to the side of the open doorway so they wouldn't be readily seen by anyone passing by, and proceeded to kiss her. She didn't try to stop him. In fact, she melted into his arms. And it was better than he could have imagined. Intoxicating, tasting her for the first time, gathering her close, wrapped in their own cocoon that excluded everything around them.

He was very tentative at first, not wanting to frighten her, but that lasted only a moment. She did seem somewhat surprised when his tongue prodded her lips open and initially swirled with hers. But she adapted quickly, was open to learning, and seemed as eager to deepen that first kiss as he was.

He had no idea how much coughing had gone on before it got progressively louder and was finally loud enough to penetrate the magical realm they had created for themselves. When he did hear it, he released Melissa abruptly, made sure she had her balance, then stepped several feet away from her before turning to face the tall young man standing there glowering at him from the doorway.

"Should I be tossing you oout the door, or was it the lass doing the kissing and in need of a thrashing?" The question was asked in a very unfriendly tone.

Melissa's chuckle, quite genuine rather than nervous, was decidedly misplaced considering what had just been said, until she told Lincoln, "Dinna look so appalled. He's no' serious. This is m'Uncle Ian. And, Uncle" – she turned to the fellow as well before reminding him pointedly – "you'll recall I've mentioned Lord Cambury tae you, aye?"

"Och, sae he's the one, eh?" Ian replied. "A wee bit tardy in coming 'round, I'm thinking, but that explains the kissing. Just dinna be practicing any more o' that until ye've yer da's permission."

The expected blush finally arrived for Melissa. Lincoln was too disappointed to have the kiss ended to feel any real embarrassment over it. And being the oldest of the three, he took control of the situation and stepped forward to shake her uncle's hand.

"A pleasure, Ian."

The young Scot finally grinned. "Aye, 'tis indeed. D'ye live here in London, then? Or only just come in from the country?"

"Neither. I was no more than a day behind Melissa in getting to London. It's taken me this long to gain entry into this fortress of a house."

"The butler doesna let in just anyone," Melissa explained to her uncle in an aggrieved tone. "If I'd known that sooner, I would've set the mon straight."

"Sae, the duchess has hindered more'n helped, eh? Now, tha's bloody well funny, if you ask—"

"Laugh and I'll be clobbering you," Melissa interrupted him to warn, which just earned her another unrepentant grin from the amused young man.

It was easy to surmise that this uncle and niece weren't merely family to each other but friends as well, and rather close ones at that. This wasn't very surprising, though, considering that they were probably fewer than ten years apart in their respective ages.

Ian looked to be in his mid-twenties, with brownish-red hair more on the reddish side, a wealth of freckles across his handsome face, and very light blue eyes. He was tall, over six feet, but other than that, he looked nothing like the MacGregor, who had to be his older brother. It had been mentioned that Lachlan MacGregor's wife was English, and this uncle certainly wasn't that.

There was something vaguely familiar about Ian, though, that Lincoln couldn't quite put his finger on. He concluded that he might have met him before, or perhaps just someone who looked like him, but either it had happened too long ago for him to retain the memory, or they'd met only in passing. It was a nagging feeling, however, as if Lincoln *should* know him.

For the moment he let it go and got a little better acquainted with Ian. It could only be to his benefit, after all, to get along with Melissa's family. Fortunately, he didn't foresee any problems in that respect, especially when he'd already passed muster with her father.

But apparently Ian was experiencing the same nagging sense of familiarity, and he brought it up. "I've the oddest feeling we've met afore."

"Now you mention it," Lincoln confessed, "I've been thinking the same thing."

"Ye've no' been back tae Scotland e'en once in the last nineteen years."

"Not once prior to this recent visit. Have you ever been to England before?"

"Nae, this is m'first trip tae these parts. One o' m'brothers, mayhap."

"One? You've more'n one?"

"Aye, a few," Ian said, and he started to laugh for some reason.

Melissa frowned at her uncle quite sternly. "Hush, you, you'll no' be scaring off another o' m'suitors afore he e'en becomes one."

"Och, he's a suitor, lass, there's nae doubt o' that, or he wouldna hae dared tae be kissing ye."

"He's right, Melissa. I am officially courting you. With your father's permission, I might add."

That got a definite blush out of her and another laugh out of Ian. Lincoln hadn't intended to be so blunt about it. But he wanted no doubt, in her mind at least, that he was serious in his intentions. He was going to marry her – and soon, he hoped. With the feelings she stirred in him, feelings that seemed equally reciprocated, he could see no reason to put off asking for very long.

"I take it you have a big family?" Lincoln said.

"Aye, big indeed," she replied.

He smiled and assured her, "I rather like that. I was an only son myself and missed the close companionship that I knew large families to have. My only remaining relatives you met last night, Melissa."

"Your cousin and aunt were both charming," she told him. "Your mother was somewhat reserved. I began tae worry that she didna like me."

"Nonsense – not that it matters. You might as well know, my mother and I are not on the best of terms. Her sending me off to live with her relatives when I was still a child and then leaving me with them pretty much severed my feelings for her. I haven't seen her but a few times since."

Melissa looked stricken, sympathy for him pouring out of her. Bloody hell, he shouldn't have been so blunt about that either. Not that he meant to keep it a secret from her, nor would he have been able to, but he needn't have mentioned it quite this soon.

He tried to shrug it off, didn't want her feeling sorry for him. "It matters little now after all these years," he said. "Don't give it another thought."

Melissa's look was now doubtful, but he wasn't very adept at lying, so he added, "In any case, she doesn't live with me and will be returning to Scotland soon, where she still resides."

"What o' yer da?" Ian wanted to know. "Had he nae say in yer being abandoned?"

"He had died a few years previously when a mine he was inspecting collapsed."

Ian went rather still upon hearing that. He was probably experiencing some sympathy as well but was hesitant to mention it. The visit ended soon after. They had errands to see to before dinner and the theater that night. Melissa gave Lincoln the name of the play in case he thought to attend. They were scheduled for a four-day gathering in the country that would last the rest of the week, to which she promised to secure an invitation for him.

Lincoln left the St James residence feeling very light of heart, with no idea that his hopes for the future were about to come tumbling down.

13

Lincoln arrived at the theater that night very eager to see Melissa again. It made no difference that he had seen her only hours earlier. That wasn't enough.

It didn't take much to realize that he didn't like being parted from her at all, nor that he couldn't see her whenever he liked. Just visiting wasn't enough either – only marriage was going to give him the access to her that he found himself craving. He would have to ask his aunt exactly how long a courtship should last, and he would be asking Melissa to marry him the moment that time was reached.

She didn't show up.

If Lincoln hadn't brought Edith along with him, he could have left to find out why. But he was Edith's only chaperon that night, and he didn't have the heart to ask her to forgo the outing, when she was receiving a good deal of unexpected attention.

Apparently having someone like Justin St James take to the floor with her last night had been precisely the sort of thing to give her that thrust forward she'd been needing. Several men came forward to introduce themselves to her before they found their seats, several more during the intermission, and one approached her twice and even asked if he could call on her the next day.

Edith was bubbling over with excitement on the way home that night. Lincoln made an effort not to dampen her mood, even though his own was filled with worry. Of course, any number of things could have happened to cause Melissa to cancel going to the theater. It wasn't as if she were missing an actual event she'd been invited to, one that would require formal regrets sent to the inviter if she couldn't attend. And he'd find out soon enough what had happened to change her plans when he called on her tomorrow.

So he thought. But he found out different when he arrived at the ducal town house the next afternoon, at precisely the same time as the previous day, only to be denied entry again, though this time simply because the duchess and her young guest were out of town. They had already departed for the country gathering that Melissa had mentioned to him and weren't likely to be back before the end of the week.

"Whose gathering were they attending?" Lincoln thought to ask, since it might be one he or his aunt had already been invited to.

The man, eager to get the door closed, said simply, "I've no idea, sir."

Lincoln found that doubtful, when most butlers

made it their business to know *everything* involving their employers. But rather than making accusations that *would* get the door closed immediately, he asked, "Is Miss MacGregor's uncle here? He might know."

"No, sir. Master Ian accompanied the ladies."

"And you really have no idea where this country party is occurring?"

A bit of stiffness now. "I'm sorry, sir, I'm not privy to such information. Her Grace's secretary might know, but he was given a holiday while she is out of town and is no longer in residence either."

That, at least, did sound plausible, so Lincoln nodded and left. In any case there was nothing for it but to wait for the promised invitation, the one that Melissa had said she would obtain for him.

It never arrived. The four days that had been mentioned for this particular gathering came and went. Invitations for the more exclusive events of the season were pouring in. But the Duchess of Wrothston and her guests didn't return to town by the end of the week, nor for the weekend that followed. And the St Jameses' butler steadfastly maintained each time he was asked, which was daily, that he hadn't received word yet when they would.

Lincoln wasn't dense. He realized that, for whatever reason, he was being avoided. Melissa didn't want to see him again, much less be courted by him. But why not simply tell him and put him out of his misery? He was kept wondering instead, and without much hope that he was mistaken, so it wasn't surprising that he would attempt to take solace in drink, which would help him to stop thinking about it, however briefly.

There was a tavern not too far from his town house, a decent establishment he used to frequent with his old crowd. He'd spent the entire evening there last night, until the landlord, whom he knew by name, finally closed down and assisted him home – at least, he had a vague memory of being assisted, had definitely needed assisting at any rate. And he'd blessedly slept away most of the day today.

But he was back there again tonight. The landlord, Patrick – or Patty as he was more often called – rolled his eyes at Lincoln when he showed up again but brought a bottle of brandy over to his table without being asked. It had been a standing joke among Lincoln's cronies that while they preferred to drink Scotch, he – the Scotsman – didn't.

Patty had tried to get him to reveal his woes last night, being of the opinion that it would be good for him, but Lincoln wasn't one to be talkative when he drank, no matter how deep into his cups he got. Getting deliberately foxed was serious work, after all. And he hoped that after a few more days of such work he'd get sick enough to put this whole debacle behind him. That was possible. And he still had to find a wife . . .

The tavern had been somewhat crowded when he arrived. Five of the tables had been occupied, if not filled, and several more men had been standing at the bar. Lincoln had recognized none of them, which was good, since he didn't want to be bothered with conversation of any sort. They were drinking quietly. He began doing the same.

He didn't notice the new crowd arriving, since he had his back to the door. The other patrons did, however, and quickly began to vacate the place, anticipating trouble from such a large group of unfriendly-looking gents, every single one of them over six feet tall.

Lincoln did notice one new fellow who sat down noisily at the table on his left. Oddly, he somewhat resembled the oldest MacFearson brother, whom Lincoln remembered, not in his coloring but in his facial features, though Lincoln had to allow that his memory of that bunch of ill-mannered, ill-tempered louts was definitely cloudy after nineteen years.

It had to be the drink. He'd had enough bad luck recently that adding running into one of *them* would go beyond the pale. No one could get that unlucky.

"I ne'er would hae recognized him m'self" was said almost cheerfully.

Lincoln turned to the speaker on his right. This one he knew. Bloody hell.

"Nor I. 'Course he was but a lad in knickers when he left the Highlands."

Lincoln turned his head around yet again. There were five more of them lined up at the bar watching him, a sixth actually sitting up on it. Poor Patty was standing nervously at the end, ready to bolt into the back room at the first sign of violence.

"There's still nae resemblance, other than his eyes and hair, neither o' which is unique."

One more had straddled the only other chair at his own table. Three more were taking seats at the table beyond. A quick glance around showed other tables behind him filled with them, at least fifteen total head count. Besides himself and Patty, they were the only ones left in the room.

"Bloody, bloody hell."

"Good tae see ye again, too, Linc," one of them said with a chuckle.

"Is this where you all pound on me again?" Lincoln remarked sourly before finishing off his current drink and quickly pouring another.

"As long as ye dinna start throwing punches as ye sae often did afore, we've nae beating planned for ye," came a new voice, contempt strong in it.

"To what, then, do I owe the distinct misfortune of seeing you all again?"

"We've come tae tell ye tae stay away from our niece" was the quick answer.

"What niece?" Lincoln snorted. "If you have one, I pity the girl for that, but since none of you had borne any children before I left Scotland, any that you bore afterward would be decidedly too young for my notice – allowing I wouldn't despise any relative of yours just by association, mind you," he added with some of his own contempt.

"This niece was born tae our only sister, older than Ian One."

"You didn't have any sisters back then. If you did, you would have mentioned it, when you were so proudly gloating over how many there were of you."

"She was one we didna know aboot, nor did our da," one of the younger MacFearsons explained. "We only discovered her existence a month or so after ye left, and she bore the MacGregor a daughter aboot nine months later."

Lincoln went very still upon hearing that. "No, she can't be your niece."

"She is."

"Bloody hell! You've ruined every other thing in my life, you're not going to ruin this as well."

"Ye give us more credit than we deserve, mon. Ye were the one who wouldna leave well enough alone."

"And who started it all tae boot" was added by yet another new voice, quite bitterly.

Lincoln turned to the last speaker. Strange how he knew exactly which one this was without having to be told, though he bore absolutely no resemblance to the lad who had been his friend for all of two years, other than sporting the dark green eyes many of them had.

A lot of them had had dark blond hair as well back then and still did, though this one didn't anymore. His hair had apparently darkened to a true brown as he aged. Dougall MacFearson. Dougi. The only person Lincoln had ever been able to claim as his *best* friend – but by choice. He'd never allowed himself to get that close to anyone again.

"Dougi—"

He had only to say the name and two of the older

brothers stepped in front of Dougall to protect him. Which was absurd. It might have been their habit when they were all growing up, to protect the younger ones whether they needed it or not. But they were all grown now, and Dougall was Lincoln's age, quite able to see to his own defense.

"I see none of you have really changed," Lincoln said in disgust. "Why does that not surprise me?"

"Insulting us already, lad?"

"Leave it go, Adam," the eldest among them suggested in a calm tone.

Ian One, the voice of reason, the voice of decision – if not always the calmest voice. Whenever this bunch fought among themselves, it was always Ian One, the oldest, who was turned to in the end to decide the matter. The firstborn – or he had been, before they'd learned of an older sister they never knew they had.

He continued in the same vein. "Ian Six was right tae be concerned and send for us. Linc here might hae behaved decently enough wi' the lass, aside from the stealing o' kisses, but if anyone hasna changed, 'tis him. If a mon canna ootgrow a foul disposition in nineteen years, he ne'er will. We hae seen what we came tae see. Now he knows she's one o' us, he'll end his pursuit o' her. He's already said he'd despise any relation o' ours. The matter ended wi' that statement, I'm thinking, sae let us leave the mon in peace."

That easily they all filed out of the tavern, just as quietly as they'd entered. Patty, wide-eyed, rushed over to Lincoln's table the moment the door closed on the last one – after grabbing a bottle for himself first.

"I've heard of large families, but never that many siblings and all so close in age – and so big!" he said in amazement.

"One father, many different mothers," Lincoln said in a tired voice.

"Ah, that would explain it, then."

"And two were missing – the eldest I didn't know about myself and the youngest, who must have finally figured out who I was when I met him last week and then sent for the lot of them."

"Seventeen in all?"

"To my grave misfortune."

14

"Did you find him?" Ian Six asked as he entered the hotel room where his brothers were gathered for breakfast that morning, trays piled high with pastries and assorted hot drinks spread out all over the place.

They had rented five rooms for the lot of them but used them only for sleeping. The Duchess of Wrothston would have opened her home to them, if she'd known they were in town. They had elected to keep their presence secret for the time being, however, since Melissa would be alarmed and want to know why they were all there, and they hadn't decided yet whether to tell her or not.

Callum, thirty-two and one of the few brothers who had a couple of sisters who were unrelated to the rest of them, answered Ian, "He was easy enough tae find, though no' sae easy tae deal wi'."

The youngest brother was surprised. "Dinna tell me he tried tae take ye all on again?"

Ian Two answered, "Nay, he was actually verra calm and quiet, just sat there stewing in hate, is all.

It was like seeing the lad all o'er again, just wi'oot the shouts and flying temper."

Ian Two was the third oldest among them, but still three years younger than Ian One. He was the most adept with his fists, however, and tended to win any fights he got into, including those with his brothers. He had restrained himself with Lincoln due to being so much older and bigger at the time, which hadn't stopped Lincoln from attacking him. He'd merely held him off at arm's length, which unfortunately caused embarrassment that just added to the lad's fury. He wouldn't be inclined to restraint now, though.

"But he'll back off, now he knows she's one o' ours?" Ian Six asked.

"There's no telling wi' a mon like him," Callum replied. "Ye'll need tae accompany her wherever she goes now, I'm thinking, just tae be sure."

Ian Six groaned. "He's no' likely tae see me as a deterrent. He's got three years on me, a few more inches, and a lot more weight."

"That doesna matter," Adam, the second oldest there, insisted. "Ye represent us, is what he'll be seeing. If he approaches Melissa wi' ye there beside her, he'll be crossing us all."

"As if that e'er stopped him," Charles said with a derisive snort.

Charles, like Dougi and Ian Five, was the exact same age as Lincoln Ross, give or take a few months. Their father had been quite fickle – and prolific – that particular year. Charles had also been somewhat jealous back then – of Dougi. Having an extraordinary number of brothers was one thing, but having your own best friend who wasn't a brother was unique in their family, and Charles had envied Dougi Linc's friendship – up until it ended. Then he'd just pitied Dougi and was perhaps relieved he hadn't won the closer relationship he'd wanted.

"I'd say we hae nothing more tae worry aboot," Ian Four put in confidently "He willna want her for wife, now he knows who she is."

This Ian was thirty-one now and, like many of them, had their father's dark blond hair and green eyes. Malcolm, who was the same age, had the same eyes but bright red hair from his mother. Johnny was but a year older than these two and took completely after his mother, with coal black hair and light brown eyes flecked with gold.

"I agree," Malcolm said.

"I disagree," Johnny said.

"And that surprises who?" Charles snorted again.

"Quiet, ye." Ian Three scowled, taking Johnny's side, as he usually did. Those two actually shared the same mother as well as father. It didn't make them any closer, really, than any of the others; it just added an additional protective instinct to this Ian, which he took seriously. "There's two good reasons why he still might pursue her."

George entered the discussion now. Thirty-three, he was the only one of them with very light blond hair instead of dark, and his eyes were sea blue. He was also one of the few of them to have married, though he'd done so only recently to the mother of his three bairns.

He said simply, "For spite."

That got a lot of nods, but Ian Three continued, "Aye, that would be one reason. The other is, he could already be in love wi' her."

Malcolm started to laugh. Ian Six, walking past him to grab a scone, kicked him to silence, remarking, "He's right. Ye werena there tae see how Linc looked at our Meli, but I was. He's a mon sorely smitten."

"Was. But we all ken how quickly a finer emotion can turn foul," Dougall said quietly.

There was a moment of silence, filled with sympathy, anger, and even some regret. They all knew how close Dougall had felt to Lincoln Ross – until that day so long ago that Lincoln started that fight with him for no good reason.

In all the years since, Dougall had never again trusted anyone outside his family. That event had caused much dissent among themselves as well. Some of them had felt sorry for Lincoln. Some didn't want to fight him, even though he insisted.

Some, like William, who'd been there the day it started, felt a measure of guilt for beating Lincoln so badly he'd had to be carried home. That would have been the end of it, however – should have been. A wrong quickly dealt with. But Lincoln just wouldn't let it go . . .

Ian One cleared his throat to break the silence. "Hae ye told her who he really is?" he asked Ian Six.

"Nae, I didna hae the heart tae. She was looking forward tae seeing him again here in London and was verra unhappy when it looked like she wouldna, then verra happy when he did finally show up. She likes him. A lot."

"As long as it was just liking, she'll get o'er it quick enough," Johnny said.

"Will she? I'm no' sae sure," Ian Six continued. "But I refuse tae be the bearer o' bad tidings for her. If she's tae be told, one o' ye can hae that honor. I did m'part, kept her away from London longer than planned, tae give ye time tae warn him off. Had tae break the duchess's poor coach wheel four times tae do it. She nearly fired her driver, blaming him. Fortunately, the last time the wheel fell off was near a friend o' hers, and she decided tae visit there, then got talked into staying o'er for a couple o' days, which is why we didna get back until yesterday."

Ian One nodded. "Then let's decide the matter here and now. Either we tell her and hope she agrees that he's no' the mon for her or we dinna tell her and just make sure he stays away from her."

"Ye dinna think our warning tae him sufficed?" William asked.

"When did he e'er back down from us?" Charles asked. He managed not to snort this time, though derision was still in his tone.

"Telling her could hae the opposite effect we'd like," Ian Five mentioned casually. "She could as likely get annoyed wi' us for warning him off, regardless that he's no' the right mon for her."

"There's that," Ian One agreed, but he added,

"And she willna be the only one. Her mother is likely tae shoot the lot o' us if we dinna handle this right. There's also the chance Meli will want him anyway."

Since it sounded as though Ian One had already decided on secrecy to keep peace with the MacGregors' womenfolk, and since most of them tended to agree with him just because he was the eldest of the brothers, Ian Six felt compelled to point out, "She's going tae be miserable if he doesna pursue her, after he told her he was officially courting her."

"Better a little misery now than a lifetime o' it living wi' a mon o' such volatile temper," Callum said.

"She'll think we're interfering if she finds oot," Ian Six warned.

"We *are* interfering," Johnny said.

"Aye, but this on top of scaring off her suitors at home? She'll be seriously displeased wi' us."

"Och, ne'er mind them," Charles said derisively. "They were afeared of a silly legend e'en afore they showed up. Merely looking at them wrong would hae sent them running. Cowards, those two. She wouldna hae been happy wi' either o' them, and she knew that."

"Linc isna a coward," William pointed out.

"Linc is sae far the opposite o' that, he takes bravery tae extremes, tae the exclusion o' common sense," Adam said. "At least, he did when he was a lad. Now, did any o' ye notice any difference aboot him last night tae suggest he's grown oot o' such foolishness?"

There was a quick round of naes. Ian Four sighed at the end of it. "And that suggests he'll ignore our warning."

"I say we've nothing tae worry aboot," Neill said with more hope than assurance. He was the second youngest, and as such he rarely offered an opinion. "Now he knows she's one o' ours, he willna want her. He'll despise her as he does the rest o' us. He said as much."

"He said that afore he heard exactly who our niece is," William reminded them. "Besides, Meli is impossible tae despise. There's no lass sweeter, kinder, more compassionate, charming, funny—"

"We've the MacGregor tae thank for that," Callum cut in with a chuckle. "Sweetness doesna run in *our* side o' the family."

"Regardless, I say he willna give up the pursuit," William continued. "And what I'm wanting tae know is, what are we going tae do then?"

"Short o' killing him?"

"Now, there's an excellent option," Charles said, tongue in cheek.

15

For such a big house, and with so many servants, it was almost amazing how easy it was to find solitude, even for meals, or at least for breakfast. The duchess slept late, of course, a necessary habit during a season when most entertainments lasted into the wee hours. Justin, on a different schedule – he'd begged off going to any more parties with them – usually spent the morning out riding in one of the city's many parks. Ian, for some reason insisting on escorting Melissa everywhere now, had started sleeping in as well.

Melissa probably would have done the same, if she could have slept. She couldn't. Well, she could, but not anywhere near as much as she was used to. Not that she needed a great deal of it, with the abundance of energy she had at her age. If anything, she would have liked to sleep a little longer just to get past the hours when nothing was planned.

At home she could go out and about by herself and find any number of things to keep her occupied. She couldn't do that here. She could just imagine the fit her uncle would have if she tried it.

Which left her a lot of empty hours spent with her own thoughts, not the most desirable thing these days.

The trouble was, she was having a lot of up and down moods, which would be fine if they weren't such extreme ups and downs. As it was, she could spend hours daydreaming, imagining all kinds of wonderful encounters with Lincoln Burnett, each of which ended most happily, as daydreams tended to do. It was a pleasant enough pastime, though she'd prefer to be having the actual encounters instead. Or she could spend hours dealing with doubts and trying to reassure herself that she shouldn't be having them.

Both were keeping her from getting quickly to sleep, and in the emotional form of excitement or anxiety, waking her sooner than intended and keeping her from getting back to sleep. The doubts were winning, though, and filling much more time than the pleasant daydreams.

But then, seeing a man only three times in nearly five weeks just didn't feel like a courtship to her. The first couple of weeks she couldn't count, when Lincoln had tried to see her but couldn't get in – at least that had been his contention. The four days in the country that had turned into a week she *could* count, but she preferred to be optimistic. She had decided that the invitation she'd arranged for him hadn't reached him, and that was what accounted for his absence. It was disappointing, but no tragedy. They could make up for lost time as soon as she got back to the city.

The optimism at least allowed her to enjoy her sojourn in the country. There had been yard games, an afternoon of golf, a picnic, riding each morning, and dozens of other activities lined up for a wide variety of choices. She'd even met two new gentlemen she'd been quick to discourage simply because they were ideally suitable, but she considered herself already off the marriage block.

Now she was having some definite doubts again about the man of her choice. She couldn't help it. If Lincoln were really interested in her, wouldn't he make an effort to see her more often? Wouldn't he at least send 'round a note to explain why he hadn't come to call?

She really had expected him to come by almost immediately upon her return to the city. He hadn't, not once. Five days later she had to own up to the possibility that he wasn't going to. She just couldn't figure out why, and she was getting more and more melancholy trying to.

"So you *are* still here?" Justin said as he entered the breakfast room, riding crop in hand.

She'd lingered longer than she'd realized, lost in her thoughts. It was nearly noon. She'd sat there for three hours with a full plate in front of her, untouched. This had to end. They were becoming unhealthy, her erratic moods.

"Where else would I be?"

"Gone home. I wasn't sure. I hadn't seen you since that ball. How's the romance going, by the by?"

She burst into unexpected tears, then was

appalled by it. But his expression turned even more horrified. It was so unlike him that it actually made her laugh. Was she going crazy? She wouldn't be half surprised.

He took the seat next to her, reluctant to say anything else, and regarded her cautiously. She gave him an embarrassed smile.

"Dinna mind me, Justin. Female vagaries."

For a moment it looked as if he'd gladly accept that excuse, but then he snorted. "Nonsense. What's happened to bring you to tears?"

"Nothing."

"I don't believe—"

"Nay, I meant . . . nothing. I havena seen Lincoln since the day after that ball. I havena heard from him. He said he was going tae court me, then . . . nothing. If he hadna kissed me, proving that his courtship was sincere, I'd be thinking he'd just toyed with me."

Justin frowned, then said hesitantly, "I hate to mention it, Meli, but kissing can have absolutely nothing to do with courtship."

She waved a dismissive hand at him. "Och, I know what you're thinking, but it wasna like that. He kissed me afore he mentioned the courting. And he said he already had m'da's permission. He wouldna have asked m'da for it if he werena serious."

Justin grinned at that point, because he had to agree. "No, I don't think any man would care to get that seven-foot giant angry with him."

"That's allowing everything he's said is the

117

truth," she added reluctantly, one of her more recent worries.

That brought Justin back to his feet rather quickly, growling, "The bastard. Of course, if he's out to seduce you, he'd be lying to do it. Comes part and parcel with the scheme, don't you know. And I wasn't going to mention this, since he seemed respectable, but I *have* heard he runs with a more . . . disreputable crowd."

"Heard?"

"I asked around. Now, don't give me that look. Just because a man's titled, that doesn't make him automatically acceptable. You're acting purely on emotion. I merely wanted to know a little bit more about him, since we'd never heard of him before now."

"What d'you mean, 'disreputable'?"

"Third and fourth sons, the sort that don't give a bloody damn if they blacken the family name, since they aren't likely to be inheriting anything from it. Nothing serious, mind you. And he's never got into mischief himself – at least, that made the gossip rounds – but some of his friends have. They're a bunch of rakehells, Meli. Now, I wouldn't personally tar and feather a man just due to association. And I did give him the benefit of the doubt. After all, many a rakehell in his youth has turned out to be an outstanding member of society after he settles down. But if Lord Cambury doesn't have a really good excuse for getting your hopes up and then ignoring you—"

"You think there can be a good reason?" she

interrupted hopefully. "I've tried tae think o' one, but the only thing I would've found acceptable was dismissed last night when I ran into his cousin Edith and she said he's still in town, if somewhat moody."

"And there's your answer, m'dear," Justin said. "People can behave quite bizarrely when moody. Take yourself, for example."

Melissa blushed. "Moody doesna keep me from normal activities."

"No?" he replied, staring pointedly at her full plate of cold food.

She blushed again, mumbling, "I wasna hungry."

"Ah, you just like staring at food all morning, then," he returned.

Her cheeks couldn't get any redder. "Verra well, I'll be agreeing with you that moody can produce abnormal behavior. But I fulfill m'schedule. I dinna lock m'self away tae brood in solitude."

"But, Meli, everyone is different in the matter of moods, doubts, or whatever. What you might do in the doldrums, another might scoff at. What they might do in the doldrums, you might find utterly appalling. A man might go out and sock someone for no apparent reason, just to try to release some of what's bothering him. Or take off riding and be so absentminded he ends up in the next county before noticing."

"Now, that sounds like you've been there." She grinned.

He gave her a sour look before continuing,

"Whereas a woman might thrash about on her bed in tears, scream out the window, snarl at everyone she passes. By the by, you're to be commended for only starving yourself."

He finally got a laugh out of her, which had the amazing effect of making her worries seem unfounded. "I take it you think I'm being silly"

"Not at all!" he replied, tongue in cheek, ending in a grin. "I merely think you've jumped the gun, as it were. Until you actually hear otherwise, assume he's got a perfectly good reason for not coming 'round. You may only have been able to think of one reason for his absence, but I can think of half a dozen. Business, other worries, estate problems, family crisis – any number of things that could be consuming all his energies, leaving him no time for socializing at the moment. Remember, you were wrong before, about why he hadn't come around to call on you."

She beamed a smile at him. "I knew there was a good reason I love you so much. Are you sure you dinna want tae marry me?"

He snorted. "When my desire is to tweak your nose rather than kiss you? Not bloody likely."

She chuckled. "Just making sure. And thank you. I should've searched you oot when we got back from the country and saved m'self four days o'. . . screaming oot the windows."

16

Lincoln opened the door to his study, where he'd been told his visitor was waiting, and only just managed to move out of the way of the fist that immediately came flying at his face. The owner of the fist wasn't as lucky. The momentum behind the swing carried Justin St James out into the hall; the smooth marble tile there kept him from stopping. He actually slammed into the side of the grand staircase, nearly flipping over the ornate balustrade.

When he corrected his posture and jerked his coat back into place, he found both Henriette and Edith standing in the doorway to the parlor just down the hall, staring at him wide-eyed. Which probably accounted for the splotches of red showing up on his cheeks.

He gave the two ladies a brief, embarrassed nod, then turned to Lincoln to say stiffly, "I'd like to have words with you."

Lincoln couldn't help it, he raised a brow. "Is that what it's called these days? Or do you always attack first and ask your questions later?"

At that point the young man sighed. "My

121

apologies. I'm not used to being kept waiting. I was beginning to think it was deliberate."

"I wasn't here. I only just got home," Lincoln replied. "But I'm inclined to think more than a simple delay prompted your greeting?"

"Well, yes, a lot more, actually." The stiffness was back. "That was merely the crowning touch."

"I'm sure you're eager to be more specific, so do come in," Lincoln said, moving into the study to take the seat behind his desk.

Justin followed him in but ignored the chairs available for his use, preferring to pace about in an agitated manner. His black hair was disheveled, as if he'd been raking it – or trying to pull it out. He seemed a short fuse ready to ignite, but whether that was a normal state for him – the impatience of youth – or related to something in particular, Lincoln was still waiting to find out.

He watched Justin for a moment before he said, "Spit it out, man. Leaving me to guess what brings you here will get us nowhere."

Justin marched over to the front of the desk, crossed his arms, and demanded baldly, "Why haven't you come 'round to see Melissa?"

Lincoln sat back in his chair and crossed his arms as well. "Is that a trick question?"

"Trick?" Justin replied belligerently. "Sounded direct. I'm sure it was direct. You bloody well can't get much more direct than that!"

"Sit down, St James," Lincoln said. "You might try *calming* down as well."

The lad didn't take well to either suggestion. He scowled. "You're not going to answer me?"

"Considering whom I've been dealing with, mine was a legitimate question. I'm not going to spill my guts only to have you repeat every word to the MacFearsons."

The scowl changed to a confused frown. "And why don't you want Meli to know?"

"I wasn't talking about her."

"Who, then?"

"Her uncles, of course."

"You've something against her uncles?"

"In self-defense, most assuredly," Lincoln replied coldly. "But the more accurate statement would be, they have something against me."

"What?"

"You're just full of questions, aren't you?" Lincoln remarked dryly.

"That's why I'm here."

"Obviously, but what gives you the right to ask them?" Lincoln demanded.

Justin started holding up fingers one by one as he ticked off his reasons. "Because I'm Meli's best friend. Because your treatment of her is now suspect. Because you stated your intent to court her, then bowed out of the running. Because she doesn't know whether to give up on you or not. Need more reasons?"

"No. And it sounds like you're unaware that I've been warned to stay away from the girl."

"What! By whom?"

"Who else? Her uncles can be quite persuasive when they show up en masse."

Justin's turquoise eyes flared. "They're *all* here? I doubt Meli is aware of that. Only one of them is staying with us."

Lincoln shrugged. He couldn't care less where the savages were staying. But if Justin didn't know that he'd been scratched from Melissa's list of suitors by her family, he had to wonder now if *she* knew and simply hadn't mentioned it to Justin – or if she didn't know either.

Lincoln found it extremely hard to believe that they *wouldn't* have told her first, before they sought him out. Or perhaps her preference in the matter made no difference to them. Actually, the latter did sound more like them. Not that it decreased his fury or made her suddenly available again.

"I believe you have the answer you came for," Lincoln said, his voice clipped.

Justin shook his head stubbornly. "What I have is more questions now—"

"Too bad," Lincoln cut in, losing some of his own patience. "Aside from the fact that it's none of your bloody business, it was an occurrence nineteen years old. Count them, lad. Nineteen years! Most of those involved were children at the time – *you* might not even have been born yet. Melissa certainly wasn't. For animosity to last that long . . . no amount of talking is going to make it go away. I've been warned off. I'm not going to end up with sixteen savages trying to break the rest of my bones, the ones they didn't get around to breaking the first go round, thank you very much."

Justin winced. "They ganged up on you?"

"A family creed of theirs. I honestly don't think they know any other way to go about it."

"So you're giving up?"

"You see another option, do you?"

"Well, no. But—"

"Go home, St James. By the by, you should work on that right swing of yours."

Justin gave him one last glare before he stalked out of the room, leaving Lincoln to curse again the day he'd met the MacFearson brothers. And what was he supposed to think now? What if Melissa didn't know that he'd been warned off. What if, as Justin had implied, she'd been left to wonder why he was ignoring her. No, she had to know. Savages that they were, even *they* wouldn't leave her in that kind of doubt. But what was going to drive him crazy was wondering if she agreed with her uncles.

One of the easier courtships of the decade? Wasn't that what the Duchess had said? What a bloody joke.

17

Justin hadn't worked on his right swing, as had been suggested – he was positive the last blunder had merely been a matter of bad luck – but he *was* better prepared this time in only having to wait for the door to open and expecting it to open immediately. It did open, and his fist connected solidly with Ian MacFearson's chin.

The blow sounded nice, but it didn't move the older man very much – barely turned his head a bit. It was still satisfying for all that. And Justin was ready to deal out more punishment. When he'd told Melissa that men sometimes chose to release what was bothering them by throwing punches, he'd definitely been thinking of himself.

Not a very good habit to get into, and one his father would most likely frown on, but at the moment it was working. He felt better already, particularly since Ian Six gave no indication of wanting to retaliate.

Justin's intention hadn't been to thrash the man senseless – he might have had a little trouble trying it, considering that Ian was older, taller, and probably much more experienced at such things. No, he'd merely wanted to make his point rather quickly and to release some of the frustration he was feeling in knowing that there wasn't a bloody thing he could do about the current state of affairs.

Ian moved aside to allow entry into his bedroom. Justin took that as a clue and lowered his fists before entering the room. He was still agitated, and it was rather deflating to have got so little reaction – even a bit of surprise would have helped – out of Ian. But the Scot seemed to have expected the attack, or at the least felt it was due.

To clarify, though, just in case Ian were used to being socked for no reason, Justin told the older man, "I went to see Lord Cambury today at his residence, if you haven't figured that out yet, because I was having trouble believing that he'd lost all interest in Meli. Imagine my amazement to find out I was right, that it was something else entirely keeping him away from her."

Ian nodded, closed the door, and moved over to the window, out of Justin's reach. His downcast look had nothing to do with a sore chin.

"Did he tell ye everything?" he asked.

"He barely told me *any*thing!" Justin growled. "So I've come to you next for some answers, because I'm sure there has to be a good reason Meli is being left to suffer with not knowing what's happened."

"I wanted tae tell her," Ian admitted. "I can barely look at her now wi'oot feeling guilty."

That was the last thing Justin expected to hear.

It just made him want to hit the man again. "You're a bastard, you and your brothers."

"Aye, we are."

"I'm not talking about the circumstances of your birth, you ass," Justin stated baldly.

"Aye, I know."

"Then why?" Justin demanded. "And I don't mean why d'you hate the man. I couldn't bloody well care less about that. I want to know why Melissa wasn't told about it, so she could forget about him."

"Because she's a mind o' her own. Because she might no' hae forgot aboot him a'tall. The thought o' her running off wi' him was weighed against the wee bit o' wondering she might be doing now."

"'Wee bit'? Have you even talked to her lately? And if it was so clear cut as that, then why are you feeling guilty about it?"

"Because I *do* ken what she's feeling, e'en if she's trying tae hide it," Ian replied. "Ye forget I know her as well as ye do, lad. And I'm the only one o' my brothers who saw Linc afore he knew who she really is. I'm no' sure we made the right decision. We ne'er gave him a chance tae prove if he's changed or no'."

"So it comes down to why you hate him after all?" Justin frowned. Ian sighed.

"We dinna hate him."

"Then what? And if you tell me you're holding him accountable for something he did when he was a child, I think I'll hit you again."

"It wasna just what he did, it was his overall re-action tae the whole thing."

"*What* whole thing?"

"He and m'brother Dougi were best friends back then. This thing started wi' Linc ending that friendship by picking a fight that Dougi couldna hope tae win. A couple o' m'other brothers took him tae task for it, but that was only the beginning. Linc took exception tae that, and for all intents and purposes he declared war on the lot o' us."

"War?" Justin scoffed. "Rather a harsh word for childish squabbles, don'tcha think?"

"Aye, except in this case, tha's bloody well what it felt like. As soon as Linc would get patched up from one fight, he'd come looking for another. Time and again he attacked us, and he didna care how many o' us he took on at once. Nine was the largest count."

"You couldn't just ignore him?"

"We tried. He wouldna allow it. We'd walk away from him, and he'd attack anyway. He proved, wi' verra little doubt, that he has a temper he canna control. There was no rhyme or reason tae it. It turned him crazed. *That* is why we dinna want tae see our Meli joined tae him. A child shouldna be held accountable for the transgressions o' his youth, but some things can stay wi' a person for-ever. A wild, unpredictable temper is one thing someone might no' outgrow."

"But what if he *has* outgrown it?"

"Were we tae put it tae the test, provoke him, see

if he's managed tae harness the thing?" Ian asked.

"Absolutely. I would have."

"Then yer no' looking at the possible results verra clearly. Risk one or more o' us – or more likely him – getting seriously hurt in the testing? We're adults now. Adults dinna fight like children. Or nip Meli's romance afore it gets started, sae no one actually gets hurt. Which would ye really choose?"

"Put that way, the latter, of course," Justin was forced to say. "Though I think it's too late to use the word 'started.' She's too dejected at the moment for her feelings to be merely tepid where he's concerned."

"Which is another reason why I havena gone against m'brothers and told her anyway. She's a lass who would follow her heart rather than common sense."

Justin sighed now. "You're probably right. But this still won't do. She's come here to get leg-shackled. That was the whole point of this trip as I understand it. But how's she going to do that, eh, if she continues to wait for a man who's not going to show up? She *thinks* he will. I even encouraged her not to give up all hope – before I found out what was going on. So she'll keep waiting and keep ignoring any other man who pays her court. And that means she goes home without a husband. You *have* figured that out, right?"

"Ye think I like any o' this?"

"I think you're going to do nothing to correct it. I'm not so restricted."

"Nae, I mun ask ye tae keep what you've learned tae yerself."

"Like hell—"

"There's no choice here."

Ian moved to stand in front of the door, crossing his arms. He no longer looked guilty. He looked damned determined, actually. Justin groaned inwardly. So he wasn't going to leave unscathed after all. So be it. St Jameses didn't back down from a challenge.

Justin put up his fists again. Ian shook his head at him, said, "Ye'd lose, sae dinna be trying it. And consider the results o' ye telling her all o' this. As compassionate as the lass is, she'll take his side. Like ye, she'll insist what's in the past should stay in the past. She'll overlook the danger tae herself that his anger could cause, because she hasna seen it yet."

"Danger?"

"A crazy mon can and will harm anything in his path, including himself, because he loses all sense o' right, wrong, logic, and all other attributes that put a harness on human nature. And I'm telling ye, I saw him m'self when he was like that. I saw him challenge m'brothers George, Malcolm, and Ian Two, all three older and bigger than him, when he had three cracked ribs already, two broken fingers, a sprained wrist, several broken knuckles, a jaw off center or – perhaps it was his nose – stitches all o'er his face—"

"I get the picture!" Justin interrupted, appalled.

"Nay, I dinna think ye do. The lad still charged

131

in, despite all his injuries. He could barely walk. He could barely see through two black eyes swollen nearly shut. Yet he still insisted on fighting us, his rage defying all reason. 'Twas almost as if he had a death wish, though I simply canna attribute such a motive tae a mere child. Temporary insanity, aye. But no matter the cause, what happens tae innocents who get in the way o' such a rage, eh? In particular, a wife partial tae the opposing side?"

"It's still all supposition. You could as easily say, What if he's nothing like that now? He could merely have lacked the maturity to contain his emotions at that age but have them well in hand now. He's not locked away, obviously. So he's managed to get to his ripe old age without killing anyone. But based on 'what ifs' and something that happened before Meli was even born, you intend to deny her a man who could be just right for her and – even if not *just* right – the one she happens to want. You took the easy path in simply telling him to get lost, when you could just as easily have tested the waters to see if they'll still churn or not."

"Ye've made some good points," Ian said. "But there are still too many question marks for this mon tae be a good choice for m'niece. Her da will agree when he's apprised o' all the facts. And that will be the end o' it. Sae all this talk and guessing is useless. The MacGregor himself will forbid the match."

Ian opened the door, signaling an end to the discussion. Justin gave him a sour look. Nothing had been resolved, in his opinion. And if anything he was even more frustrated now than when he'd arrived, when he'd thought he could make a difference. Some difference. Melissa was still to be left in the dark, and that wasn't right. If anyone should have a say in this arbitrary decision her uncles had made, it was she.

"I'll say nothing for now, but her father had better be arriving soon to decide the matter, because I *don't* think you MacFearsons have handled this well a'tall."

"Believe it or no', lad, I'm hoping the same thing," Ian said. He rubbed his chin as Justin passed him into the hall, adding, "You should work on that right swing. Get some strength behind it."

Justin turned, gave him a hard look and said, "Actually, I'm left-handed."

The door was closed quickly enough in his face to finally give him a reason to smile.

18

"You're late, m'boy, and for once you really shouldn't have been," Henriette said the moment Lincoln walked into the parlor where the ladies in the house gathered each day for afternoon tea.

"My apologies," Lincoln replied. Though it wasn't his habit to take tea with them, and though he avoided the lower regions of the house altogether during the afternoon "calling" period, he was usually in residence just in case he was needed. "I was detained by an old school friend I haven't seen in years. He insisted on chewing my ear off about his travels. Did I miss anything in particular?"

"Indeed yes," Henriette said with a distinct tone of triumph.

And Edith added, "You'll *never* guess who paid us a visit today."

Lincoln's curiosity should have been piqued by then, but that seemed to be lacking these days, along with most of his other emotions. Ennui was an odd experience for him. Safe, if quite boring. And now that he'd acquired it, he couldn't seem to get rid of it.

"The queen?" he asked rather dryly.

"Don't be silly," his aunt admonished. "The Duchess of Wrothston was our esteemed visitor, and you simply can't imagine what an honor this was. She couldn't have timed it any better if we'd asked her to, since we already had several callers when she arrived, including one of *the* biggest gossips in town. *That*, m'boy, will put the topping to Edith's amazing success this season."

"You should have seen her, Linc," Edith continued in the same excited tone. "She's *so* socially adept. She completely took over our little gathering. No awkward silences around her, no indeed. She led the conversation and kept it going, right up to the end."

Eleanor was sitting there quietly, not sharing even a little in their general air of excitement, though that seemed to be a normal state for her. If she wasn't looking sad, she wasn't looking . . . anything. She apparently had far less emotion at her disposal than Lincoln's ennui was leaving him with. She was watching him, though, and somewhat intently, as if expecting something.

"I'm pleased for you, Edi," Lincoln said. He really was. He just wished he could sound like it. "Was Her Grace just making the rounds of her new acquaintances, or did she stop by for anything in particular?"

"No particular reason. At least, none mentioned. Of course they did ask after you and seemed somewhat disappointed that you weren't home."

"They?"

"Miss MacGregor was with the duchess. Oh, my, have we finally piqued your interest? Why else would I say you *should* have been here?"

"She actually came *here*?"

"Isn't that just what I said? And you shouldn't be so amazed. You *do* have female relatives, after all, making it perfectly acceptable for the women interested in you to come calling. Speeds up the courting process, indeed it does. Why, more'n half our visitors are ladies hoping to get better acquainted with *you*, m'boy. You really should make more of an effort to join us for tea."

"With her uncle?"

The question was too out of context for Henriette not to be confused. "Eh?"

"Was Melissa's uncle along?"

"Oh – no, they were alone, no male escort a'tall. Were you expecting an uncle? They did seem somewhat surprised when I mentioned that the duchess's son had been by to see you just the day before. I refrained from telling his mother about his . . . odd behavior," Henriette added in a whisper, only to finish quite loudly, "which *you* haven't even explained yet. Why *did* he try to hit you?"

Lincoln sat down in something of a daze, too many questions rolling around in his head at once – his own questions. As for his aunt's, he'd avoided any direct conversations since yesterday because he really didn't want to discuss Justin's visit, any more than he wanted to talk about Melissa's entire family showing up in London, which he hadn't mentioned either. His family knew that something was wrong, though not exactly what. They attributed his new silences to moodiness, but then his courtship of Melissa hadn't been going well from the beginning, which they also knew, and they probably assumed he was having another setback or two. What an understatement.

He hadn't wanted to talk about it, because to say it out loud – that Melissa's family wasn't going to allow him to marry her – would put a finality to it that he simply didn't want to face yet. Moving into a limbo of indecision instead wasn't helping, of course. He'd tried not to think about it. He'd tried to wash it from his mind with drink. He'd moved into a state of ennui that put his emotions on hold – as well as his questions. But this visit of *hers* most definitely cracked the ennui.

How in the hell did she end up being related to *them*? A sister, an unknown sister – bah, as if there weren't enough of them already. But he'd met the MacGregor, who was nothing like them. And this older sister of theirs obviously hadn't been raised with them, so she probably wasn't like them either. Melissa certainly wasn't like them. She was like no one he'd ever met. So as much as it would relieve his dilemma and help him to forget about her, he couldn't lump her into being "one of them."

"I suppose I should have mentioned this sooner," Lincoln told his aunt, "but it seems I have a closer association with Melissa's family than I realized, and not a good one. I don't have many enemies in this world, but the few I do have are all in the same family – hers."

"Rubbish," Henriette said in his defense. "Who could possibly not like you?"

"Nonsense," Edith agreed. "Or is it that *you* don't like *them*?"

"Melissa is related to the MacFearsons?" Eleanor guessed aloud.

He glanced at his mother, somehow not surprised that she would connect the word "enemy" to the MacFearsons as well. She'd been involved – to a degree. At least, she'd known about the conflict, if not what started it. And she was quite pale at the moment.

"Yes, the tribulations of childhood, coming back to haunt me – again," he said. He missed Eleanor's stricken look as he turned back to his aunt to add, "I had some major conflicts with that family when I lived in Scotland that haven't been forgotten or forgiven. Suffice it to say they've told me clearly to stay away from their niece. So her coming here doesn't make much sense to me at the moment."

"Perhaps she isn't required to follow their dictates?" Henriette said with a serious frown. "She might even be estranged from that side of her family?"

"No, one of those uncles escorted her here. When I first met her, she was with another of them."

"But you *did* have her father's permission to court her," Edith pointed out.

"I don't believe he knows about the conflict –

yet," Lincoln replied. "Though I'm sure they'll inform him at the first opportunity."

"I don't understand how something that happened so long ago can still bear such consequences."

Lincoln almost laughed, though there would have been no humor in it. "Oh, it can, Aunt Henry. To a great degree it shaped and molded me into the man I am today."

Which was nothing to be proud of, though he didn't add that aloud. How he felt about himself he would keep to himself. And he didn't dare look at his mother just then, when he held her mostly responsible.

Henriette sighed in disappointment. "I suppose she might have wanted simply to offer her regrets. You did have your mind set on her, after all."

Could the reason for her visit have been that simple? Yes, he supposed it could. Justin had probably told her about his visit. If Melissa hadn't known about her uncles' interference before, she undoubtedly did now.

"And yet," Henriette added thoughtfully, "the duchess brought Miss MacGregor here, and I find it extremely difficult to believe that she wouldn't have been informed of what's what in this matter, her being the girl's sponsor. In that case, this could be their way of telling you that you needn't abide by her uncles' dictates – or that they've changed their mind about you. Just saying so would have been *most* helpful instead, but . . . well, they might think you've changed your mind also, now that you know whom the girl is related to, so wanted to proceed cautiously, to avoid embarrassment if you have. Have you?"

It was a good thing Lincoln had years of practice in deciphering his aunt's convoluted way of getting her points across. He was able to answer immediately, "No, I haven't changed my mind. I might have implied otherwise to her uncles, but that was before I knew they were her uncles. But I did let this throw me."

"Yes, it *does* explain your being out of sorts this last week," Henriette sympathized. "What a dreadfully unexpected wrinkle."

Lincoln actually smiled. "I've called it much worse, believe me. And it still pertains that if she wants nothing more to do with me now, there's not much I can do to change that. But it's time I stopped thinking the worst and find out what Melissa thinks about all this."

19

Find out what Melissa thinks? Much more easily said than done. What Lincoln did find out, however, was that he was denied access once again to the Wrothston residence. This he had actually expected, which was why he hadn't come around sooner to have it confirmed. But he should have tried sooner, since the butler was quite informative now, possibly because he was himself annoyed over the restrictions placed on him.

He'd volunteered in a stiff, distinctly angry tone, "I have been warned, sir, that I will be shopping for a new nose, as the young Scot put it, if I let you past this door again. The young lady, however, is unaware that you are no longer welcome here and has requested that if you should come by when she's not here, I let you know her plans for the evening."

Lincoln now had Melissa's agenda for that evening and, checking with his aunt, even had an invitation to the rather large dinner party himself. That, of course, was no guarantee that he'd get to talk to her. If one of her uncles was with her, then he would be directly defying their wishes if he approached her, and that would lead to a distinct hell he wouldn't wish on anyone, much less himself.

Until he knew, without a doubt, whether or not she was going to abide by her uncles' wishes as well, he would be prudent not to give the impression he was thumbing his nose at them. However, if she gave even the slightest indication that she would still have him, nothing was going to keep him from her.

He saw her the moment he arrived at the dinner that night with his aunt and cousin. It was being held in a private home. He'd moved directly to the parlor while his aunt stopped to talk to the hostess in the hall. And there she was. He felt like a man starving, and Melissa's presence was a feast, filling him with all manner of sensations that were simply beyond his normal experience. He'd missed seeing her more than he realized.

She was across the room, talking with Megan St James. They seemed to be alone for the moment. Could he be that lucky? No . . .

"Leave, afore she sees ye," Ian MacFearson said at his side.

Lincoln turned slowly to the younger man, who was leaning against the wall. His defenses rose abruptly, as did an anger so acute he could nearly taste it.

None of which showed, however, when he asked with commendable calm, "What were you doing, guarding the door just in case I showed up?"

"Aye, actually, and no' the most pleasant duty either," Ian admitted in a surly tone. Then, "Dinna start this again, mon. Leave now."

Just like that? When Lincoln was so close to her he could call out her name and she would hear him? "I happen to have been invited here."

"Ye happen tae hae been asked tae stay away from Meli," Ian reminded him. "If that means adjusting yer own social calendar—"

"What difference?" Lincoln interrupted. "If she wants nothing more to do with me, what does it matter if we're in the same room at the same gathering? She'll ignore me, I'll ignore her. That is what happens when two people no longer have any interest in each other."

Ian's frustration was clear in his expression. "She hasna been told yet."

"So I was beginning to suspect, after being taken to task by young St James for ignoring her. Which leaves me in something of a dilemma that I'm sure you'll appreciate. You see, I happen to care enough about her to not leave her guessing, whereas you apparently don't."

Ian flushed with color. "She'll be told as soon as her da arrives."

"And when will that be? If it's not tomorrow, then you'd better do something about it – or I will."

Lincoln was so furious he was close to causing a scene. He turned to leave, before he did something he would regret. He had planned ahead, though, for just such an occurrence. If he hadn't, he didn't think he would have had the willpower to walk out without speaking to Melissa first. To have gotten so close to her . . .

He stopped long enough to tell his aunt that he was leaving and would send the coach back for them. She was astute enough to realize why, since they had discussed the possibility on the way there, so she didn't barrage him with questions. He also nodded to his cousin, giving her the go-ahead to carry out his contingency plan.

He'd written a note for Melissa ahead of time. Edith was to deliver it inconspicuously, or at least without Melissa's relatives noticing. He'd admonished her not to read it herself, for which she'd blushed furiously, which said clearly without words that she'd already been thinking about it. But she assured him thereafter that she wouldn't peek and wouldn't let him down, that she'd get the note to Melissa even if she had to drag her aside to do it.

Outside, he paused, took a deep breath. The night was warm, clear, a good night for a rendezvous. Unexpectedly, excitement swept immediately through him with the thought. This was going to be much better, he realized, than trying to talk to Melissa in a crowded room. He'd have her alone, to himself. If she came. There was the possibility that she wouldn't. It was asking much of her, was asking her to be clandestine, to do something highly improper.

Ordinarily she would undoubtedly refuse for just that reason. But she'd been left in the dark. She'd been left to wonder. He was counting on that to be the deciding factor. She'd have her answers. She wouldn't like them, but she'd have them. And he'd have his. One way or another they'd both know whether there was any hope for them after tonight.

20

Melissa actually considered climbing out the window of her bedroom, two stories up, when there was a perfectly good staircase just down the hall. But that merely showed the current condition of her mind, which was in a very odd state of confusion. She'd like to blame it on having spent yet again three hours over breakfast without eating anything, for the second day in a row, but today had just gone from dazed to worse.

The "worse" started when Justin showed up again before she'd left the small dining room where breakfast was served. He looked as if he'd only just got up. He looked quite agitated. He said as much.

"Didn't get much sleep mulling this over. Do yourself a favor, pay a visit to the Burnett ladies today. Take my mother along with you. Don't mention it to your uncle. And don't ask me why."

He'd said no more than that before he turned on his heel and was gone from the room. By the time Melissa thought to go after him for an explanation, he was nowhere to be found. But she was capable of reading between the lines, despite the cryptic nature of his suggestion. He knew something she didn't, but for some reason he wouldn't or couldn't tell her about it. She was likely to find out for herself if she paid the Burnett household a visit.

She spent some time berating herself for not thinking of a visit like that herself. And Megan was certainly willing to accompany her. But it hadn't gone as she'd figured it would, their visit to the Burnett household. Merely bad luck that Lincoln hadn't been home when they arrived, nor had he shown up before they left. At this point Melissa couldn't begin to guess. But something *did* come of it, or at least she assumed that the note in her possession now was a direct result of her visit.

Edith Burnett had slipped the note into her hand, without a single comment and when no one was watching them. Very secretive of the girl, but considering the note's contents, Melissa understood why.

Instead of calling on her in an acceptable manner, Lincoln wanted to meet her privately, late that night, without chaperonage. He was waiting outside for her at that very moment. The note said he would wait all night if necessary. A lovers' rendezvous? Nonsense, they weren't lovers. Yet this meeting had all the earmarks of just that.

What was she to think? She shouldn't think, she should just follow her instincts. And her instincts told her to meet him no matter what, if for nothing else than to find out why he'd changed his mind about courting her in the traditional manner she'd expected.

She'd never in her life had to sneak about for anything, though. It felt very wrong to do so. Still, she did it, tiptoed down the hall, down the stairs, around to the music room, and out the French doors there. Every noise she heard along the way stopped her cold and caused her heart to pound and her palms to sweat. She expected at least for the butler to be lurking around every corner. But no, the house was completely silent, except for her own footsteps.

Outside, the night was still as clear as it had been earlier in the evening. She saw his coach immediately, down the street out in front of the house, waiting in the shadows between lampposts. She found herself running toward it, whether in eagerness or simply to avoid detection, she couldn't honestly say.

It had been nerve-racking, the sneaking, which produced a number of illogical thoughts in her. One new thought stopped her in her tracks before she reached the large coach. What if Lincoln weren't it in? What if *he* hadn't sent the note to her? Someone else, someone completely unknown, could have given it to Edith and merely said to deliver it on Lincoln's behalf. A wild plot – to what end?

But the coach's occupant, whoever he was, had heard her approaching, or had been watching for her. He stepped out of the coach. The shadows didn't reveal him fully, though. He was the right height, the right build, but she just couldn't see his face clearly yet, so she remained where she was.

He waited, but he must have realized she wasn't coming any closer. He closed the distance between them, took her hand, said merely, "Come, before we're seen."

She'd follow him anywhere now that she knew for sure it *was* him. Ironically, all nervousness fled with that certainty, too. It probably shouldn't have. She should at least be leery of the reason for their meeting in this fashion. But she was too trusting. Some might see that as a fault. She didn't. And she was sure he'd have a good explanation. She was looking forward again to hearing it.

The coach was well lit inside, the windows tightly covered to contain the light. A tap on the roof, and the driver set off at a very slow pace, too slow to indicate he had a destination to reach.

Lincoln confirmed that by saying, "He'll drive about until told otherwise . . . I wasn't sure you would come."

Melissa glanced at him fully now, which was probably a big mistake on her part. It was so *good* to see him again, too good. Her first instinct was to throw her arms about his neck and tell him how much she'd missed him. She restrained herself. They hadn't progressed that far in their relationship for her to be that bold. Yet, oddly, it *felt* as if they had.

At any rate he was here, in her presence again. The thing that had kept him away was apparently resolved – or maybe not, considering the strange way they were meeting. But whatever it was, she was sure they could overcome it. If she didn't believe that, she'd be truly devastated at the moment, because he was looking at her again in a way that said clearly that he wasn't going to give up the pursuit.

That had been her main worry. And certain now that it was unfounded, she could relax. Calm was back, and with it her teasing nature.

So she *was* merely teasing when she said, "Is this how we're going tae proceed? One meeting every few weeks?"

"Not if I can help it."

Not a very promising answer.

"You're no' sure?" she asked, the teasing note gone from her voice.

He was looking too serious by half now, and he even sighed. "I have a lot to tell you, not much of it good. But before I go on, can I assume that you still have no idea why I haven't called on you?"

"Nay, none," she replied. "Was someone supposed to have told me?"

"Yes, at least in my opinion you should have been the first to have been told. And after my warning to your Uncle Ian tonight, you should have been told immediately. Surely before you reached home. But I suppose I wasn't taken seriously when I said that if they didn't enlighten you, then I would."

"You spoke with Ian tonight?"

"At the dinner you attended. I was asked to leave before you saw me."

"Och, you're right, this doesna sound good. I've been deliberately kept from knowing . . . what?"

"Why I've stopped courting you."

"Which is?"

She'd lowered her eyes, was holding her breath. His hand touched her chin, raised her face to look at him again. There was tenderness in his gaze.

"Not by my choice, Melissa," he said quietly. "I was asked – ordered would more aptly describe it – to stay away from you."

"By whom?"

"Your uncles."

She frowned. "You mean Ian?"

"I mean *all* your uncles."

"But where? How? They're in Scotland."

"No, they're here in London, all of them. Another thing they've kept from you."

"Did they tell you why?"

"There was no need to tell me. It's who I am. It's who they are. It's that we have history together, a rather violent history"

Her frown increased. "But Ian One said he ne'er heard o' you, that the only Lincoln he knew was the Ross lad . . . Och, nae, you're him?"

"So you were told about me?"

"Nae – I mean, aye, but only a brief tale tae explain why I should hope you werena the same lad."

"There are two sides to every tale. I'm sure the side you heard showed me at my worst."

She nodded with a wince. "I know why they wouldna want you courting me. They think you're crazy."

He managed a smile. "I probably did seem to be, back then."

"Could they no' see you're no' like that now?" she demanded.

"Would it matter to them? Once you define a person in your mind, that definition tends to stick. I think of them as savages. They think of me as crazy. There isn't much middle ground there."

"Nonsense. You were a child when you knew them before. Whatever you did then, you're no' likely tae do something like that now, aye?"

He didn't answer immediately, which was somewhat alarming. Was there more to it, then, than just simple actions?

She added hesitantly, "Perhaps I should know what it is I'm asking you tae confirm or deny."

He smiled at her gently. "Emotions, which so rarely come with guarantees. And memories, some of which are so vague and distorted I'm no longer sure if they were real or imagined. But, yes, you are due an explanation."

He was suddenly looking so full of dread that her compassion rose. "You dinna have tae speak o' it, if the memories are so painful."

"Are there any other kind?" he said with a half smile. Then, "Forgive me, that was biased and not even true. I do have other than bad memories, it's just that the bad ones have dominated a good deal of my life. If I sound bitter, it's probably because I am. But I'm not talking now just about what happened with your uncles. They were merely the start of it and the catalyst for the rest – but I digress."

Despite her curiosity, she tried once more to stop

152

him, because it was so obvious he didn't want to stir up such memories again. "Lincoln, this was sae long ago. Is it really necessary tae bring it all into the open again?"

"For you, yes. The truth is, I've never spoken of this in any depth with anyone before. My Uncle Richard, who raised me after I came to England, knew some of it but not all. Perhaps that was a mistake, to keep it all contained and to myself. But I do need to tell you about it, Melissa, and all of it. If it changes your mind about me, I'll understand."

And now she was filled with dread as well. If he thought she might change her mind, then what he was going to tell her was going to show him in as bad a light as it might her uncles. But could something that happened so long ago really have any bearing on today? She truly hoped not, but she wouldn't know until she heard it. So be it.

21

Melissa sat back in the coach opposite Lincoln. It was plush. The interior was spacious, would seat eight, perhaps even ten, very comfortably. But she wasn't comfortable. Neither was he. Their dread was contagious.

She sighed. "Tell me, then. And if you turn out tae be a monster, I swear I'll be really annoyed wi' you."

He blinked, then laughed. "Thank you. I *was* beginning to sound too serious, wasn't I?"

"A wee bit, aye," she mumbled.

"I'll try to keep this in perspective and not bore you with incidentals. You do need to get back before dawn, after all."

She rolled her eyes at him. He did seem a little more relaxed – less tense, at least – after such silliness. There was value to teasing – occasionally.

"Some background first, or it will seem very odd, my reaction to your uncles. You see, what I felt back then went beyond anger. It was more desperation, but there was a reason. I was left with a void in my life after my father died. I didn't lose only

154

him, I lost my mother as well, since I rarely saw her after his death."

"She went away?"

"No, she just wasn't available anymore. She tended to lock herself away in her room, where I wasn't allowed, to mourn in private, so I rarely saw her. Being an only child, I was left starved for companionship."

"You had no schoolmates?"

"I wasn't enrolled in the local school, it being so far from home. I had a tutor. An excellent teacher he was, but he was a dour sort of fellow who didn't encourage personal conversations. And then I met your Uncle Dougall. He filled that void, became my best friend – my only friend, really. I loved him. He became the brother I'd never had."

"Aye, I'd been told you were good friends wi' Uncle Dougi but that you started a fight wi' him that ended it. Why did you do that?"

"I didn't – at least, it wasn't intentional. We were at the swimming hole where we had first met – where I met you as well," he added with a smile.

She grinned, was relieved that she felt like grinning. "I know that my uncles had been going there for years. I didna know it was such a popular meeting place though."

"It wasn't, really. I never knew anyone else ever to use it, other than the MacFearsons and myself. That day there were four of us – two of his older brothers had joined us. They'd been talking about a fight they'd witnessed recently. Dougi was claiming he could do better. I teased him that his fists were the size of a girl's and would be better left to swatting flies. I was in the habit of teasing him. He was used to it. He usually enjoyed it and gave as good as he got. To this day I don't know why he took offense that time. The only thing I could reason was that it was because both his brothers had heard the remark and laughed over it. But for whatever reason, Dougi got angry and insisted on putting it to the test."

"So *he* started the fight?"

"If you can call his taking a swing at me 'starting it,' then yes," Lincoln said. "But not in my mind, because he couldn't do me any real damage. We were the same age, but in the two years I'd known him, I had grown a great deal and he hadn't caught up yet."

"Aye, Ian One said as much, that Dougi couldna have won the fight and you knew it."

Lincoln nodded. "I would never have fought him, no matter the provocation. My hands were up only to hold him off. I was trying to assure him I'd only been teasing, when he tripped and fell into me."

Melissa's eyes flared wide with the realization, "Dinna tell me he broke his own nose on your fist."

Lincoln blushed somewhat. "I know it sounds silly – sounds impossible, actually – and his nose *wasn't* broken. It had merely started bleeding. It was the worst luck, that he should fall at that exact angle, just as I was raising my hand to push him back, and his nose should connect with my hand. It surprised me more'n it did him. I was frankly

156

appalled and started to apologize, even though it wasn't my fault. I didn't get a chance to. The blood running down to his upper lip took the humor out of it for his brothers, and they both jumped me."

Melissa winced, but she offered, "If you knew them at all, that shouldna have surprised you."

"It didn't. It infuriated me, because I wasn't given a chance to set things straight with Dougi immediately, but it didn't surprise me. They were always quick to stick up for each other, especially the older brothers for the younger. I actually admired that – when they didn't take it to extremes. With me they took it to extremes."

"Perhaps because they saw it as a betrayal."

"I came to that conclusion as well, though not until years later. I don't know how I got home that day – at least, I have no memory of it. Because I was beat up pretty badly, for once I even had my mother's attention again. I do remember that, and I even let her coddle me in bed for a day. That was a strange mixture of feelings, being glad that she was noticing me again but angry that I had to get hurt for it to happen. Yet there was also an urgency. I still had to set things right with Dougi. And the urgency won out."

"So you sought Dougi oot, wi'oot giving yourself a chance tae mend first?"

"Tried to. Unfortunately, all his brothers had heard what had happened by then – their version anyway – and were up in arms about it. I got to see Dougi, though not alone. Four of his brothers stood there to keep me from getting close to him. Their attitude didn't make it easy to apologize, but I did so, only to hear them scoffing that I wasn't sincere. Whether Dougi believed them or not, he wouldn't accept my apology. And his brothers wouldn't even let me see him after that, to try again. Which was when I lost my temper with the lot of them."

"You didna think tae let the matter settle down first afore you tried again?"

"Do you really think that would have made a difference with your uncles?"

"It might have. It was at least another option tae try. But perhaps that didna occur tae you?"

"No, I admit I wasn't thinking very clearly at the time. I was devastated. As I saw it, I'd lost the best friend I'd ever had over some stupid teasing that had gone awry, and the rest of the MacFearsons weren't going to allow me to correct it. My rage over their interference just got worse and worse. And my mother added guilt to the issue, ordering me not to leave the house and to stay away from them, neither of which I could do at that point. It was paramount that I get to Dougi to make things right with him."

"Sae you felt guilt for ignoring your mother's directives, sorrow for the whole mess, and rage because m'uncles united tae keep you from fixing it. Aye, some powerful emotions tae be plaguing such a young child."

He gave her an odd look. "You make it sound so very simple."

She blushed. "Nae, I'm no' trying tae make the matter seem trivial, just trying tae picture what all o' that would do tae a young laddie."

"I wasn't complaining about your assessment, I'd just never looked at it from such a simplistic view myself. At the time, however, I wouldn't have been able to if I'd tried. There was also some pain involved – quite a bit, frankly – since I'd ended up with a few broken bones from that first encounter and a few more from the next. Looking back, I *know* that pain clouded my reasoning, but I just couldn't see it happening. To anyone else it probably did make me seem somewhat crazy. But in my mind I had a goal that *had* to be met, to get to Dougi, even if I had to plow through his brothers to do it."

She leaned forward until she could touch his hand. "Pain can do strange things tae you – aside from hurting."

He smiled at her. "I suppose it can. To be honest, my memory is rather vague on what happened after that. I'm sure I kept trying to see Dougi. I know there were more fights. I vaguely remember pounding my fists bloody on a locked door – I assume it was my own – and climbing out the window eventually, which broke another bone or two, because my hands hurt too much to be able to grip the sheets I'd tied together. I remember my mother crying over my injuries. I just don't remember which ones or at what point. But I probably could have brought tears to a stone by then, I was so beat up. I remember the pain being constant, that nothing would make it go away, and it was too great to even allow sleep. I think the lack of sleep may be why my memories are in such a jumble."

"But you did finally sleep?"

"Yes, if you can call being drugged sleeping," he replied sourly. "And for a very long time I was kept that way. He was a very gruff doctor we had, the only one available in that area. His motto seemed to be 'If you can't reason with a patient – then don't.'"

"For how long?"

"I have no idea, really, though when I finally came out of it, I was almost completely mended."

"But you could think clearly again after that?" she questioned.

"Oh, yes, and was met with the amazing news that I'd lost my home. I was to live with my Uncle Richard in England thereafter."

Melissa sat back with another sigh. It was impossible to miss the bitterness that had entered his tone. It didn't surprise her. To grasp everything that had occurred to him, and at such a young age – it was more than she could stomach.

"Perhaps that was for the best. Or were you done butting heads wi' m'uncles?"

He shrugged. "I'll never know. It wasn't something I had time to think about, when I was told as soon as I awoke that I'd be leaving the next day. It was apparently easier for my mother to ship me off than to deal with my problem."

"But what could she have done?"

"Got the matter resolved."

"How? You think she could've reasoned with the MacFearsons, when there's no Scot more stubborn than they are? They decided you were crazy, or capable o' crazy actions, which is pretty much the same, aye. You could've behaved like a saint from then on, but they wouldna have trusted you tae no' go crazy on them again, and for that reason they wouldna have let you near Dougi again."

"Is it because you're a woman that you're taking my mother's side? Or do you really believe that?"

She rolled her eyes at him. "Neither. I merely know my uncles. And I'm telling you, you could ne'er have left Scotland, could have lived there till now, just miles away from them, but they would've kept you away from Dougi. The only way you could e'er have talked tae him again would have been tae find him alone. And even if *he* forgave you and wanted tae go on as before, it wouldna have happened. They would have forbidden it, and then they would've been the ones fighting – wi' each other. Sae I'm thinking that if you couldna leave the matter go and forget you e'er met them, then 'tis better all around that you went tae live elsewhere."

"But I was never given a chance to make that decision. I can't say if I would have given up or not. But I'll never know, because I wasn't there to find out."

"Ah, sae *that* is the bitter root you still carry? No' that m'uncles put a wall 'tween you and Dougi, but that you werena there tae try tae break it down or no'."

He made such a sour face over her conclusion that she laughed. He might have taken offense, but he didn't. He even smiled at her.

"I rather like it that you aren't afraid to disagree with me," he said.

"Och, glad I am tae hear *that,*" she said with a show of exaggerated relief, then added seriously, "But there's nothing tae disagree about in this case. Hearing the whole o' it, wi'oot being one o' the participants, I can only guess at the causes. The ifs and maybes are redundant. What happened back then canna be changed. It happened. That it's come back tae haunt you in an unexpected way is what needs tae be discussed."

"Indeed," he agreed. "Being told who you are related to was a shock, but nothing in comparison to being told to stay away from you."

"I take it you've been abiding by their wishes?" she guessed.

He nodded. "Only because I assumed you'd been talked to as well and were in agreement with them. But when Justin paid me a visit—"

She cut in, "Ah, so that's why he suggested I call on your womenfolk."

"He didn't tell you why?"

"Nae. I can only assume he spoke wi' one o' m'uncles and was asked tae stay oot o' it."

Lincoln sighed. "Apparently. But what I cannot comprehend is why they would go to the trouble of seeking me out to warn me off, yet make no effort whatsoever to tell you they'd done so and why. Do *you* know why they would neglect to mention any of this to you?"

"That's easy enough tae guess."

"Then enlighten me, because it seems as if they

don't care what state of mind this has left you in, and if that's the case, then why do they care who courts you?"

She suggested, "You're letting your opinion of them color your assumptions. Tae answer why they might think it best no' tae mention this tae me, you should know that there were a few lads who showed up tae court me at home. M'uncles managed tae scare them off, no' intentionally, but the lads had heard the 'legend,' o' course. M'uncles could've merely looked at them wrong, and they'd have run for the hills. But because o' that – and 'twas only recent – they'd probably rather I didna know they'd done it again, this time intentionally."

"That's it?" he said incredulously. "They'd rather let you think the worst of me – that I could state my intentions and then proceed to ignore you – rather than simply explain why they don't think I'm the right man for you?"

"Well, there's also the fact that although I love them dearly, they have no real control o'er what I will or willna do," she replied.

"You mean you're not obliged to obey them?"

"That's a wee bit inflexible, tae put it that way. I'd hear them oot, o' course, and if they make sense, I'd likely agree wi' them. But when it comes tae the rest o' m'life, nae, those decisions are mine tae be making."

"And your father's? Your uncles seem quite certain that he'll change his mind about me and do some forbidding of his own."

She winced. She hadn't had time yet to think

how her parents would view all this. For that matter, *she* hadn't had time yet to mull it over, other than to consider her first instincts, which were that he wasn't crazy, just a victim of a strange set of circumstances that had got out of hand. But her uncles could be quite persuasive when they were all of them banded together in a common cause. Not that her father would bend under such heavy odds if he were of a differing opinion. But still, Lincoln would have to have something strongly in his favor for her father to support him against such odds.

22

"Your silence isn't very encouraging," Lincoln said with a great deal of disappointment. "I take it I won't like your answer?"

She hadn't meant to prolong his suspense or give him the wrong impression. But it had occurred to her that once again her uncles were going to keep him from a personal goal. Was the past going to relive itself? Would he butt heads with them again because of it? No, they were all adults now, and adults talked their way through such things, without resorting to violence. Well, they *ought* to.

"I willna lie tae you, Lincoln. I've ne'er in m'life disobeyed m'da. Ne'er wanted tae, ne'er felt a need tae. Sae ordinarily I'd obey him wi'oot question."

"Ordinarily?"

"Well, there's m'feelings tae take intae account. There's also m'mother's opinion, which has been known tae change his on occasion."

"Wouldn't she be inclined to agree with her brothers?" he asked.

"Nae, just the opposite." Melissa finally had a reason to grin. "She was raised English, which is no' tae argue wi' your elders, but anyone younger is fair game. And they're all younger than her, as it happens."

He chuckled. "I probably should disagree, since I was raised English as well."

"Go ahead, I'm younger than you – by all o' twenty years as I recall you thinking."

He smiled at the reminder of the teasing they'd done about her age when they first met. That particular smile, though, affected her senses in an extraordinary way. It made her blush – and feel other things. She almost wished he weren't so handsome. It was strange for her, having a man's looks disturb her in such unsettling ways.

It seemed to be contagious, too. Her reaction to his smile, being somewhat visible – truly, a lot visible – affected him as well. His expression softened, his gaze turned sensually admiring. She was reminded quite potently that for all intents and purposes they were completely alone. And she'd better stop thinking along *those* lines . . .

She quickly got back to the matter at hand. "M'da is a fair man, extremely so. He's been the MacGregor since afore I was born, and making decisions that have bearing on many, no' just himself. My uncles are reactionary, as I'm sure you know. They'll swing first and talk about it after. M'da is just the opposite. Probably because o' his great size, he tends tae give any conflicts careful thought first."

"He gets along well with your uncles?"

She chuckled. "Let us say he tolerates them.

Being wed tae their only sister, who they're pledged tae guard and protect no matter what, you can imagine he's had his differences wi' them, and no' just a few. They've had many fights, both physical and verbal, o'er the years."

"Now, *that* is encouraging."

She made a face at him. "Bah, dinna be thinking that's tae your good. As I said, he *listens* afore he reacts. He'll be hearing everything they have tae say aboot you, you can be sure, which I hope willna be anything more than what you've said yourself."

"I held nothing back. If there's more to it, I simply don't remember it."

"That's fine," she replied. "Having already heard the brief version from Ian One, I'm thinking there canna be anything worse tae add tae it. I'm also guessing it's your temper they're most worried about, since it got sae oot o' hand that it made you seem crazy. Have you had any problems wi' your temper since that time?"

He shook his head. "I tend to keep such feelings to myself now."

She frowned thoughtfully. "That's no' always a good thing, but . . . well, never mind. Tae keep tae the subject, though, I think you mun convince m'family that you're no' crazy, is all. And since *I'm* sure you're no' crazy, that shouldna be too hard for you tae do."

"Sure, are you?"

She noted his grin. She would have swatted him if she were more familiar with him. A few more

167

meetings and she wouldn't hesitate. She settled on a scowl.

"This whole thing is going tae come down tae perception on their part, and if you get your foot in the door, I dinna doubt a testing. Your temper will be under close scrutiny by one and all, since it is the bone o' contention. Now you've told your side wi'oot once raising your voice and wi' only a couple sour looks, so I'm thinking you've outgrown any wild tendencies you may have once had. But I havena tried tae provoke you. Dinna doubt m'uncles will. And how will you be holding up under such fire?"

"With several buckets of water at hand."

She stared at him, then burst out laughing. "Aye, Mr Scot turned lordly English, I'm thinking you'll do verra well – that's assuming you get let in the door again. You can be sure I'll be having words wi' m'uncles that they willna like, o'er their high-handedness on m'behalf. But I've a feeling they'll stand by their decision until m'da gets here tae say otherwise. In the meantime—"

"In the meantime," he cut in as he sat forward, his elbows on his knees in a relaxed manner. "My problem, as I see it, is, how am I going to get you away from your despicable uncles to continue my courtship, short of abducting you?"

"Abducting, eh? Why is that no' sounding a frightful experience?"

He grinned and reached forward to caress her cheek. "Would you like to be . . . abducted?"

Now she knew they were talking not about

abducting but something entirely more intimate, and her pulse was racing as if he'd said the real word he meant. Somehow he'd just gotten far too close to her. She could smell him, could see the minuscule gold flecks in his brown eyes that made them not quite so ordinary. And though his fingers on her cheek were hot, nor did he remove them.

She had no idea what she would do if he suddenly kissed her. And then she found out. No question about it, she was kissing him back.

She was thrilled, just like the first time, but able to enjoy this kiss more. Without the fear of discovery that had been present before, she was able to relax, experience more fully the taste and feel of him. But she didn't stay relaxed for long. Hot, determined, wicked his tongue was. And too many were the sensations it evoked.

He was sharing the same seat with her now, and holding her close. She hadn't thought this would happen. The possibility had been there, surely, but they'd had too many things to discuss first. They were done with that for the moment, but nothing had been resolved and wouldn't be until after her parents got to town.

She could hope for the best, but her future wasn't guaranteed to include this man. She wanted it to, she really did, but the odds were currently against it. And the thought came, wickedly, that to make love with him would definitely better those odds – if her parents found out about it. Not a very fair way to go about it – rather underhanded, actually, not to mention highly embarrassing – but in desperate situations desperate measures could be examined.

Now there was no time to examine anything, though. They both got carried away very quickly, and it became a matter of need rather than decision.

Melissa stopped thinking about it. She was too caught up in the pleasure of his touch. He began innocently enough, caressing her cheeks, her arms, and, when she was too deeply involved in the kiss to notice at first, her breasts. But she did notice, and quickly. How amazing. She could touch her own breast and feel absolutely nothing. He merely rested his hand there and her heart slammed beneath it. And when he squeezed, ever so gently, there was a corresponding tug in her belly – and then lower.

Her breathing became deeply labored. The sensual tension was mounting fast, too fast. She had a fistful of his hair in one hand, and her nails were digging half-moons into his neck with the other – probably all the encouragement he needed to move his hand on to even more intimate regions. Her long skirt was hiked up by degrees as he cleared a path, and the sudden scalding heat of his palm on her bare thigh set off a wealth of coiled churning deep in her core.

And then he stopped.

It took her a while to realize he'd gone perfectly still, had removed his hands from her skin, was just holding her now, albeit a bit tightly. Her breathing calmed down somewhat, but her thoughts began a frantic whirl.

Had she done something wrong? Was her inexperience more than he wanted to cope with?

It was probably going to embarrass her terribly, but she had to ask: "Why did you stop?"

"Because I want your father to have a good opinion of me, not want to break my neck."

He'd tried to inject a light note into his voice, but his own breathing hadn't quite calmed down yet. "Is that the only reason?" she ventured.

"No. Because I want to do this right. And stealing your virtue before I'm absolutely sure that I'll be allowed to make you mine would make me the worst sort of cad. It's my intention to marry you, Melissa, not dishonor you if the unthinkable should occur and you be forbidden to me."

Such warmth filled her heart, she wanted to squeeze him until it hurt. If the unthinkable should occur. Well, she simply wouldn't let it.

23

Melissa was amazed, looking at the clock in her room when she got back to it that night, that it was no longer night, that dawn would be arriving within the hour. Of course, Lincoln hadn't taken her right home after deciding he wouldn't dishonor her. He had been loath to end what would probably be their last moment of privacy for a very long time. She'd been equally reluctant, for that matter. So they spent some time just talking about the things young couples talk about when getting better acquainted – which included no further mention of her family – and holding each other.

The holding part was so very nice. He took pains to keep it impersonal. If they thought about any more kissing, they kept these thoughts to themselves. Though he did kiss her good-bye, and very passionately, before he gently swatted her behind and pushed her toward her door.

She wasn't exhausted, however, even after being out all night. She still had too many things on her mind. So she was quite surprised to find she had fallen right to sleep as soon as she climbed into bed, and not a bit surprised that she didn't wake until noon.

Dressing hurriedly, she went immediately in search of her youngest uncle. She found him having lunch in the formal dining room and not alone. Justin was there as well. They'd been arguing, or at least Justin had been raising his voice, since she'd heard him from down the hall.

They sat at opposite ends of the table. It was a very long table. That could be why Justin's voice had been raised, but she doubted it. When they noticed her arrival, they fell silent, both offering her a smile as if they hadn't just been scowling at each other.

"I'm verra glad your mother isna here tae witness this, Justin."

He blushed to his roots. "We were merely having a difference of opinion."

"I dinna mean that, I mean this," she replied and picked up a very pretty flower arrangement in the center of the table to throw at Ian.

Her uncle leaned out of the way of it. His reflexes were very good. Fortunately – at least in her opinion, though probably not in his – there were other things at hand, and a plate went flying at his head next. He ducked that, too, and was on his feet by then, raising his hands toward her in a conciliatory manner.

"Now, Meli, I can guess what this is aboot, but if ye'll be giving me a moment tae explain—"

"Two seconds you have, until I reach that water pitcher," she huffed.

"I wanted tae tell ye!"

"Did you? Well, since you ne'er got around tae it, that doesna count for much, does it now?"

"It was Ian One's decision!"

"As if I havena figured that oot? And since when do you do everything he says?"

"When he makes sense."

"Och, sae there was sense tae this?" she said, crossing her arms while she glared at him. "Verra well, I'm waiting tae hear it."

"He's a mon capable of severe violence, Meli. There's no way we could allow him tae continue courting ye."

"Severe, eh? D'you realize the same can be said o' you and every one o' your brothers?"

He blushed. "There's a difference. We've ne'er gone crazy like he has."

"Rubbish," she replied with a snort. "He's no more crazy than you or I."

"He has no control o'er his temper."

"I've yet tae see him angry. But I've seen every one o' the MacFearsons demonstrate a fine temper. Does that make the lot o' you crazy?"

"Ye dinna know what he did," Ian insisted.

"Now, there you're wrong," she returned. "I do know. He told me, all o' it, which, as it happens, is probably more'n you know."

"But was it the truth?"

"Do you realize it doesna matter, Ian? He's no' like that now."

"Ye canna know for sure, Meli, that it willna

happen again. How could we trust him wi' ye, knowing what he's capable of?"

"Sae you thought tae protect me? That's fine. That's acceptable. I even thank you for your intentions. But I'll ne'er forgive you for no' explaining that tae me and giving me a chance tae find out if your protection was warranted or no'. Do you ken what it's like tae want tae see someone sae bad, you canna think straight? Tae listen for and get hopeful at every footstep you hear, then die inside a wee bit when they dinna belong tae who you'd hoped? Tae wait and wait, unaware that you're waiting in vain? *Do you?*"

"I *told* you it was too late," Justin said to Ian in a half-accusatory, half-smirking tone. "She's already in love."

Melissa rounded on her younger friend and spared a glower for him as well. "I'll be getting tae you next, Justin St James, since I know that *you* were also aware o' what they'd done and didna share that wi' me. But I'll be hearing from m'uncle first, about why I'm the last tae know about what they've been up tae on m'behalf."

"We thought it for the best," Ian said. "We took into account that yer da isna here yet tae put his foot down, and that ye might be doing as ye please in the meantime. Yer running off wi' him was one o' our fears. We also wanted tae prevent ye getting any more attached tae the mon, sae it wouldna hurt sae much that ye canna hae him. And when did ye see him, tae find oot aboot all o' this?"

"I snuck out in the middle o' the night like a common criminal!" she said hotly. "But what other choice did you leave me, when you prevent him from courting me in the traditional manner?"

"Ye saw him alone?" Ian demanded, red-faced, imagining the worst.

Melissa narrowed her eyes on him. "Aye, and he was the perfect gentleman – for the most part."

"What do ye mean, 'for the most part'?"

"I mean there was some kissing, which I would've started if he didna, since I absolutely adore his kissing. And dinna be preaching tae me about what I can or canna do, Ian. I'm going tae marry that mon."

He shook his head at her. "I dinna hae the heart tae deny ye, hinny," he said, giving her a moment's hope before he added, "I'm going tae fetch Ian One."

"Gather all the reinforcements you need," she grumbled. "You're no' going tae change m'mind. And dinna think m'da will side wi' you either. He wants me tae be happy – unlike the rest o' m'family."

"I'm thinking he'd rather ye be safe."

24

Lincoln didn't try to delude himself that Melissa's uncles would see the error of their ways and back off from the stance they'd taken. They'd given him warning. He'd ignored it, had even told the youngest Ian that he would. Melissa had also said she'd be talking to them, so there'd be no doubt in their minds that he'd defied them.

He expected them to retaliate – and soon. He was braced for it. He even stayed away from home the next day because he didn't want his family to witness the ensuing violence. Knowing the MacFearsons, he anticipated nothing less than the worst from them.

He left word where they could find him, though. Avoiding them was out of the question. Oddly, he was even looking forward to the confrontation. He couldn't win, he knew that. There were simply too many of them. But they weren't going to escape unscathed either.

It seemed as though he'd been preparing most of his life for this one confrontation. He was in supreme condition. He'd sought out some of the best fighters in the realm over the years to teach him their tricks. Never again was he going to be at such a disadvantage, as when he'd last butted heads with the MacFearsons. He'd made sure of that, even though he'd never really expected to run into them again.

Three or four at a time he could take on easily now. More than that, though, and he'd succumb to sheer numbers – which was how the MacFearsons fought. They didn't know the meaning of the word "fair."

Ah, well, he'd go through it as many times as he had to, if it meant Melissa would be his in the end. That was, *if* he survived. There was always the chance he wouldn't.

They showed up at his private club late that afternoon. He'd bored himself most of the day playing billiards with a couple of the older regulars, so he was actually relieved when the MacFearsons got there. They couldn't get inside, not being members, but he was informed of their arrival and went outside to meet them.

Only half of them had come. Well, eight was still a few too many to handle, but only a few, since it seemed only the younger MacFearsons had come, though the youngest Ian and Lincoln's ex-best friend, Dougall, weren't among them. The elders *were* getting a bit old for this sort of thing, he supposed. But the younger brothers were more likely to lack the skill, at least up to his standards, which was something in his favor.

So as not to draw too much notice, he was

going to suggest they adjourn to a sporting club, since there happened to be one handy just down the street that should still be open, even though evening was approaching. Londoners frowned on public exhibitions of fisticuffs in their streets. The streets in good neighborhoods anyway.

Lincoln never got a chance to open his mouth. He was pushed, shoved, and otherwise tossed into the large coach they'd brought along. They had a plan, apparently, and it didn't include playing nice. Before they were done, he was bound hand and foot, gagged, even blindfolded, and left to stew on the floor of the coach at their feet.

Amazingly, they'd said not a word to him, nor did they even after he was fully trussed and helpless. He gave them credit for surprising him. Considering their numbers, underhanded tactics like this weren't called for and hadn't been anticipated. But they *did* have a plan, obviously, since they would have been arguing about what to do if they didn't. They just weren't sharing it yet. And whatever it was, he knew instinctively he wouldn't like it.

It was perfectly natural, as the hours passed, for Lincoln to start imagining the worst. They'd bribed a jailer to toss him in prison and keep him there, and they were just waiting for the rest of the prison to be asleep before they snuck him into it. Who, after all, listened to a prisoner's plea of innocence? Or . . . they'd already dug a hole somewhere and were going to summarily execute him and cover him up in it. They were just having trouble locating it now that it was getting dark.

Tying him up was one thing, merely a way to keep him from fighting back. But the gag? Simply because they didn't want to hear his opinion of what they were doing? Or didn't want anyone else to hear him? The blindfold also wasn't necessary to restrain him. In fact, he couldn't think of very many reasons that one would be needed. So he couldn't see where they were taking him? So he couldn't see who was helping them, if anyone was? More likely so *they* couldn't see the extent of his fury.

Oddly, he wasn't angry – yet. Uncomfortable, yes. A bit worried, certainly. But mostly curious. This just wasn't like them. They never avoided fights. If they wanted to do him serious harm, they were more apt to do it with their fists. If they merely wanted him out of the way so they didn't have to deal with him anymore . . .

Wherever they were transporting him, it was taking a very long time to get there. Scotland came to mind. They could be taking him to their home to confine him there indefinitely, he supposed. They were a close-knit clan, after all. None among them would question it. And they could keep him confined until Melissa forgot about him and married someone else.

Or perhaps they weren't actually leaving the city. He was reminded that he'd had his driver circle around last night with Melissa, just to be on the move, not to get anywhere. They could be doing the same thing, simply to kill time. But he'd lost count of the hours. His best guess would be that it was nearing midnight, or even later. And waiting until the wee hours of the night couldn't bode well for him. It meant secrecy was needed, because whatever they were about wasn't lawful.

They still hadn't spoken, not once, not even to argue among themselves, which wasn't a good sign either, since they liked to argue among themselves. He would almost think he'd been left alone in the coach if he didn't occasionally hear the shuffling of their feet.

His own feet had gone numb, his hands, too, tied behind his back. Lying facedown, his cheek against the cold floorboard, he probably had a few splinters by now from being jostled by the occasional deep rut.

When the coach finally came to a halt, he stiffened – and soon regretted it as life came back to his sleeping limbs. He was pulled out of the coach and helped to stand on his feet, but only for a moment. One of them tried to get him up onto his shoulder to carry him, but that didn't work out well. Some were as tall as he was, but most weren't as hefty. He was solid weight and muscle, and broader than any one of their shoulders could manage.

He was put back on his feet clumsily, but not to be untied so he could walk. He was lifted by two of them now, feet and shoulders, and they were even having trouble with that because of his weight – and his unwillingness to make it easy for them. But they carried him along for a while, and finally they were no longer outside. The abrupt end of a salty breeze he'd felt indicated that.

He was thankful for being indoors, wherever it

was. He'd been able to smell the water on the way. Though he couldn't tell if it were river or ocean, he had seriously thought he was going to be dumped into it. That would certainly solve the problem, as they saw it, that he presented. And he wouldn't be able to do a damn thing to save himself.

But they weren't murderers. He hadn't *really* thought they were. Savages, yes. A law unto themselves, yes. But though they wouldn't hesitate to join forces to beat him to a pulp, they drew the line at killing – at least intentionally. Accidentally, on the other hand . . .

Whatever he was laid down on was hard, but not solid hard, and not flat. It was rather lumpy actually. He waited to be untied. He wasn't. And he could hear them leaving. They had delivered him and were just going to leave him, still trussed up. Without any explanation. He had an idea now where he was – the sounds around him were rather distinct – but no confirmation was forthcoming from them.

But one of them was still there. He tsked, and said in a complaining voice, "Ye wouldna listen, arranged tae see Melissa anyway, though we warned ye tae stay away. She's here tae get herself wed. We're here tae make sure it isna tae ye. Wi' any luck both will be accomplished afore ye find yer way home. Pleasant sailing, Linc."

More hours passed. Lincoln slept at some point. He'd been left completely alone, closed into the hold or storeroom of some ship. His bed could be sacks of grain or flour. In London Harbor or some harbor down the coast, he had no idea which. And what was going to happen come morning? Would he be released and put ashore at the next port of call?

Not by the sounds of that parting comment. Nor by the remark of the fellow who showed up at some point late the next day to let him out.

It was a storeroom he'd been dumped in, rather than the hold. Fewer rats to contend with, at least. And the chap had apparently been paid to assist in his being shanghaied. Whether the ship was short of crew or not, Lincoln was going to be added to its ranks.

"There's no point in complaining about it, so don't," he was told by the big lout as he was untied. "We're at sea, on our way to China. You won't be seeing land for several years. Get used to it, mate. Do your work like the rest of us, and you might even get to like it. It's a healthy life, that of a sailor."

With all restraints gone, and feeling finally returned to his limbs, Lincoln got to his feet and decked the fellow. *Now* he was angry, but it was contained, like the quiet before the storm.

25

"We took care o' it."

Ian One was greeted with this announcement as soon as he left his dressing room. In the short time it had taken him to have his morning bath, all his brothers had arrived in his room for breakfast as they usually did. No stragglers, though. They'd apparently collected each other on the way there so they'd show up together.

"Breakfast?" he hoped Charles meant.

"Nae, Lincoln."

He'd been afraid of that. Charles had sounded too smug with his remark. But he wasn't the only one yet to be informed of how they "took care o' it." Half his brothers were staring at Charles, waiting to hear more.

"How?" Ian asked simply.

"Ye dinna want tae know," Neill said. "I tried tae talk them oot o' the plan they'd settled on, but they'd no' listen tae me."

"*What* did ye do wi' him?" Adam demanded in an alarmed tone.

"It's no' what ye're thinking," Callum offered quickly. "He's still alive."

"Then what did ye do?" William asked.

"Sent him tae China."

"I'm really hoping ye mean a china shop, though I wonder why I doubt it," Ian Three said dryly. "D'ye e'en know where China is?"

"On the other side o' the world, ye dafty," Ian Two added. "And though that may no' sound sae far away, it takes years just tae get there."

"Exactly, that *was* the point," Callum replied.

"He *agreed* tae go tae China?" William exclaimed, his expression incredulous.

"Well – no. We didna exactly ask him."

Charles, who wasn't one to hedge, bragged, "We tied him up and delivered him tae a ship scheduled tae sail with the morning tide, sae he's oot tae sea by now. Any ship would hae served the purpose, but we just got lucky finding one departing for China. Did it wi'oot a single bruise, tae," he added in a mumble.

There were several groans before George said, "Och, God, ye'll be looking o'er yer shoulder the rest o' yer lives now, cause he'll definitely kill ye for that."

"What the devil could ye be thinking, tae do that tae a mon, e'en him?" Adam added.

"It was better than beating him senseless, which was what Charles wanted tae do," Malcolm said.

"I'd rather be beat senseless," Ian Two replied with a scowl.

"Sae would I," Ian Three agreed.

"And whose brilliant idea was this?" Adam wanted to know, glaring at each of his younger brothers in turn.

"Mine," Jamie admitted, looking rather shame-faced by that point.

But Ian Four put in quickly, "In Jamie's defense, Linc happens tae like sailing. He's mentioned more'n once he'd enjoy the life of a sailor, sae Jamie didna think he was doing Linc that much harm."

"But for those – like us – who dinna like it, it'll be pure misery," Adam said. "George was right, he'll be killing everyone o' ye when he gets back."

Ian sighed and sat down on the edge of his bed. He'd gone to talk to Melissa yesterday, after Ian Six had apprised them that she'd spoken with Lincoln. He'd taken several of the eldest brothers with him. It wasn't that he felt he'd have trouble dealing with a lass young enough to be his daughter, but he hadn't felt completely comfortable with his decision to keep her in the dark and had merely wanted his brothers' support on that issue.

He came back from that meeting angry, not at her but at himself, because he saw her point. They should have told her who Lincoln was as soon as they found out. She would more than likely have agreed that it was better to let sleeping dragons alone and just move on. And Lincoln would have stayed away, because her family didn't approve of him and she was in accord with her family. He *had* been staying away – until he found out she didn't know the reason. So Lincoln had sought her out because he wanted her to know why he wasn't coming around. They should have told her, if only to keep him from telling his side of it, because he obviously had her full sympathy now.

And hearing a bit more of his side of it, from her, Ian was beginning to wonder if they hadn't made a serious mistake all those years ago. Lincoln's temper *had* gone beyond reason. Dougi *did* need protecting from it. But not one of them had thought to ask why he'd gone off the deep end. Not that they would probably have done anything differently, but they could have been less forceful about it.

"I canna say I'm no' glad to have the matter done," Ian said with another sigh. "Those o' ye who decided on this will tell Meli what ye did. It'll be a long time afore she forgives ye, but at least she'll agree now tae forget aboot Lincoln Ross. Three tae four years is too long tae wait for a mon tae show up tae finish a courting. When, or if, Linc does return, we'll hae a new problem, but at least our niece willna be part o' it. I'm thinking we can go home now and let her finish what she came here for."

"Ye're taking this awful calm, Ian," Adam said, voicing what most of them were now thinking.

"Nae, I'm anything but calm," Ian replied. "But I'm also glad tae hae the matter oot o' m'hands for the time being. I'm thinking Kimber will be laying into me for letting this get oot o' control, and Lachlan will likely take his fists tae me for the same reason, but I'll deal wi' that as it happens. The fact is, I wasna looking forward tae another feud wi'

Lincoln. The first one went beyond good sense, and no' just on his side but ours as well."

"Ye would've done nothing, after he defied us and spoke wi' her anyway?" Callum asked.

"He'd been abiding by our wishes because he *thought* she was in agreement wi' them. He defied them only because he found oot she'd been told nothing aboot it."

"What did Meli hae tae say aboot it?" Johnny questioned. "Ye came back from talking wi' her yesterday and didna say much."

"Because I had a lot tae think aboot," Ian said. "And because she'd agreed no' tae speak wi' him again until after her da arrived tae settle the matter. Sae there was no hurry for any action."

Jamie blushed guiltily. "I'm thinking ye should hae told us that."

"I'm thinking I should've, too. But the reason I'm glad it's no longer an issue is Meli still wanted him for her mate, despite what we had tae say aboot him. And she was confident that Lachlan wouldna deny Linc's suit, after he heard the whole of it."

"Ye think that's possible? Wi' as crazy as Linc once was?"

Ian shook his head. "Nae, she would've been sorely disappointed. Lachlan is no slouch in protecting his own. Though she thinks the past has no bearing, he'd see it otherwise."

"Ye're sure that's no' just wishful thinking on yer part?"

"Ye know better. Wi' e'en the slightest possibility that the mon could go crazy again, Lachlan wouldna turn his only daughter o'er tae his care."

"I'm sure we'll be finding that oot soon enough," Ian Two put in, with another disapproving look sent toward Jamie, before he added, "No' that it matters anymore, wi' Linc now oot o' the picture."

Jamie blushed yet again but said defensively, "I thought it was a bloody good plan. It settled the matter. He's gone, and gone for long enough that she's no choice but tae forget him. She'll be wed and wi' several bairns, no doubt, afore he gets back tae cause any more trouble. And she'll be thanking us someday."

"Ye're dreaming if you think she'll e'er be thanking ye for having her mon shanghaied," George said. "And that's how she sees him, ye ken. In her mind he's already hers – or he was. But at least there's that. She *does* hae no choice now but tae forget aboot him."

26

It was much easier to rant and rave at her younger uncles than it was at the elder group. When Ian One and those of his brothers closest to his age showed up later that day, after Melissa had lit into Ian Six, she'd known she would be at a serious disadvantage. They reasoned with her just as her father did, calmly, with assurance that they were right and she was wrong. She'd been forced to listen to them, especially after they began by apologizing for not telling her everything to start with.

When the younger bunch of brothers showed up the day after, she was expecting more of the same from them – apologies first, then the reasons they thought Lincoln wasn't a good choice for her. She'd already decided that she wasn't going to repeat herself, at least until her father showed up. She'd already told Ian One that although his concerns were sound, she simply didn't, nor ever would, believe that Lincoln Ross Burnett was capable of hurting her.

She did have some doubts now that her father would see her side of it, though. *I'm thinking he'd rather ye be safe.* She hadn't been able to get that parting remark of Ian Six's out of her mind.

Ian One had pretty much said the same thing, reinforcing those new doubts. She hadn't counted on seeing Lincoln again before her father showed up. He had agreed to stay away until then. So she wasn't going to have any further opportunity to bolster her certainty, to counter theirs. And she expected to hear more of the same now from her younger uncles, which was only going to intensify her doubts. With so many of them set against Lincoln, it was seriously daunting, the thought of changing their minds.

Her first clue that this meeting with her younger uncles wasn't going to be as she assumed came when she arrived in the parlor where they were waiting to find Ian Six going about the room, gathering every object that might be throwable. She raised a brow at him in question. He blushed but continued to pick up a few more items – and then couldn't figure out where to put them all so they'd be out of her reach.

In a teasing gesture, she held out her skirt, forming a deep pocket, indicating that would be a good place. He gave her a stern frown. She shrugged, leaned back against the doorframe, crossed her arms in a relaxed manner. He decided simply to hold on to the items for now.

"Well, then, who's tae be the spokesman today?" she said nonchalantly.

They were all contained in one area of the room, filling up the two sofas and two chairs in the center grouping of furniture. It was a large room, though. There were three other, smaller groupings, each with several chairs along with a table and lamp, spread about the room. These were designed for more private conversation, far apart from each other. And there were still more single chairs set here and there, just in case a large crowd showed up.

After posing her question, her uncles glanced at each other for a moment. One by one, they all pretty much cast their eyes down, silently telling each other they were passing the buck. Neill realized with chagrin that he hadn't been quick enough to lower his own eyes.

Melissa grinned at her second-youngest uncle because he just happened to be the shyest of the lot. "So it wasna decided ahead o' time, and now you're elected by default, eh?" she teased.

Neill lacked confidence in himself. He knew it, his brothers knew it, yet not one of them spoke up to get him out of this fix. Which, come to think of it, was quite alarming in itself.

All humor gone, she gave him a steady look and said, "Just say it."

He nodded, cleared his throat. "Ian One ordered us here, and rightly sae, tae make a confession. We've done something we're no' proud o', on second thoughts, though we had the best intentions."

" 'We'? As in . . . ?"

"Just those of us here."

"Correction," Ian Six put in, giving Neill a

baleful look for starting off in error. "I wasna part o' this, Meli, nor would I hae been had I known o' it. Only just heard aboot it m'self. But I'm thinking ye should sit down afore more is said."

She came away from the door, stiff now with dread. "I dinna want tae hear this."

"We wish ye didna hae tae hear this either, but it has tae be said."

"Nae." She shook her head, repeated adamantly. "Nae. Go back tae your hotel — back tae the Highlands for that matter. There's no reason for you tae be here any longer. I already told Ian One that I'd let m'da decide the matter."

"But our older brother, in his *infinite* wisdom, neglected tae mention that tae us," Charles said in his typical sarcastic fashion. "All we knew was that Linc scoffed at our warning tae stay away from ye and sought ye oot anyway, and something had tae be done aboot that."

"But that was your fault, for no' telling me tae begin wi', what you'd done," she replied. "Lincoln felt that *somebody* should've told me, and rightly so."

"Aye, we're sorry for that," Johnny offered.

A few more of them piped up with the same, but it was too late for apologies on that score, when they'd apparently done something much worse. Or was she simply letting her imagination run wild? They could just be so guilty about that oversight that having to add a little something to it now was too much in their minds.

She sighed and moved farther into the room, sat

down between Ian Five and Callum on the first sofa. "So tell me, then, what did you do now?"

Complete silence and more downcast looks. She stiffened again. Was it so bad that not one of them could get the words out?

Ian Six, not sharing their guilt, didn't have a problem ending the suspense. "They had Linc shanghaied on a ship bound for China. They paid a crewman to make sure he canna leave the ship at any ports it stops at on the way. Sae he'll be making the complete journey, which can last from two tae four years – or longer."

She stared at Ian Six, then at each of her other uncles in turn. Not one, other than Ian, would meet her eyes. Ian apparently believed what they'd told him and what he'd just shared with her. She didn't.

"This is a joke, right? You just want me tae think he's gone sae I'll forget about him. You found out he had tae leave town for some reason, and you're using that. I canna believe you'd lie tae me like this."

There were so many hot blushes after that, the temperature in the room rose a notch. "It was my idea, Meli. I take full blame," Jamie said, looking miserable.

"Yours, was it? But you're all here, so you all were in agreement, and I havena heard the end of the story yet. I'm still waiting."

Ian Four and Neill, sitting on both sides of Johnny on the other sofa, nudged him to speak up. At thirty-two, he was the oldest there at the moment, and they figured if she'd believe any of them, it would be him.

He didn't like being put on the spot, however, so his tone was a bit surly as he said, "Ye were right on one count, Meli. Ye know verra well we wouldna lie tae ye." She started shaking her head, but he had more to say. "No real harm has been done other than showing Linc a life he'd probably ne'er thought tae pursue. It's a grand experience, going tae sea, according tae Jamie, who'd like tae do the same. And since yer da would hae forbidden ye tae wed the mon anyway, we've assisted ye in getting o'er the notion o' having him that much sooner. It's done. No one was physically hurt, which is what it would've come tae wi' Linc defying us. Which is no' tae say we dinna regret doing it. We didna give it enough thought, or take into account just how furious Linc will be."

Melissa's mind went numb. They'd put him out of her reach. They'd decided the matter for her, when they didn't have that right.

27

When Ian Six reported that Melissa had locked herself in her room and wouldn't speak to anyone, even the duchess, the MacFearson brothers began to fight among themselves. Their arguments came close to blows on several occasions. Charles came under the most fire, since no one was able to stomach his sarcasm when tempers were already short. Guilt turned them all defensive.

Ian One took it upon himself to visit Megan St James and explain to her what had transpired, so she wouldn't worry unduly over Melissa's seclusion. Receiving a severe tongue lashing from that beautiful, if formidable, lady had put him in a foul mood again.

He'd mellowed in his older years, but it was hard to tell that week. And although he should have sent a detailed letter to Lachlan, because of his mood, he was very brief in the missive he sent off, telling him merely that they'd interfered with Lincoln Burnett's courtship of Melissa and suggesting that Lachlan come to London sooner than planned, since she was upset about it. He didn't include a note to his sister. He was really not looking forward to explaining to her what they'd done.

Because they expected Lachlan and Kimberly to show soon, the brothers elected to stay in London for the time being – to face the music, so to speak. They spent a lot of time at the St James residence, waiting, or at least hoping, that Melissa would get over her shock and come down to rail at them, and *before* her parents arrived. They deserved it. It would be good for her. And she could then get on with having her season – and Lachlan and Kimberly then wouldn't be quite as furious with them.

The duchess tolerated them in her house and after a few days even began inviting them to dine with her, since they seemed at such a loss for what to do with themselves. She was still too annoyed with them to invite them to be her houseguests for the duration, but she made a small effort to entertain them, gracious lady that she was. They *were* Melissa's relatives, after all, though at the moment the poor girl was probably wishing they weren't.

They were having dinner with her tonight, had almost finished, when the butler arrived to say, "An *un*expected guest, Your Grace." Then, to Ian Six, "If you even *look* at my nose, Master Ian, I shall quit my post, which is likely to annoy the duchess."

Megan glanced at the youngest MacFearson, who was already starting to blush, and said, "Yes, extremely annoyed, as it happens."

His blush got much worse, but no one noticed,

because the mentioned "visitor" now stood in the doorway – filled it with his large size, actually – and had everyone's attention. Silence reigned. Shock had a way of doing that.

Megan was least affected. She left the table, cordially offered her hand to Lincoln Burnett. "You're back? Somehow that doesn't surprise me in the least. But you will avoid . . . disturbing my furniture while you're here, won't you?"

It was an order, not a request. No fighting in her house under any circumstances.

Either way Lincoln would have replied, "Yes, Your Grace," and did.

"Very well, I'll leave you to your business, then," the lady said and with a signal to the butler, who had hoped to witness the ensuing theatrics and was disappointed that he wasn't going to be able to, left her guests to iron out their numerous differences.

The silence continued, probably because Lincoln's expression was completely inscrutable, giving them no clue to the degree of his rage. He looked fit, no worse for wear, but that could be deceiving.

William was the first to break the uncomfortable spell, remarking, "Och, Linc, I'm amazed tae say I'm actually glad tae see ye."

"You'll forgive me if I doubt that," Lincoln replied quietly.

William chuckled. "I *did* say I was amazed."

Callum wasn't amused, but he did reiterate, "Actually, I'd say we're all relieved that a mistake we made got rectified somehow. Sae, aye, for that reason alone, we're glad tae see ye. It has nothing tae do wi' anything else."

Lincoln accepted that explanation with a nod. "I have an aunt and a cousin who depend on me. Did you even think to inform them that you'd arranged for me not to be around for a number of years? Or were you going to leave them to wonder indefinitely over my 'disappearance'?"

Ian One answered, "I sent them a note, that due tae a lack o' good judgment on the part o' several people, ye were sent tae China for a number o' years. Ye havena seen them yet tae find that oot?"

"I only just got back a few hours ago. I wanted to know if I would have the authorities to deal with or not, in case they had reported my absence."

Ian nodded. "They may not have believed the note and summoned the magistrate anyway. Are ye implying ye'd rather no' deal wi' the authorities o'er this?"

"It's a personal matter that I'd as soon keep that way," Lincoln replied.

They'd thought as much, knowing him, or thought at least that having the law to answer to hadn't been one of their worries. His retaliation was, though, and his display of calm was making more than one of them nervous.

"Ye didna like the sea at all?" Jamie asked with genuine curiosity.

"Is he serious?" Lincoln said to no one in particular.

"Aye," Adam replied. "It was his idea, 'cause he has a hankering tae sail."

"Then he should have got on that ship instead," Lincoln replied simply.

"I'm wishing I had," Jamie mumbled.

"How'd ye know we'd be here – or was it Meli ye came tae see?" Johnny asked.

"I gave my word that I'd stay away from Melissa until her father arrives. Whether you believe it or not, I tend to keep my word."

"Had *some* of us known that ye had agreed tae stay away, we wouldna be having this conversation right now," Malcolm said with a frown sent toward Ian One.

Ian One explained to Lincoln, "Melissa did inform me o' that. Whether I believed it doesna matter. I'm afraid I wasna quick enough tae let the rest o' m'brothers know."

"Which exonerates no one," Lincoln replied in the same quiet tone. "Be that as it may, to answer your question, I went to your hotel first. It took me less than an hour to find your name in the register. I had a feeling I'd find you here. I assume that you haven't told Melissa about the little trip you planned for me?"

"Nay, we told her," Ian four said. "She's taken to her room e'er since."

Lincoln shook his head in disgust, the first bit of emotion he let show. "You don't tell her when you should but do tell her when you shouldn't. Is there no end to the idiocy that runs in your family?"

Usually the MacFearsons wouldn't stand for an insult like that. Usually they'd all be leaping to their feet and swinging fists almost immediately. Not one of them moved, however, likely because they'd said as much to each other more than once in the last few days.

"Frankly, it will be m'pleasure tae let her know ye somehow cut that trip short," Johnny said. "How did ye, by the way? It's only been five days."

"I was put ashore in France. I would have been back sooner, but it took an extra day to find a harbor with a ship departing immediately for London."

"Aye, but how'd ye talk yer way off the China-bound ship?"

"A bit of extreme luck that you picked a ship captained by an old schoolmate of mine. I'd only just run into the chap a few days prior to hear how he'd taken to the sea. He was rather put out that one of his men was taking on crewmen against their will. Almost dumped the fellow overboard."

"We still canna let ye court our niece, but ye're due retribution if ye're wanting it," Adam remarked.

Lincoln surprised them by saying, "I want none."

"Then what are ye doing here?" Ian Four asked warily.

"I spent quite a few boring hours on that ship with nothing to do but consider my options. Dealing with my bride-to-be's parents is expected, part of the process, as it were. Dealing with the rest of her relations is not. And there's only one thing that you MacFearsons actually understand. So here's an address," Lincoln said, tossing a card onto the table. "Be there tomorrow morning at nine, the lot of you. I want you off my back."

28

Curiosity prompted the MacFearsons to arrive early at the address they'd been given. The name of the establishment would have given them a clue – or not – to what Lincoln had in mind, but it hadn't been included with the address. A sporting hall, complete with a roped-in ring for fighting matches and three sides of the large room filled with benches to accommodate a great many spectators. There was also a training room with an assortment of equipment in it and another room for fencing. Out back was an archery range. They arrived so early, at 8:00 A.M., that they were there long before Lincoln, and even a few minutes before the owner of the place arrived to open the doors. But they were informed, grouchily, that they couldn't enter unless they were there to rent the hall. Apparently it was rentable at a hefty fee between the hours of eight and noon each morning, for the use of discerning gentlemen who preferred to train in private, then open to the general public for the remainder of the day.

They guessed that Lincoln planned to rent the

place, so, rather than wait outside for him, they paid the fee. They also guessed that he'd gone crazy again. To invite them, or rather insist they come to such a place, could only mean he meant to take them all on again. They even began to relax. Dealing with the crazy Lincoln was actually much easier than dealing with the quiet one that had showed up last night. He should have been foaming at the mouth. He should have been railing at them. That he'd shrugged off their blunder just wasn't . . . natural. At least for him.

However, they had time to discuss what they were each expecting and how to handle it. The brothers spread out on the benches, some sitting backward to face the rest, some stretched out, since there was lots of room. Ian Six even fell asleep. He wasn't used to getting up so early, being on the "season" night schedule since he'd come to London.

"We should refuse tae fight him," William said to start the discussion.

"That's been tried. It doesna work."

"He was a child when it didna work. He might be made tae see reason now."

"Him?" Said with a snort.

"I've no desire tae hurt him. I feel bad enough aboot the shanghaiing."

"Sae do we all, but what are we supposed tae do when he starts throwing punches, eh? If you havena noticed, he's no small laddie now. I've no desire tae get m'self hurt either, trying tae keep him from getting hurt."

"Is there something else he could hae in mind in a place like this?"

About seven naes came in answer, but Ian Three suggested, "He could be verra good at fencing and have guessed correctly that none of us are."

"Tae take us all on is crazy or stupid, which doesna say much for him thinking of an advantage like that, does it now?" Charles replied.

"Linc isna stupid," Dougall remarked in his ex-friend's defense.

"Exactly, and crazy folk dinna think of advantages," Ian Three said.

"There's crazy and there's desperate," Malcolm pointed out. "Hae you considered he just wants Meli sae much he's willing tae try anything?"

Charles scoffed, "He hasna known her that long tae want her that much."

"What's time got tae do wi' it?" Callum wanted to know. "Malcolm didna say 'love,' he said 'want.' Personally, I've ne'er wondered if I want a lass or no'. If I do, I'm knowing it immediately."

There were a few chuckles before Malcolm added, "Aye, but there's more'n that involved, when ye're wanting a lass for wife, as he wants our Meli. If he was only lusting after her, we wouldna be having a problem. She would've told him tae get lost, and that would've been the end o' it."

"I wish that was all he was wanting," Ian Two said. "Then I'd hae good reason tae smash his face in."

"And ye dinna now?"

"Nay, 'cause he's done nothing tae warrant a

good face-smashing yet. In fact, he's been doing everything *right*, more's the pity. E'en making sure Meli knew what was going on was the right thing tae do."

"We've been trying tae avoid fighting him, which may hae been a mistake," George said. "Gives him the impression we're no' serious."

"I know Linc," Dougall put in. "He merely wants tae deal with her da, no' all o' us as well."

"But will he listen tae Lachlan?" Ian Five asked. "I'm guessing he'll still try tae pursue Meli, e'en if her da turns him away."

"Guessing isna productive," Adam said. "Until that actually becomes a fact—"

Adam was nudged to silence as their nemesis came through the door. Lincoln had already removed his coat, had it hooked on a finger over his shoulder. With his other hand in his trouser pocket, he looked too nonchalant, certainly not a man anticipating a serious beating.

When he stood below the benches where they had gathered, Johnny was the first to ask, "Sae what's this aboot, Linc? Ye canna be thinking o' taking us all on again."

"Can't I?"

"Ye're fighting for her?"

"Correct," Lincoln said.

"*All* of us?" Ian Five wanted clarified.

"Yes – but there's a catch," Lincoln replied. "We're going to use the ring here, but there'll only be two of us in there at once. Line up if you like, pick your own order. The only time anyone else comes into the ring is to carry the loser out if necessary. And I'll have your word on it. One at a time. There's no excuse for ganging up on your enemy now, no disparity of age or size as there was when we were children. To do so would be cowardly, and you know it."

"Let me get this straight," William said. "Ye're willing tae fight each o' us, one after the other? Ye're no' asking for a break tae recover?"

"I won't need it."

There was a round of laughter. Ian One cut it short, saying, "Ye realize how crazy this is, Linc? Ye willna last verra long. Sae what's the point?"

"The point is, you lose, you bother me no more. I'm willing to pay for that in blood."

"We'll likely be going home as soon as the MacGregor gets here," Johnny pointed out.

"He's not here yet, so that's not soon enough for me," Lincoln replied. "And besides, I'm not talking about the immediate future, I mean permanently. I never want to see any of you again, for any reason – ever."

"Now, that's an unrealistic expectation, for a mon who wants tae marry into our family."

"Not unrealistic at all. I live in England. You stay in Scotland. We all live happily ever after."

Ian Six had been poked awake when Lincoln arrived, and he chuckled now. "That would be fine wi' us, if ye're giving up on Meli."

"I'm not."

"I didna think sae," the youngest Ian continued. "But what ye havena found oot yet, or just havena considered, is how close she is tae her family. E'en if the unthinkable should happen and ye manage tae marry her, ye canna keep her away from her relatives for verra long. And I'm no' saying they willna stand for it. *She* willna herself."

"I didn't say I'd try to keep her away from her parents," Lincoln replied. "You MacFearsons, however, would never be welcome in my house."

"Enough talk," Charles said in an annoyed tone. "Let's just oblige the mon and get this o'er wi'. And ye start, Ian Two. That will put an end tae this nonsense afore it gets messy."

Lincoln smiled and climbed into the ring. His smile unnerved a few of them. Sending in their best fighter first was a good strategy. Lincoln even knew that Ian Two was their best fighter. It should have put a dent in his confidence, but if it did, he wasn't showing it.

They faced off in the ring. There was no one there to start the match – or break it up. Ian Two was known for quick, brutal jabs that could demolish an opponent within seconds. Lincoln never gave him a chance to get one off. Few of them even saw the blow to Ian's throat that laid him out flat on the floor, it was so swift.

"Next?" Lincoln said.

Johnny was angry enough now to climb into the ring, while another brother pulled Ian Two out. "Sae ye mean tae fight dirty, eh?"

Lincoln grinned. "Is there any other way against the lot of you?"

"We'll be on tae yer tricks soon enough," Johnny said with a snort.

"We shall see, won't we? Now, are you going to fight me or bore me to tears?"

Johnny raised his fists, but the blow came in a wide arc and caught him squarely on his ear. The pain was momentarily excruciating, dropping him to his knees. He was coherent enough – just – to roll quickly out of the ring before any more blows fell on him.

Ian Five climbed in next. He was Lincoln's age and a few inches taller. He said not a word, was more prepared, went immediately on the offensive. He landed the first blow to Lincoln's cheek, which staggered him back. That gave him the advantage, but he lost it when Lincoln plowed into his belly, headfirst, and tossed him over his shoulder. Ian Five landed hard, winded, dazed for a second, and didn't even see the punch coming that finished him off.

George entered next. Thirty-three, he was a little overweight due to his new wife who spoiled him with extravagant cooking. That, added to his normally stocky build made him a hard one to topple. So Lincoln went for the area George had recently been pampering, his belly. He had to land a few blows, though, to set up the punch to where it would be least anticipated and so do the most damage. It worked. Bent over, breathless, George was at his mercy. Lincoln didn't bother to finish him off, merely signaling for someone to help George back to the benches.

Dougall surprised everyone by moving to enter the ring next. Neill tried to stop him but was shrugged off. Many wore a worried frown. This was the pairing that had started it all, the two friends who had been so close. Lincoln's expression turned inscrutable for a moment, but then he actually grinned – whether with real humor, though, it was hard to tell.

"So you think you can do more'n swat flies with those fists now, Dougi?"

Hot color began to climb up Dougall's cheeks, but his loss of consciousness kept it from getting very far. The blow had been incredibly fast. Dougall had seen it coming but hadn't been able to block it in time.

"If his nose isn't broken, it wasn't for lack of trying," Lincoln said, and then he looked directly at William, who had been there that eventful day at the pond, to add, "And be sure to tell him when he wakes up – *this* time was deliberate."

The remark managed to get most of the brothers angry. They even argued over who would be next into the ring, each wanting a piece of Lincoln now, all guilt forgotten for the moment.

Anger might work against some men, making them careless. It was usually a good tactic to use, to get your opponent enraged to the point of stupidity. That wasn't the case here. An angry MacFearson was a man who ignored pain, as Lincoln found out during the next four rounds. If he didn't get in a lucky early punch to knock each of them out, or at least disable them, then he started taking some serious blows himself.

Lincoln was no stranger to pain, though. And he had such self-discipline he could almost will himself not to feel it. However, the damage he was taking was still wearing him down, not in clarity of thought so much as in simple exhaustion. The irony was that, just as before, there were *still* too many of them. He'd defeated nine, but with seven to go and its becoming an effort just to get his fists up now, his confidence that he could finish this was pretty much gone.

And he still had to fight Ian One, who appeared to be saving himself for last. The eldest MacFearson brother was no clod when it came to fighting. He hadn't been the one they all deferred to just because of his age. He wasn't as fast as Ian Two, but he was known to hit twice as hard due to his heftier build.

Charles was up next, the wisecracker, the one voted most likely to get his mouth smashed. Even his brothers were known to have that urge on occasion – well, quite frequently, actually. But Charles got lucky. He landed a blow to Lincoln's left eye, which was already half swollen shut from another punch he'd taken there. It dazed him for a moment, letting Charles get in two more solid blows, one to Lincoln's midsection, one to his jaw. Lincoln recovered enough to retaliate by grabbing the hair on Charles's temples to slam his head down on the knee he shot up to meet it. The maneuver didn't smash his mouth, but it did knock him out.

After that round, Lincoln needed a few minutes – or more – to get his mind clear, but he'd called it himself. No breaks. And although he was willing to go until he couldn't stand on his feet any longer, the anger he'd incited in them had petered out enough that when Jamie reluctantly started to climb into the ring, Ian One stopped him.

"I'm thinking we're done, Linc, if ye are," the eldest told him. "Ye got much, much further than any o' us expected. Ye dinna see us laughing now. But enough is enough. There's no point in going on, when ye canna finish it. Show some reason this time and admit defeat."

"Defeat? No, I don't admit defeat until I am defeated. But I do admit this wasn't such a good idea after all and, yes, enough is enough. Dare I hope that at least those of you who lost will go home now?"

Ian One chuckled. "Now, that's pushing it, when ye didna really win. But afore ye change yer mind, recall ye were told that we'd be going home soon as the MacGregor gets here. That could be today. He's due."

29

Melissa was still too angry to feel just relief. Megan had brought her the news last night, that Lincoln had returned to London. She wouldn't have believed it if one of her uncles had told her. But the duchess wouldn't lie to her. Lincoln was back. The last five days could be forgotten. But they wouldn't be.

Her shock had lasted only a couple of days. The anger had set in after that, so much that she didn't trust herself to speak to anyone. And rather than test her willpower to keep from saying something she'd regret, she had remained safely locked in her room, speaking only to the maid who came by with her meals each day.

Continuing her season had been out of the question. Even to think of marrying someone else just then, when it was Lincoln she wanted . . . well, maybe in a few years, but definitely not now.

She had finally decided to go home, had actually been packing for it, when Megan told her that Lincoln was back. She'd given up hope herself, another reason she'd been so angry. She was usually optimistic, could see a bright side to just about anything. Not this time.

But Lincoln was back. She now had to worry again about butting heads with her father over him – that was, if he still wanted her after what her family had tried to do to him. And she couldn't even blame him if he wanted nothing more to do with her. Another reason she was still so angry. She had no idea where she stood now, nor would she know, until she saw him again.

She should try to find out. She'd said she wouldn't see him until her father arrived, but that was before her uncles had decided to act like barbarians.

She was debating whether to visit the Burnett ladies again as she went downstairs for lunch. Seeing Ian Six coming in through the front door almost turned her around on the stairs. He noticed her, moved to the bottom of the stairs to wait for her. She stiffened, glared at him, and continued down the stairs and on to the dining room.

He didn't take the hint, or perhaps he simply chose to ignore it. He followed behind her, remarking in a chipper tone, "Ye're still no' talking tae us?"

"Nae," she said as she took a seat and nodded to the servant waiting to serve the meal.

"It ended lucky, wi' Linc managing tae get off that ship afore it sailed too far," Ian reminded her as he took the seat across from her.

"Lucky for you," she mumbled.

"Why? If ye're no' talking tae us, there's no' difference, I'm thinking."

"Because I'd no' be talking tae you e'en more if that wasna the case."

"Ah." He grinned at her. "Put that way, I see yer point more clearly. If it's any consolation, he got revenge on some o' us. Though since ye're no' talking tae me, I guess ye dinna want tae hear aboot it."

She ignored him. She'd said too much to him already. If he weren't her friend as well as her uncle, she wouldn't have said a word.

"Now, that's commendable willpower ye're showing, Meli," he commented cheerfully after a few moments of silence. "Ne'er seen the like."

"Oh, shut up and tell me."

He laughed this time before he replied, "Ye're a veritable font o' contradictions today, lass. But as it happens, we all o' us met Linc at a sporting hall early this morning – at his request, mind you – where he proceeded tae make short work o' more'n half of us."

"How badly was he hurt?"

Ian rolled his eyes over her first concern. "Ye should be asking how badly yer kin were hurt."

"At sixteen-tae-one odds, I dinna think so. How badly was he hurt?" she repeated.

Ian snorted. "Barely a'tall, which canna be said for some of us."

She raised a brow at him, pointing out, "You're looking fit and too amused. I take it you werena in the half that got beat on?"

"No indeed. Lucky for me, he gave up the notion o' defeating us all afore it was m'turn."

"Your turn?" She frowned. "Sae this wasna him against all o' you at once?"

"Nay"

"Bah, why'd you no' say that tae begin with?" she admonished him. "You had me picturing a grim repeat o' what happened years ago."

"It was nothing like that," he admitted. "Though his intention was still crazy, tae take us on, one after the other, wi'oot any respite. Had he suggested one of us a day, that would hae been reasonable."

"But would you have agreed tae that?"

He considered it for a moment, then replied, "I dinna see why not. In sixteen fights the odds are still that one of us gets lucky. No' that it matters. He called it, proving he's just as crazy as e'er."

"Nonsense. It was actually the honorable way tae do it, if he was determined on revenge. No surprise visits tae catch any o' you alone. Even if he didna expect tae win, he made his point."

"Och, now, that's just it, he *did* expect tae win. And in fairness tae him, I should mention he *claims* it had nothing tae do wi' revenge, that he wanted no retribution for his wee boat trip."

"Then what?"

"It was for ye," he said in a scoffing tone. "Or rather tae get us tae back off sae he could finish his courting wi'oot our interference."

She ignored the tone, gave him a brilliant smile. "Was it?"

"Bah, none o' us believed that, Meli. We e'en told him we'd be going home as soon as yer da got here, which could be today, for that matter. Sae there was no point tae his fighting us, other than he wanted tae inflict some suffering for what had been done tae him."

"No' if you look at it from his point o' view. He sees no' just one but sixteen men standing in the way tae what he wants. He's still got m'da tae deal wi', which is daunting enough. But here's sixteen others, and doing things unthinkable like shipping him off tae China. Aye, you better believe he'd consider getting rid o' you and your brothers o' more importance than any revenge."

Ian frowned, conceding, "When ye put it that way, I suppose he might've been speaking true."

She nodded pertly. "Who did he defeat?"

He named off the names. Her eyes widened over a few. "Ian Two?"

"Aye, in one punch."

Her eyes widened a lot more. "Really?"

"Dinna look sae amazed. That was his strategy and, come tae think of it, the only thing that would hae made it work, tae take us each oot in short order, afore he took tae much damage himself. Had there been a few less of us, he would hae fought tae the end, I dinna doubt. But he was running oot o' steam wi' seven of us tae go."

"And that's the mark of a sane man, tae retreat when you know you canna win," she said triumphantly.

Ian snorted at her. "I ne'er said he didna hae his sane moments."

"Bah, you. I *told* you he's no' like the child anymore. Admit you're trying tae see things in him that just are no' there now."

"The only thing I'm admitting is it was a pleasure tae watch him in action today. He's become a damn fine fighter. Unfortunately, that's another mark against him."

"How?"

"Because now it's no' that he might hurt ye if he should lose control. He showed us all today he could well kill ye if he e'er took one o' his fists tae ye."

She stood up, furious with him again, and snarled on her way out the door, "If, if, if! I refuse to live m'life based on ifs, Ian. Tell *that* tae your brothers."

30

Kimberly was annoyed with him. Well, in truth, steaming mad would better describe her mood. Lachlan had tried to cajole her out of it, but that didn't work. Which didn't surprise him. Concern for Melissa could make her very unreasonable, and she was very concerned after they'd received Ian's note.

She had wanted to leave for London immediately to find out what was going on. He'd already adjusted his schedule to accommodate their planned trip the following week, had crammed everything that needed doing into that week, including several important meetings. The soonest he could leave would be the end of the week. That wasn't soon enough for his wife, which was why she was mad at him.

She had even started to leave without him. He put his foot down about that, which only made her madder. Unlike her, he wasn't that worried over Ian's note. It was probably no more than some silliness, the same as had happened at home when they'd chased off Melissa's first suitors. Lincoln

Burnett wasn't like them. He'd met the man, liked him. And he knew that Kimberly's brothers could and most often did overreact. Whatever was bothering them about Lincoln Burnett could be worked out, he didn't doubt.

But that wasn't Kimberly's concern either. It was that Melissa was upset. That was the key word that had set her off. Her anger with him was nothing compared to her present anger with her brothers. They'd let their protective instincts get out of hand. They all shouldn't have gone to London. Only Ian Six was to have been Melissa's escort. And this time they'd upset her baby. Whatever they'd done, they shouldn't have done it, and she was going to make sure they never did it again.

She'd said all that before she stopped talking to Lachlan. It had been an uncomfortable journey south. He sighed every once in a while. She ignored it. His Kimber all stiff, prim, and glaring was usually an amusing sight. He just didn't like it when she got angry with him for something that her brothers started. A most frequent circumstance over the years, unfortunately. So he wasn't too pleased with them at the moment either.

He'd often wished Kimberly's father had never gathered all his bastards under his roof. Separate, they would've been rarely heard from. Banded together, they were a distinct pain in the backside.

Kimberly's mulish expression didn't change even when they rolled into London that afternoon. However, she was showing some signs of renewed impatience the closer they got to the St James residence.

Ironically, they arrived to the sound of laughter – a lot of it – including Melissa's, which they easily recognized. Hearing it, Lachlan gave Kimberly an I-told-you-so look. She snorted at him and moved toward the parlor, where the laughter seemed to be coming from.

The duke and duchess were there, along with their son, Justin, plus Melissa and Kimberly's youngest brother, Ian. Devlin St James had been regaling them with a few of the more amusing mishaps that had occurred during his long trip across Europe. He'd apparently only just arrived home himself.

Melissa squealed in delight when she noticed her parents standing in the doorway, and she rushed over for hugs and kisses. Ian Six was looking for the nearest exit, but they were blocking it. Only Lachlan noticed his obvious desire to be gone and wondered about it.

There was a round of greetings. Megan remarked in an aside to her husband, "What perfect timing. I was afraid you would get involved in the drama of Melissa's courtship, but with her parents here now, you won't have to."

He raised a brow at her. "Why would I want to?"

"Because it's quite a mess. Her suitor, Lord Cambury, is severely outnumbered by her uncles, and I know how you love to champion the underdog."

"I could have sworn that your sponsoring of her was to have been a simple matter."

The duchess winced. "It was. But how was I to know that all sixteen of her uncles would come to town and start undoing my good efforts?"

While Megan filled Devlin in on what had transpired during his absence, Kimberly pulled her daughter aside, asking in a whisper, "You're not upset anymore?"

"I am," Melissa said with a contradictory smile.

Considering the smile, as well as the laughter they'd walked in on, Kimberly couldn't be faulted for assuming, "Then it's not really serious?"

"It is."

Kimberly's brow knitted in confusion. "So you're just taking a break from being dejected?"

"Nae, I was just expecting you to show up soon, and I was thinking everything would be fine once you did."

Kimberly rolled her eyes. "I'm glad you have such confidence, Meli. I could have used some of it myself this week. Now, what's this all about? Ian's note said only that you were upset and that he and the rest of my brothers were the cause of it."

"They've been busy, your brothers. Ian Six figured out that they knew m'Lincoln personally, e'en though it's been nineteen years since they've seen him. He let the rest of them know, and they all came tae town wi' their prejudice firmly in place. They've no' given Lincoln a chance tae show them he's no' like the lad they once knew."

"What is it they have against him?"

"They think he's crazy or, more precisely, capable o' going crazy. That he seems perfectly sane doesna matter tae them. They're basing their objections on ifs. *If* he gets angry, he could go crazy again. *If* he goes crazy, he could hurt anyone in his path, including me. And now that they've seen him fight and how good he is at it, they've changed that tae *if* he goes crazy, he could kill me."

Kimberly was seriously frowning by then. "What led to all these . . . ifs?"

"That thing that happened nineteen years ago. I've heard both sides o' it and can see how it got out o' hand. You and Da should hear Lincoln tell it. And I'm sure your brothers can't wait tae be giving you their account."

"Are they talking real crazy?" Kimberly asked. "Or just seems crazy?"

"O'er the deep end for real, tae hear them tell it," Melissa said in disgust.

"I think I'd rather hear you tell it."

"Nae, tae be fair tae them, I'm biased. I've heard it all, and I still want Lincoln for m'husband. But tae give you the gist, your brother Dougi was Lincoln's best friend back then – his only friend. His da had died, his mother secluded herself because o' it, so Dougi was all Lincoln had in the way o' companionship. But that ended when some teasing atween them went bad. Dougi took it wrong and started a fight that more o' your brothers finished."

"Bah. Now, why does that sound just like them?"

"Because it is just like them. And they beat

223

Lincoln pretty bad. That should've been the end of end. It would've been for them. It probably would've been for Lincoln, too, 'cause he knows how they are. But they wouldna let him set things right wi' Dougi. And that's when it got out o' hand, because in his mind Dougi was all he had."

"Out of hand how?"

"There were a lot of fights, wi' Lincoln taking on more'n one o' them at a time and getting hurt worse and worse. He wouldna stop trying tae get tae Dougi. But they blamed him for that first fight and felt they had tae protect Dougi from him. He was angry by then, but in so much pain he doesna remember e'en half of it. Sae aye, he probably did seem crazy, when all he was was desperate to make things right wi' Dougi."

"How did that end?"

"He got sent tae England, where he's lived e'er since," Melissa said.

"So he never set things right with Dougall?"

Melissa shook her head. "Your brothers make a good solid wall when they've a mind tae."

Kimberly sighed. "Aye, I know it. And how does your Lincoln feel about it now?"

"Bitter," Melissa replied with a sigh. "He apparently lost his mother o'er it as well, since she stayed in Scotland when he was sent off tae live wi' her relatives. I dinna think he's forgiven her for that."

"So he hates them all?"

"If he didna hate them when they all showed up here just tae tell him he couldna have me for his wife, he probably does now."

Kimberly winced, knowing her brothers, and asked, "What'd they do?"

"Aside from no' telling me that they'd warned him off, sae I was waiting and waiting for Lincoln tae get on wi' courting me, and didna know why he stopped coming around, they had him shanghaied, actually dumped him on a ship tae China."

"Shanghaied!" Kimberly exclaimed.

Ian Six bolted out of the room upon hearing that, so when Kimberly turned around to pin him with a baleful look, he wasn't there to receive it.

Across the room Lachlan excused himself from his chat with Devlin and came over to his wife and daughter to ask, "Is there something I should know about?"

Kimberly was too incredulous to answer him immediately. Melissa didn't answer either, at least not his question. She put her arms around his waist, hugged him, and said, "After you've heard it all, Da – and you will as soon as m'uncles find out you've arrived – keep in mind that their worries are no' based on anything current but on the past. And keep in mind, too, that Lincoln Burnett is the only mon I'm wanting tae wed. I've heard both sides. I trust m'instincts, that he'd ne'er hurt me. But I'll abide by your decision. At least – I hope I will."

31

"D'ye realize that Melissa actually said she might no' obey me?" Lachlan grumbled to Kimberly as they changed clothes for dinner that night, the first moment they'd had alone together since they arrived. "Ye did hear that? I wasna imagining it?"

"Do *you* realize that she's been with us only eighteen years, but in all likelihood she'll be with her husband three times as long at least?" Kimberly replied.

"And what has that tae do wi' it?"

"Everything, or at least it puts the matter of 'husband' at a higher priority in her mind."

"But she's ne'er disobeyed me, Kimber. No' once, no' ever."

"Of course she hasn't. She's a good daughter. We couldn't have asked for better. But this is the rest of her life we're talking about. And it's not as if we'd disown her if she didn't do as we say, like my father – or rather – who I thought was my father – threatened to do to me. And besides, put yourself in her shoes— Well, maybe not you, since you weren't all that eager to marry me—"

"I was."

"You weren't," she insisted. "The decision sort of took you by surprise. It wasn't something you thought about for the longest time."

"Kimber, dinna ye dare tell me I didna want tae marry ye. Once I realized I did, getting ye wed was all I could think about."

"Faugh, you didn't let me finish. I was going to say 'at first.' Which is neither here nor there. My point was, what would you have done if a parent – yes, I know, yours were no longer around – but if you still had one at the time, would you have stood for being told to forget about me and find someone else?"

He scowled at her. "The choice was mine tae make, either way."

She narrowed her eyes on him. "Because you're a man? Your parents wouldn't have interfered because of that?"

He gave her an aggrieved look. "Ye know it's different for a woman, Kimber. There's no point in arguing about that. She's only eighteen. And if for some reason she's set on a mon who really isna right for her, then it's our duty tae see that she makes the right choice."

She scowled at him now. "You know how I feel about this, Lachlan. My mother made the wrong choice, obeyed her parents and married a man she despised rather than the one she loved. Because of that she lived her life miserable until the day she died. I do *not* want that happening to my daughter. I named her after my mother as a sort of second chance for her, *not* to have history repeat itself. So be very, *very* careful in your decision about this young man she wants."

"Ye're saying ye'll side wi' her if I forbid the match?" he asked.

No comment, but she did present her back to him to get her dinner gown fastened, which meant, in her mind, she didn't think it was going to come to that. He didn't think so either, but then, he hadn't heard yet what had her brothers so set against Melissa's choice. Kimberly knew, but when he'd asked her for a full account, she'd merely told him she hadn't been given one, just a few facts, so he should wait and hear what her kin had to say. Since they were going to be chewing his ear off over the matter, he didn't need to hear it a dozen times or more.

She'd added only, "Melissa has heard both sides and still wants the fellow. That's a lot in his favor, you must admit. And remember your own first impressions of him. You *did* give him permission to court her, after all."

Lachlan had said no more on that account, because he hadn't wanted to admit that his first impression of the lad had been influenced by his own preferences. Lincoln was a Scot, and he had an estate nearby, which meant Melissa wouldn't be moving so far away, at least not permanently. That alone had put Lincoln Ross Burnett in his good graces.

He didn't know enough about the man to judge him by anything else. He'd given him his blessing to court his daughter, leaving it to her to decide if she wanted him or not. And that would have been the end of it if Kimberly's brothers hadn't found something wrong with him.

Once Kimberly finished fastening her gown, Lachlan put his hands on her shoulders before she could move away. He rested his chin on the top of her head.

"Are we done fighting?" he asked.

"Yes, I do believe we are," she replied in her prim, English manner. But then she turned and wrapped her arms around his waist. "We weren't really fighting, you know. I just couldn't *stand* not being able to help our daughter. It's the first time we weren't able to fix immediately something that upset her."

"This 'upset' doesna come close tae the upsets she had growing up, Kimber," he replied cautiously. "This is one we may no' be able tae fix."

"I know." She sighed. "And that's part of it, that she's grown up and the problems she has now aren't the kind that can be soothed away. This is such a far cry from what I expected. She's a pretty girl. She had a sponsorship other girls could only dream about. I expected us to come to London, give her 'choice' our blessings, and go home and plan a wedding. The thought of not approving her choice never once occurred to me. She's a sensible girl. How could she *not* make the right choice?"

"We dinna know yet that she hasna. Just because all o' yer brothers dinna like the mon—'

"But that's just it, Lachlan," she said in a worried

tone. "They overreact, true. They go overboard. But when have you known them *all* to agree on something? There's always a few dissenters and reason for them to be fighting among themselves. But they're all opposed to Lincoln Burnett. That doesn't say much for the man."

"Except that Meli still wants him anyway."

"Well, yes, there's that." She leaned back, frowned at him. "Did we suddenly reverse our positions?"

He laughed at her. "Nae, we just see eye tae eye where our daughter is concerned. We've both the same worries. We both want what's best for our lass. If this Scot-turned-Englishmon isna right for her, we'll know it and agree on it, I dinna doubt. There's no need tae be arguing o'er it afore it comes tae that."

"I know, and I'm sorry for taking my worry out on you," she said, giving him a hug.

"Ye didna. Ye bottled it up instead," he scolded lightly. "Next time spill it out as ye should, so we can mop it up."

She chuckled. "Let's hope there isn't a next time. And let's hope my overprotective brothers show up for dinner, so we can get this matter settled and done with."

"I'm all for 'settled'," he said and kissed her cheek, then the side of her neck. "Are ye sure ye were wanting this gown fastened?"

"Well, now that you mention it . . ."

32

"She's angry," Ian Six cautioned his brothers before they entered the dining room where the MacGregors and St Jameses were already gathered. "She arrived angry, I could tell. Which means Lachlan probably isna in a good mood either."

William, first to pass through the doorway and take note of the congenial atmosphere in the room, whispered behind him, "Kimber looks tae be in a good mood tae me."

Charles, the second through the door, whispered next, "Her cheeks are blooming, and we know what that means."

"She's caught cold?" Neill said.

"Nae, ye ass, she probably made love afore coming down tae dinner. Bless Lachlan, he couldna hae picked a better time."

The room fell silent as the rest of them crowded through the doorway. The duchess stood up to welcome them. Now that she knew them better, she wasn't joking when she cautioned, "No arguing until after sweets."

That started a few blushes. Kimberly said

nothing yet, simply looked them over. Her eyes passed Dougall, then came immediately back to him.

The first words out of her mouth weren't a greeting. "What the devil did you do to your poor nose, Dougi?"

"Lincoln smashed it for him again," Neill volunteered.

"Again?"

"We'll get tae that – after sweets," Callum said with a sheepish look cast toward the duchess.

"And your eye, Malcolm? Did he smash that, too?" Kimberly asked.

"As it happens," Malcolm mumbled.

"You, too, William?"

A blush in answer. Lachlan burst out laughing then, which caused sixteen scowls to turn his way.

He ignored the dirty looks as he usually did. "I'm impressed," he said.

He inspected the rest of them as they took their seats. There were four of them with black eyes – Jamie even sported two. A few more were wearing split lips and assorted facial bruises.

"Verra impressed," Lachlan continued. "I wouldna want m'daughter tae wed a mon who couldna defend her, who'd wet his breeches if I looked at him wrong. But it's a decided plus, in my opinion, that he no' be afraid o' the MacFearson side o' her family either."

"There's no' afraid and then there's too stupid tae be afraid," Adam pointed out.

Lachlan nodded thoughtfully. "Aye, but ye'd

respect the first and be leery o' the second, sae either way I'm still impressed. And ye likely are as well, though I'm thinking ye willna admit it."

Silence. Lachlan chuckled again, but ended with a cough when he noticed that all three women at the table were frowning at him. "In deference tae our hostess, we'll be discussing her fine cuisine, the awful state of overcrowding in this city, and the appalling state o' the roads getting here."

"Must we?" the duke said dryly. "This was just getting interesting."

And Megan replied with a sweet smile directed at her husband, "If you weren't sitting on the other end of the table, Devlin, you'd be wincing. Do keep in mind how pointed the toes of my new shoes are."

He winced anyway. The others at the table began to relax. Servants started arriving with the first course. And if Lachlan's three subjects didn't get discussed during that long and excellent meal, neither was any more mention made of Lincoln Burnett.

After sweets were served, however, Devlin stood and announced, "My wife has reminded me – without words, mind you, she's quite good at that – that I do *not* want to get involved in what is essentially a family matter. So if you will excuse us, Megan and I have a great deal to catch up on after my extended absence."

Several of her uncles glanced Melissa's way, expecting her to take the hint and leave as well, but she crossed her arms and said stubbornly, "I'm staying. I've heard it all, sae dinna hold back on m'account. You'll no' embarrass me by talking about me, and I'll try no' tae interrupt – easy enough tae do, since I'm no' talking tae any o' you anyway. I've heard the other side as well, but I'll be letting Lincoln get tae that. Uncle Dougi, though, has a confession tae add, I'm thinking, which is going tae come out when m'da talks tae Lincoln, sae he may as well mention it now."

That, of course, had everyone turning to Dougall, who merely looked confused. "What confession?"

Melissa sighed. "Well, when you hear Uncle Ian – I'm assuming he's going tae be your bearer o' bad tidings – give his account o' what happened, you'll be figuring out what needs tae be added. I'm saying no more."

She ended by staring at Ian One, who took the cue and cleared his throat, addressing his sister and brother-in-law. "First, we made a number o' mistakes since we found oot who was courting Meli and came tae London tae put a stop tae it. We warned Linc tae stay away from her, which, tae give him his due, he was doing – until he found oot we neglected tae let her know what we'd done."

"And why didn't you tell her, when *she* was the one being courted?" Kimberly asked.

"There were two good reasons – at least we considered them good at the time. We didna think she was sae set on him yet that she couldna easily forget aboot him and find someone else, wi'oot having tae be told the nasty details o' why she should. But Linc went and told her everything."

"So that's why she was upset?"

"Nae, she got o'er that – anyway, she said she'd wait on yer decision and wouldna see him again until then. Then there was m'own personal mistake, in no' letting all o' m'brothers know her decision soon enough. Half o' them took it upon themselves tae get rid o' Lincoln, since he obviously wasna going tae abide by our warning."

"Rid o' how?" Lachlan asked with a frown.

Ian explained about the trip to China, and before Lachlan could blow up about it – and he looked as though he was about to – quickly added that Lincoln managed to get back to London on his own. "I sent the note off tae ye afore he returned, when Melissa was sae upset she was locking herself in her room and speaking tae no one."

Kimberly scowled at her brother. "Can ye blame her?"

"Nae, it was a blunder all the way 'round. However, afore ye disown them for it, keep in mind that in their view Lincoln had defied us. He was going to continue courting Meli e'en though we'd warned him off. They didna know yet that a standoff had been agreed tae. They figured that getting him oot o' the country was better than beating the tar oot o' him. They were attempting tae be civilized and avoid violence."

"From the look o' some o' ye, violence was certainly avoided," Lachlan said dryly.

"After Linc got back tae town, he made an attempt tae get us tae leave it," Ian One said, explaining the bruises. "It didna work."

"He figured if he could whip us all, the matter would be done," Adam added.

Charles snorted. "As if a mere whipping would get us tae stand down from protecting one o' our own."

"He was wanting tae fight *all* o' ye?" Lachlan asked incredulously.

"It wasna such a crazy notion as we first thought it was," Ian One allowed. "He damn near pulled it off. Wi' just a wee more luck on his side, he might hae succeeded."

"What was crazy aboot it," Ian Three added, "was that he took damage and dished it oot for no good reason. He said it wasna for revenge for the boat trip. He said it was for Meli and tae get us tae stop interfering wi' his courtship. But we assured him we'd leave the matter tae ye, and ye'd be arriving soon. Sae there was no point tae him fighting us. It was purely a crazy thing tae do."

Melissa started to open her mouth but then clamped it shut again. Ian One noticed and smiled at her.

"Ye dinna hae tae hold yer tongue, Meli, just because ye said ye would. If ye can think of a reason Linc would insist on fighting us when he didna hae tae, we'd be glad tae hear it."

Charles added first, "He denied it, but revenge is the only sane motive."

Melissa shook her head. "He had no reason tae lie about it. He was owed retribution. You expected it. He declined tae take it. That says much for him. And mayhap it was no more than that once again

236

you are trying tae keep him from something he really wants, only this time he's more capable tae deal wi' it than he was nineteen years ago."

"Sae you're thinking, it was just a demonstration? Tae show us he's now a mon tae be reckoned wi'?"

"Let me ask you instead, what made you think you could come tae town and warn him off and he'd simply back off and forget about me? That he'd no' fight for me? Because there are sixteen o' you and only one o' him? That he did stay away at first was because he thought you had the right tae be making such decisions and that I would meekly abide by them. Well, you're m'uncles, and I love you, and I may e'en talk tae you again someday, but you dinna have the right tae be deciding m'life for me. And perhaps he was showing you that you dinna have the right tae be deciding his life either."

There were a few guilty looks, but no one spoke up to say they were wrong in their original intention. To a man, they all still felt justified in their stand against Lincoln.

"Before ye confuse me e'en further wi' all o' this," Lachlan said impatiently, "dinna ye think it's time ye told me what ye're talking about?"

33

It took nearly a half hour for a full accounting. Ian One started it, but his brothers added to it from their own personal observations and participations. Melissa heard new information herself – a more detailed list of Lincoln's injuries, that he'd only skimmed over in his telling, described in full by those who caused them.

They were leaving nothing out – how they'd befriended him and then how he turned on them, starting that first fight and every fight thereafter. Melissa was a bit pale by the time they were done. Even she could see clearly now why they didn't want him in the family. She'd made her own assumptions, had come up with her own reasons for what happened, but what if they were right and she was wrong? What if he really *had* gone crazy during that period – and could again?

Melissa thought that for only a moment, then scoffed at herself for thinking it at all. They knew him only from before. She knew him now. Nineteen years had come and gone without any similar incidents. Whatever had caused his abnormal behavior back then was an isolated occurrence, no more likely to happen again than she was to go crazy herself. Why couldn't her uncles see that?

She wasn't the only one to have lost some of her coloring. Dougall did as well, hearing much of the account for the first time himself. He'd been kept out of it back then, since he was the one they were "protecting."

"Why was I ne'er told all o' that when it happened?" he asked Ian One now.

"Because we didna want ye feeling sorry for him and befriending him again, after what he did tae ye. Ye're too softhearted by half, Dougi."

"But he ne'er did anything tae me."

"He broke yer nose," William remind him. "Ye were bleeding like a stuck pig."

"It wasna broken that time, merely bleeding a lot. Ye know how easily I bleed."

"He started the fight. He knew damn well ye couldna win it, him being sae much bigger than ye."

Dougall slumped down in his chair and said in a meek voice, "I'm thinking I started it."

"Like hell ye did," Callum replied. "I was there, remember? I heard what he said."

"He insulted me, aye, but knowing him, he was probably only teasing. Ye e'en laughed yerself, as I recall. Any other time and I'd hae laughed it off, too, but Charlie and Malcolm had just teased me

239

aboot the same thing the day before, aboot how pathetic I am at fighting. They would hae beat the crap oot o' me if I'd tried tae prove them wrong, but I knew Linc wouldna hurt me too bad if I fought him."

"Ye call all that bleeding ye did no' hurt too bad?" Callum demanded.

"Ye're missing the point. He didna really start it, and he didna e'en bloody m'nose. Och, I'm glad tae hae this oot in the open finally. For a long while I was too embarrassed tae mention it tae any o' ye, then it didna matter anymore, after Linc was sent away. But, aye, he didna bloody m'nose, it was m'own doing." He paused, his cheeks filling with bright color, before finally admitting, "It happened when I tripped and fell into him."

"Ye didna think tae tell William and Callum, before they lit into him?" Adam said.

"They were too quick, already beating on him, but I did try," Dougall said. "They were just in a blood rage and didna hear me."

"Jesus, Dougi," William said in disgust. "I felt guilty for the longest time for whipping him sae bad that day, and now ye tell me I shouldna hae whipped him at all? I've a mind tae break yer nose again."

"The start doesna cancel the end," Ian One reminded them. "I'd like tae say it does, but it doesna change the fact that Linc displayed behavior far beyond normal, that can only be called crazy. He was seriously hurt, yet he still tried tae get through us tae get tae Dougi."

"Probably tae wring his neck," Callum said, glowering at Dougi as well.

"It was tae apologize," Melissa said. "I'm sorry, I know I said I wouldna interrupt, but that's all Lincoln wanted. He was desperate tae make things right wi' Dougi, but none o' you would let him."

Dougall flushed guiltily. Some swearing made the rounds. A few arguments started. Before it got too loud, Lachlan stood up to draw their attention.

"What a sorry mess," he said, looking around the table. "He knows ye and still wants tae join our family – aye, he mun be crazy!"

"We protect our own, Lachlan, ye know that," Adam said in their defense.

"Aye, and that's tae be admired, but in this case ye were protecting a friend from a friend."

"We saw just the opposite. Lincoln had betrayed Dougi's friendship – or sae we thought." Another glare was sent Dougall's way.

Lachlan sighed. "Who's really tae blame and what started it doesna concern me sae much as what happened after and if it can happen again. I'll be sending off a note now tae ask Lincoln Burnett tae come by in the morning, tae hear what he has tae say for himself. I'd like ye tae be here, Ian," he said, glancing toward Ian One. "I'll need tae be sure I willna be hearing anything that will later be contradicted. Did any o' ye e'en think tae ask the lad why he was so determined tae get tae yer brother?"

"He was a fuse already lit," Johnny put in. "Ne'er in m'life have I seen anyone that angry. And it's rather difficult tae talk tae someone swinging broken fists at ye."

Lachlan sighed again. "I suppose it is."

34

Lincoln couldn't remember ever being so nervous. During those few days at sea, when he'd had nothing to do but think, he'd realized that history was in a way repeating itself, that once again the MacFearsons were standing between him and what he most wanted. He'd realized also that Melissa wouldn't just make him an ideal wife, wouldn't just give meaning to his life. She was much more than that now. She had to be his. There was no other choice.

But he saw clearly the similarities between now and the last time something had been this import-ant to him. The consensus was that he'd gone crazy that first time. With so many holes in his memory of those events, he couldn't even deny it. Between then and now nothing had ever occurred to bring his emotions to that extreme level again . . . but he couldn't help the nagging fear that had surfaced. If Melissa were denied to him, what would he do?

The nervousness arose because the decision wasn't his to make. His future happiness was going to be decided by Lachlan MacGregor – who in turn was going to be influenced by the MacFearsons. Melissa's assurance that her own opinion and that of her mother would be taken into account wasn't all that reassuring when you came down to it. It was still going to be her father's decision in the end.

His appointment was 10:00 A.M. He arrived at exactly that time and was let in immediately. Melissa came flying down the stairs a moment later, running up to him in the hall.

"You came!" she said breathlessly.

"You didn't think I would?"

"After what m'uncles did tae you, I wasna sure you'd still want me," she admitted.

He gave her a tender smile. "Of course I still want you. Your family hasn't changed that – nor will they," he added meaningfully

She beamed at him. "They're waiting for you in the parlor."

"They?"

"M'mother and her oldest brother are wi' m'da," she warned him.

"I feel as if I'm going on trial."

"Just be yourself."

"You aren't coming in?"

"Nay, I was there last night, for m'uncles' account o' it. M'da put his foot down about m'presence in this meeting. But I'm no' worried."

"Liar." He smiled at her.

She didn't answer, just pushed him toward the parlor door. He took a deep breath and went ahead.

Ian One was there, looking solemn and dwarfed by Lachlan's great size, who was standing next to him in front of the cold fireplace. Melissa's mother was sitting on the sofa nearby, in the process of pouring tea as Lincoln entered.

She stood, smiled at him, and introduced herself. She was not quite what he expected, nothing like Melissa, who apparently favored just her father. Tall for a woman, with dark blond hair and dark green eyes. She was no beauty and probably never had been, but her smile changed all that and gave her a unique radiance that could be startling it so transformed her appearance.

He turned toward Lachlan and began by stating the obvious. "I want to marry your daughter. You already know that. Since I came to London to pursue her, nothing has altered that simple desire, not even who her relatives are."

Lincoln looked pointedly at Ian as he said that last part. The oldest MacFearson brother merely stared back stoically, unaffected by the left-handed slur.

Lachlan cleared his throat. "Some issues have been raised."

"Yes, I'm sure they have," Lincoln replied. "I never realized that the old adage about how your past can come back to haunt you could be so true."

"M'wife's brothers have filled m'ear wi' their version o' this 'past,'" Lachlan explained unnecessarily. "I'd like tae hear yer version, if ye dinna mind."

Lincoln nodded. It wasn't as if he hadn't expected to have to lay his guts on the table before them. Leaving a man to his own personal demons didn't apply when that man wanted to marry your daughter.

Calmly, sparing himself nothing, he told them everything he could remember, everything he'd already told Melissa. It took nearly an hour, because they interrupted with questions here and there. Even Ian asked a few.

He ended, "What happened back then was caused by many odd circumstances. Some of it even had to do with my father's death. I didn't mourn properly when he died. Like most boys that age, I felt that crying wasn't manly. Instead there was a lot of rage, because he was gone. And my mother was gone, too – not physically, but she might as well have been, since I rarely saw her after his death. So I lost them both, and had no one to take their place – no siblings, no other children in the area around my age – until I met the MacFearsons, and Dougi became the brother I never had. Losing him, and over something so stupid, brought the rage back."

"He ne'er told us that he hurt himself falling against ye," Ian said. "He only fessed up tae that last night. He claims he was too embarrassed tae mention it at the time, but then he didna know that ye were still trying tae reach him either, or that we were still preventing it."

"None of which makes any difference to the real issue, I suppose?"

"Nae, yer rage – understandable, given all we know now – still made you crazy. There's no other

246

word tae come close tae describing a lad sae injured he could barely stand up, which was yer condition by the time I saw ye, still charging into the fray. Ye were asked tae stand down, tae leave it go. I asked ye that m'self, the one time ye tried tae get past me. Do ye e'en remember that?"

"No." Lincoln sighed. "I recall William telling me to go home and mend at one point, but I was far too desperate for Dougi's forgiveness to do that. However, I'm aware that my memory is too vague, or completely devoid of some of those encounters. There were two things in control of me – pain and my need to make things right with Dougi. It has been suggested that the pain caused me to be unreasonable."

"Ye forget the third thing – yer rage," Ian reminded him. "It was there and well lit on each of those encounters. The pain ye were in might hae had some tae do wi' it, but it was yer rage that had ye throwing yourself against unbeatable odds, again and again. Ye had no care for what stood in yer way, Linc. Ye tried tae crush everything in the path tae yer goal – unsuccessfully, aye, but only because ye were too injured yerself tae do anyone else serious damage."

"Ian, I know what you're thinking, and you're wrong. I'd never hurt her. Nor do I think I was crazy back then. I do agree I behaved abnormally, but whatever caused it – the pain, the rage, a combination of both, my desperation, whatever – has never beset me again. That alone indicates it was an unfortunate but isolated occurrence."

"Can ye honestly say it will ne'er happen again?" Lachlan asked quietly.

Lincoln would have said yes immediately, if it weren't for those missing chunks of his memory. "No," he had to allow, and even as he said it, he knew he was cutting his own throat.

"Then I canna give m'daughter tae ye, mon," Lachlan said with genuine regret. "I'm sorry."

Lincoln's throat closed with emotion. He'd known that this was a possibility, but he really hadn't thought that it would become reality. Did they really think that anything in life could hold such guarantees?

He was so crushed he could barely get the words out. "I understand. Actually, I don't, but I suppose that doesn't matter. I bid you good day."

As soon as Lincoln was out of the room, Lachlan told his wife, before he even glanced at her to see her scowl, "Dinna look at me that way."

"I'm with him," she growled. "I don't understand either."

"Ye heard him. He canna guarantee he'll ne'er go crazy again."

"I can't guarantee I won't someday buy me a gun and shoot you either," she replied hotly. "Both are extremely remote possibilities, and since when do we live by such extremes?"

"Ye ne'er bought that gun when ye were a child and shot someone wi' it, Kimber. But he did go crazy as a child. There's yer difference, and it's a big one, I'm thinking."

"Rubbish. And you better tell me you were just testing him, or I'll be ordering a gun."

"Now, Kimber. . ." Lachlan began.

But Ian put in, "He'd hae tae be half dead wi' injuries for a true testing."

"Don't *even* think it. In fact, you both think too much. That's the problem here. So stop it."

Out in the hall, Meli was waiting. Lincoln wished she weren't. He didn't have the heart to tell her. But he didn't have to. Her expression had been eager, excited – until she got a look at his.

She still had to hear it. "He turned down your suit? He willna let you have me?"

"No."

She didn't cry. He felt like crying. She didn't rail. He felt like railing.

She said simply, "Then take me wi' you."

He wasn't expecting that, any more than he'd expected to be denied her, but hearing her say it, he could breathe again. He still had to ask, "You're sure?"

"Aye, I've already thought about it, in case he decided against you. I e'en wrote a note for my mother, sae she willna worry. I really thought I'd be tearing it up and throwing it away, instead o' having it delivered. But m'parents will see reason – after we're wed. Sae take me with you, and be quick about it, afore they come out tae try tae explain tae me why they're being so silly."

35

Melissa had wanted to hurry, because she'd assumed, like most young couples deciding on elopement, that they'd be heading to Scotland to accomplish it, where there was no waiting for banns or licenses or anything else. Speed was of the essence, because she didn't doubt that her family would follow and try to stop her from making a "mistake," as they saw it, so they needed a good head start.

Lincoln didn't seem that concerned with speed, however. When they left the city heading south instead of north, she merely thought he must know of a different way to get to Scotland, other than the normal route. And then she stopped thinking about it entirely . . .

He'd been holding her hand ever since they'd left the mansion. He hadn't released it in the coach. She'd been anxiously staring out the window, until she felt his lips brush against her fingers.

She turned to him, caught her breath. Looks had to be guarded in public, but there was nothing guarded about the look he was giving her now. It was filled with unmasked longing. It drew her forward, until she was clinging to his chest, their heartbeats meshed. He kissed her brow, her temple, finally her lips. She'd missed him so, thought she'd lost him for good. Those feelings and more were in that kiss – a desperation, because they weren't wed yet, and something could still happen to prevent it.

He didn't kiss her for long. More would have started something they couldn't have stopped. She wouldn't have minded, but she knew his thoughts on the matter, knew he wanted their first mating to be perfect. But he didn't let her go either, held her tightly, possessively. It was soothing and frustrating at the same time, but she consoled herself with the thought that in a few more days, there'd be no more need for restraint.

When she noticed again, several hours later, that they were still heading south, she finally remarked on it. "We're no' going tae Scotland?"

He smiled at her, more a grin actually. "No offense meant, Melissa, but you have sixteen bloodhounds in your family that I don't doubt will divide themselves to cover every avenue north. They'll be in Scotland and barring the door to every kirk along the border before we could even cross it."

"Then where are we going?"

"To my estate. They won't think to look there – at least not for a long while, and then it will be too late. We'll be wed in the morning."

She beamed, because it took longer than that just

to reach Scotland, so she hadn't expected to be wed quite so soon. "You've a special license then?"

"No, a special vicar, which will do just as well," he replied.

"Eh?"

He chuckled at her confusion. "He's a Scotsman born and bred. I built him a church on my land many years ago, where he's lived happily ever since with his English wife. He's a bit unorthodox, though, at least in his disagreement that a country should butt in to the Lord's business, with their governing rules and regulations. Since he was raised in Scotland, one of those disagreements is the reading of banns. He feels that if people want to get married, they should do so and brag about it afterward, not beforehand."

"But is that legal? In England, that is?"

"If it came down to it, I'm sure he'd swear he's read the banns the requisite three weeks in a row."

"He'd actually lie about it?"

Lincoln coughed. "He'd tell you the Lord works in mysterious ways."

She burst out laughing. And relaxed after that – for all of twenty minutes. Which was when it sank in fully: She was going to be married *tomorrow*.

They arrived at his home late that afternoon, while it was still light enough for her to see how lovely the estate was. The manor house was large, not on the grand scale of Castle Kregora but just as big as the St Jameses' mansion in London. There were parklike gardens behind it, with a small pond for ice-skating in the winter and a larger pond farther away – more a lake – that was man-made and well stocked with fish, since both Lincoln and the previous Lord Cambury enjoyed fishing.

The stables were extensive. Melissa was already thinking of having her horse delivered. But that was assuming they would be living here for a while. He had that estate in Scotland as well that she fully expected to be their home for at least a part of each year.

After a brief tour of the house, she was shown to her room so she could rest before dinner, while Lincoln went to make the arrangements for their wedding. She didn't want to rest. She was too wound up with excitement even to consider it. They were going to be wed in the morning. Lincoln would be hers finally, hers to kiss whenever she liked, to touch whenever she liked, to make love with whenever . . . well, whenever *he* liked. No, even that could be by her choosing. Hadn't she seen her mother drag her father upstairs on more than one occasion?

Soon, very soon, she'd know what that was all about. Waiting, even another day, was going to be a test of willpower she wasn't sure she could pass, nor did she even want to try. Why did they need to wait, when they'd taken the matter into their own hands?

Lincoln probably wasn't thinking along those lines. After all, he'd been the one to show restraint before, not wanting to compromise her just in case something prevented them from marrying. But that was before they'd decided to marry no matter who objected. Would he still insist on waiting if she suggested there was now no need to? Did she even have the nerve to suggest it?

She shouldn't have been left alone with her thoughts. By the time she went down to dinner, she was a bundle of nerves, wanting to make love with him tonight, afraid he'd think her too forward if she let him know. But it seemed that since she'd met him all she'd done was wait: for him to show up in London, for him to start courting her as he'd said he would. One thing or another – mostly her uncles – had kept them from progressing in a normal manner. Yet now they were beyond that. They both knew they were right for each other, had known it from the start. And nothing else was going to stand in their way. That was why waiting any longer, even one more day, seemed so unnecessary.

It was a pleasant dinner, cozy, just the two of them at one end of a long table, with candlelight and servants going out of their way to please without intruding. Melissa would have enjoyed it more, though, if she could stop thinking about love-making. But she found herself watching Lincoln's mouth too much as he ate, and reading sexual innuendo into his every expression. It was all in her own imagination, of course. Actually, he seemed to be more circumspect than ever, making a concerted effort to keep his eyes off her for the most part. Was he having the same problem she was?

By the time sweets were served, distraction was mandatory. And despite her hectic thoughts, she'd heard it during the tour of the house, now again during dinner – "Lady Henriette this," "Lady Henriette that" from the servants. This was Henriette's house, had been hers first, always would be hers, no matter whom the current Lord Cambury married. As long as Henriette lived in it, the servants would go to her for their instructions. Melissa wanted her own house, where she wouldn't feel as if she were usurping someone else's domain. It would be the same at his house in Scotland. His mother lived there, so that wouldn't do either.

Bah, what a pickle, to think of such a thing at the last minute, but it was welcome as a distraction, and Melissa didn't hesitate to broach the subject. "We'll be living here? With your aunt and cousin?"

"It's a big house, Meli, certainly big enough to accommodate a large family."

"Aye, but it's your aunt's house. What if I'm wanting a house o' m'own?"

"Do you?"

She blushed, glanced down in her embarrassment. "I'm thinking I do."

"Then I'm thinking we'll have to build you a house of your own."

She blinked up at him. "You mean it?"

"Contrary to what you apparently assumed, I see your point. So, yes, you shall have your own house – ten houses if you like. I mean to make you happy, Meli, whatever it takes."

She smiled at him. "One will do nicely, but can it be wherever I like?"

"Wherever you like. Within reason."

"In Scotland?"

He rolled his eyes, but then he chuckled. "I can't say I didn't see that coming. Very well, in Scotland, as long as it's nowhere near the . . . obnoxious side of your family"

"As it happens, there's a nice parcel o' land no' too far from Kregora that's been vacant for as long as I can remember. M'da thought about buying it once, but I dinna think he e'er located the owner."

"I wouldn't be surprised if I'm the owner."

"You're no' sure?"

He shrugged. "One of my father's passions was buying property, empty or otherwise. With the large estate my uncle left me, and my reluctance to deal with my mother, who's been handling my father's estate, I never got around to finding out the extent of my Scottish inheritance. But I vaguely recall going with my father, when I was around four, to look over some land he was buying in the direction of Kregora. Though it may not be the same. There are quite a few miles between Kregora and my father's house."

"And it could be exactly the same – and perfect!" she said with delight.

He smiled. "We shall see."

And then, out of the blue, "Can we be wed tonight, Lincoln?"

36

Melissa had taken Lincoln by surprise with her question. Herself as well. She hadn't meant to ask that, which left her open to be asked in turn why she couldn't wait until the morning. She blushed immediately.

She started to say "never mind." In fact, she was just about ready to run out of the room, she was so embarrassed. His answer, bless him, was without inflection and simply to the point.

"1 thought of that myself," he admitted. "Until I had to follow the vicar's trail to locate him and remembered this is the one day a week that he's never at home. It's his day for visiting the sick and injured in his parish. Because it's a set day, they expect him. And he's been known to spend half a night with some, if he thinks it will help."

"Well . . . damn," she replied.

He coughed. Her blush got worse. "I mean, och, never mind. You wouldna understand."

He stood up, moved behind her chair to pull it out so she could as well. "Now, there you are incorrect," he said, and he lifted her in his arms to carry her from the room. "I understand perfectly, and I am in complete agreement."

"You are?" she asked a bit breathlessly, a lot hopefully.

"Meli, you've agreed to wed me. Will you agree to having our wedding night a day early?"

"And here I was going tae ask you that – or I wasna . . . well, I didna really think I'd have the nerve."

"Is that a yes?"

She nodded, burying her face against his neck. He clasped her tighter, hurried his step. It was his room he took her to, a large room, but she barely saw any of it, couldn't take her eyes off him after he set her down carefully on the edge of his bed. He removed his coat. She started to remove her shoes, but he shook his head.

"I want to do that," he told her. "If you knew how often I have undressed you in my mind, you would know how much pleasure I'm going to get from the simple matter of removing your clothes."

She lay back, crossed her arms behind her head, gave him an impish grin before admitting, "And if you knew how often I've pictured you undressing *yourself* – I'll just watch, if you dinna mind."

He didn't mind at all, apparently, and even slowed down his efforts slightly. Her breathing became more labored with each piece of clothing he tossed on a nearby chair. She hadn't been joking. She really had imagined this moment so many times but, never having experienced anything like it, couldn't have come close to the actual reality of seeing him get naked.

He was more muscular than she could have guessed. Clothes could be so deceiving. Thick arms, black hair sparsely covering his chest, a bit more down the line of his belly. For all the injuries he'd had in his youth, none had deformed him. He was perfect in every way – if a bit bruised from his recent clash with her uncles.

When he unfastened his trousers, she almost lost her nerve. This was getting into the area of the unknown for her. But her fascination wouldn't let her close her eyes, though there was a moment of natural fear. His manhood, rampant with desire, was simply too big, in her opinion. There was no possible way she could accommodate him, or so she was thinking.

He guessed that from her expression, said gently, "You were made for me, Melissa MacGregor. We will fit perfectly, I promise you."

"Really?"

He joined her on the bed, gathered her close to soothe her fears. "Really. Men come in all sizes, if you haven't already figured that out. But the female body is a wondrous thing, made to take that into account. With the right preparation—"

"What kind o' preparation?" she interrupted.

"The kind that will make you wild to have me inside you," he said.

"Oh." She blushed, then said, "Show me."

"As it happens," he said huskily and began kissing her, "I was going to do just that."

It was very odd, how his kind of kissing could make her feel things in other parts of her body. A restless yearning built so quickly, she was impatient to get as naked as he was. But he was sincere in his desire to remove her fears, and so immersed her in the taste, scent, and feel of him, that by the time he sat up to undress her, she was no longer wondering if he would fit. She was instead thinking, how soon?

And it wasn't just an undressing. Everything he did to her was sensual in the extreme: kisses along the skin he bared, cloth removed so slowly it was a caress in itself. But then the real caressing began, that drove her as wild as he said it would. His lips caught each of her gasps, and there were many, as his hands traveled the length of her body and back, stopping in the most intimate of places.

She was more than ready for him when he moved into position above her. She was hot, wet with need, making his entry smooth. Then once again he stopped his movements completely, panicking her. She thought of that other time. He wasn't going to insist on that piece of paper with their names on it coming first, was he? When, in her mind, he was already hers?

She was about to ask when he said hesitantly, "This is the part that will hurt a bit. No, don't stiffen. Do I need to explain . . . ?"

"Nay, m'mother did. I just forgot for a bit."

She actually relaxed. Waiting, even another day, was worse in her mind than some little pain she would feel with this first experience of lovemaking.

She clasped his head, kissed him. "You've showed me so much. Now show me the rest."

"I love you," he said tenderly, filling her heart with joy just before he filled her body.

She didn't have time to respond. Her cry was brief, and the relief that followed, relief that it hadn't been so bad, allowed her to more fully experience the thickness filling her. It was wonderful, knowing they were truly joined now. And the pleasure as he began to move in her again . . . it took her by surprise, built swiftly to a crescendo, and then an explosion of pure sweetness that had her crying out again. His own climax followed almost immediately.

Replete, satisfied beyond her expectations, she drifted off to sleep in his arms. The morning would see them wed for real, but in her heart they already were.

37

Lincoln woke with the same feeling of euphoria with which he'd fallen asleep. Melissa was his, come what may. That simple knowledge made such an amazing difference to his peace of mind. Making love to her had been an incredible experience, a new experience for him, like nothing gone before. There was simply no comparison to satisfying a need – an experience that could be easily forgotten, it was so lacking in depth – to making love with the full spectrum of emotion, as he'd done last night. But making love to her still paled in importance to knowing she was his now, for all time.

He'd told her he loved her, but that didn't come close to describing his feelings for her. She filled every aspect in his life that he'd been missing for most of it. His feeling of being alone was gone.

That he woke up alone, the bed empty beside him, was only mildly disconcerting. There was no thought that he might have dreamed of bringing her to his home and making love to her. Last night was stamped in his memory for all time. She was about somewhere, he merely had to find her, and he quickly dressed to do that.

The last thing he expected, though, was to see her sitting huddled on the top step of the stairs, her arms wrapped around her knees, and looking absolutely miserable. He did panic then. Such dread filled his heart that it hurt.

He dropped down beside her, put his arms around her, held her so tightly she moaned. He relaxed his frantic grip, but he didn't release her.

"Tell me what's wrong," he said.

She sensed his fear, quickly soothed him. "Shh, it's no' what you're thinking."

He leaned back to stare at her but couldn't get rid of his dread. "Then what?"

"When I woke and dressed, it came as a shock tae realize I'd be wearing the same ordinary dress I wore yesterday tae m'wedding, that I've nothing nice tae wear for what is one o' the most important occasions o' m'life."

He sighed in relief, said, "I ought to throttle you for scaring me like that." Then, noting that she didn't smile, he asked, "That's not all, is it?"

"I have a fine wedding gown in Scotland. It's extremely lovely. M'da sent all the way to Brussels for the white lace. It took several months to locate the finest white satin, so shiny that, in contrast tae the white lace, it appears a glowing silver. M'mother and I spent weeks designing it."

"Melissa, getting married has nothing to do

with what you wear to accomplish it. You'd be a beautiful bride in my eyes even if you were wearing sackcloth."

"I know, but—"

"But?"

"I canna do this, Linc."

The panic was back, was about to run rampant. "You can't *not* do it. We've made love. I've compromised you beyond redemption."

"Nae, you misunderstand. I want tae wed you more'n anything, but I want tae be wed in Scotland, at Kregora, where I always expected tae be, with m'friends and family gathered 'round. I need m'parents' blessing. I want them tae agree that you're the right mon for me."

"We tried that," he reminded her.

"I know, but we mun try again, and again if necessary. They can be stubborn, but they're no' unreasonable."

"They're holding my past against me. Do you think it's even possible to change their minds?"

"Certainly! M'da has just let m'uncles rile his protective instinct, is all. That will settle down as soon as they get tae know you better. But I canna bear the thought o' them worrying about me as I know they're doing right now. And I want them present for my wedding, tae be there tae share in m'joy. I'm too close tae them, Lincoln, tae no' have them be a part o' this grand moment in m'life. I'm no' sure you can comprehend just how important this is tae me, when you havena been that close tae your own parents."

He flinched, but he wasn't going to get into that at the moment. He *had* been very close to his parents – before his father died. Which had been part of the rage. He'd been too close. They'd been everything to him – as her parents seemed to be to her.

"What you're saying is you want to go back and get this settled with them *before* we marry?"

"Aye," and then, guessing accurately, she added, "You're disappointed?"

"Most assuredly."

"But you understand?"

"Yes." He hugged her tight again, then admitted his thoughts. "I just can't help the feeling that I'm going to lose you in the effort."

"No!" she exclaimed fervently. "No, you've missed the whole point, Lincoln. I'm still going tae marry you, no matter what. I'll marry you today if you insist. I'll e'en leave the decision tae you. I'm just hoping you'll agree that a wee bit more effort wouldna hurt, tae convince m'parents that our marrying is an occasion for celebration, for us as well as them. It's them that need convincing you're the only mon for me, no' me. If they prove stubborn, we'll elope again. Dinna doubt that."

He cupped her cheek, kissed her gently. "That's all I needed to hear. Let's get something to eat, and then we'll be on our way."

"You mean it?"

"Meli, I *told* you I mean to make you happy. If it means doing this first, then we do this first. Whatever it takes, I'll get your father to like me."

"Och, I'm thinking he already likes you."

Lincoln rolled his eyes. "I know, he just thinks I'm crazy."

38

It was still early afternoon when they arrived back in London. The St Jameses' butler gave them a quick account of who was in residence before he dispatched a footman to notify Melissa's mother that they'd returned.

Melissa moved into the parlor, disappointed that her father wasn't home. She'd been hoping to have the matter settled before the end of the day. An unrealistic hope, but even more impossible without her father's presence.

Lincoln, noting her expression, guessed, "You really didn't think he'd be scouring the countryside looking for you?"

She gave him a sour look, since he obviously expected no less. "When, as you'd put it, I've plenty uncles tae make good bloodhounds, no, I expected him tae leave the looking for me tae them and be here comforting m'mother."

He put his arm around her shoulder to do some comforting of his own, reminding her, "You left your mother a note, told her not to worry.

"Aye, but that wouldna stop her from worrying anyway. Mothers are like that."

"Some are, I suppose."

It was his tone that had her wrapping her arms about his waist to take over the comforting, "Och, that was thoughtless o' me. I'm sorry."

"Don't be," he replied, admitting, "It had been my hope to diffuse that old bitterness, prior to marrying. It's why I went to Scotland."

"It didna work?"

"No, I hadn't counted on all the old rage returning with just the sight of her. But never think you need to guard your words from me or tiptoe around the few old wounds I carry. Always speak your mind to—"

The sound of running footsteps ended their conversation abruptly. They had just enough time to move apart before Kimberly rushed into the room. Her eyes went immediately to Melissa and stayed there for several long moments, looking her over from top to bottom.

"Yes, I knew you were fine, didn't have a single doubt," Kimberly finally said.

That statement was belied, of course, by her hasty entrance and the close examination that had followed. Neither Lincoln nor Melissa cared to point that out.

"Did you marry?" Kimberly said next.

"No," Lincoln replied, but then he added meaningfully, "not yet."

"Why not?"

Lincoln's expression showed clearly he wasn't

expecting that question, at least not so bluntly and in an almost accusatory tone, as if Kimberly were saying, "You should have."

Melissa stepped in to explain. "We were going tae be wed, were able tae be. Nothing would have prevented us – but Lincoln saw that m'happiness wouldna be complete without m'family and friends present for the ceremony. He brought me home so we can do this properly, because it means a lot tae me, and m'happiness means a lot tae him."

Kimberly nodded. "I knew there was a reason I liked him – aside from the fact that you do."

Lincoln wasn't expecting to hear that either. "Then you aren't against our getting married?" he asked.

"Not a'tall. I'm on your side, have been from the moment Meli said she wanted you. Besides, I listened to your heartrending story and watched you walk out of here after being delivered a devastating blow, without the least show of abnormal behavior from it. I don't share my husband's worry on that score."

"I am grateful for your support," Lincoln said.

"Don't be. Lachlan is known to put up his defenses and get stubborn when I argue with him, so my opinion could be more harmful than beneficial."

"What she means is, arguing wi' her makes m'da verra unhappy," Melissa said.

"Nevertheless, I appreciate her faith in me—"

"Hold on, now," Kimberly interrupted with a stern look. "That I support your marrying my daughter is based on *her* instincts and feelings for you – and the fact that you have acquitted yourself admirably under opposition. Don't think I'm not displeased with you for running off with her, but also don't think I'm not delighted with your reasons for bringing her back either. I simply don't know you well enough to have an opinion of you that isn't influenced by her opinion. For this to go forward, I think that we need to correct that major lack. I *know* it needs to be corrected, if there's to be any hope of swaying my husband in this matter."

Lincoln nodded solemnly. Melissa gave him an encouraging smile. "That isna as bad as it sounds."

"I know. Your family has no knowledge of me, other than of my past. Had that past not occurred exactly as it did, and had I remained in Scotland, I've no doubt we would have met sooner, might even have been childhood friends."

It was his tone that had Melissa quickly say, "Och, dinna be bitter about that, too. It's just as likely we wouldna have met any sooner than we did, if you'd been there and still friends wi' m'uncles. I've ne'er been introduced tae many o' their friends."

"Probably because they don't have any, other than each other."

Her expression turned sour over that somewhat sarcastic observation, because she couldn't dispute it offhand. Kimberly did, though not in the exact context.

"They had friends, just not the close kind you mean. Having sixteen brothers means you don't need any other close associations, I suppose. That one was formed with you, Lincoln, is a credit to you. But what followed is done, can't be changed. And still you two met. Fate, as it were."

"Aye, we did." Melissa beamed, but her mother wasn't finished.

"Now, back to the matter at hand," Kimberly said. "Is my daughter compromised?"

Melissa groaned inwardly, the blush already starting. She and Lincoln had discussed this subject on the ride back to London, and both had agreed not to mention what they'd done last night, that it would only embarrass everyone all around – as it was doing now. There was also the possibility that it could make things worse, that her father would think Lincoln had done it to force a wedding.

The lack of immediate response, as well as the blushes, had Kimberly adding, "I see that she is. Well, we won't tell her father that – *if* it can be helped. And hope he doesn't ask, because denying it won't do you a bit of good when it's written all over your faces."

"When do you expect him?" Melissa asked, more to change the subject than anything else.

"There's no telling—" Kimberly started to say.

But they each clearly heard Lachlan's booming voice from the direction of the front door – "Where is she?" – and assumed that the butler just informed him of Melissa's arrival.

Kimberly amended, "Now would be my guess."

39

Lachlan stormed into the parlor. He was unkempt, dusty, tired-looking, but, more important, very much enraged. A giant on the warpath was intimidating indeed. Nor did the first words out of his mouth give any hope that his anger could be easily defused.

"Give me one good reason no' tae rip yer head off," he said to Lincoln.

Melissa answered first. "Because I like his head where it's at."

"Then ye give me one good reason why I willna be locking ye in yer room for the next ten years – or until ye dinna like his head where it's at anymore."

"Because you'd be unlocking m'door yourself after only one day, since you canna bear tae punish me."

"Aside from that," he growled.

Melissa took a step closer to Lincoln. She knew she had nothing to fear from her father, but she was already instinctively turning to Lincoln for emotional support – and protection. Kimberly noted this, even if Melissa wasn't quite aware of it herself.

"He brought her back," Kimberly said calmly. "That's reason enough. And they aren't married. They could have been, but he brought her back instead—"

"You don't want her now?" Lachlan demanded of Lincoln incredulously, about to go off on a different tangent.

"On the contrary, I want her for my wife more than anything. But her happiness means more to me than my own, and since that includes your blessing, I'll do whatever I have to do to obtain it for her."

"This was his decision," Melissa put in. "I would've married him either way – still will. But I'd prefer the wedding I've always dreamed of, wi' you there giving me away, wi' all m'family there tae share in m'happiness, and he took that into account. I know he's the right mon for me. I want you tae have that same certainty."

"I could as easily say I know he's no' the right mon for ye and I want ye tae see that. Ye're letting emotion color yer judgment."

"And what is marriage if no' emotion? Does love no' count, then?"

"If it's going tae hurt ye, then, nae, it counts for nothing."

Melissa gasped. "I canna believe you said that!"

"Ye're m'daughter," Lachlan replied. "Yer welfare comes first, afore yer wants and wishes. If ye're lying dead because he goes into an uncontrollable rampage again, plowing through everything in his path, what is left tae say, eh? That ye died *happy*?"

"He wouldna—"

"I *know* he wouldna hurt ye intentionally. I need no convincing o' that," Lachlan admitted. "It's unintentional harm that I fear."

"You're asking for the impossible. It's enough that I trust his feelings, deep as they are, to stay his hand, if it should e'er come tae that – no' that I think it e'er *would* come tae that. But he hated m'uncles when he tried plowing through them, was enraged at them. There's your difference and why he'd ne'er hurt me."

Lachlan shook his head. "He wasna able to guarantee that, Meli – neither can ye."

Melissa threw up her hands in frustration. "Bah, stubborn!"

Into the fray, Kimberly said dryly, "Would anyone like tea?"

It was a clue that they were getting nowhere arguing and should calm down. Lachlan ran a hand over his face and moved to stand stiffly by the fireplace.

Kimberly tried a new subject – though she unfortunately picked the wrong one – asking Lachlan, "Why are you back so soon? I didn't expect you for another day or so."

"I had a feeling she'd be here, but then I know m'lass well, and that she couldna bear tae hurt us like this for verra long."

The scolding in his tone had Melissa replying defensively, "That's true, Da, but I know you well also, which is why I canna understand how you could so casually dismiss the one thing I'm wanting most. Or did you no' take into account just how much that would hurt me?"

"That's a bit unfair, Meli," Kimberly protested.

"Stop it," Lincoln said angrily. "All of you. I didn't bring her home to fight with you. You're saying things none of you mean and will only regret. It's all so unnecessary. I want to marry her, she wants to marry me – that should be all that matters. But it isn't. Because of my past, you think that I might be a danger to her. If there is any way to prove to you that that isn't so, I'm more than willing to do it. Think about it."

"Well put," Kimberly remarked.

She gave her husband a look that said, There's a solution, take it. He didn't grasp her meaning instantly, but soon he did. He sighed, willing to make this one concession to keep the peace in his family.

"Verra well, I've a suggestion tae make," Lachlan said, then added, in case it occurred to anyone, " and it's no' because it will get me oot o' this town I hate any the sooner. Come home wi' us, lad, tae Kregora. Be our guest for a while, so we can get tae know ye better."

"Certainly," Lincoln replied.

"I'm no' saying m'opinion *can* be changed," Lachlan cautioned when his wife and daughter began smiling at him. "But it canna hurt at this point tae observe and see what happens."

40

The journey back to the Highlands of Scotland wasn't as tense and uncomfortable as it might have been. They departed late the next morning. None of the MacFearsons had returned yet from their pursuit of the eloped couple, but runners had been dispatched to find them and let them know all was well and that the MaeGregors were on their way home, Melissa and her ardent suitor in tow.

Lincoln brought his own coach to accommodate his luggage, as well as his own horse, which had been left behind last time. His vehicle was also used for most of Melissa's baggage, so they wouldn't have to bring along a third coach just for that. And he spent several hours each morning, and again in the afternoon, riding with the MacGregors. There was no point in waiting until they arrived in Scotland, after all, to begin getting better acquainted.

By unspoken agreement no mention was made of the past, their aborted elopement, or anything else that might be the makings of an argument – at least while they were on the road and forced into close proximity. There were even a few moments of laughter, not many, but a good sign. But there was absolutely no opportunity for Melissa and Lincoln to speak privately. Her parents were keeping too close an eye on her, whether intentionally or merely as a result of the worry she'd recently put them through.

Six of the MacFearson brothers joined them en route, the runners having caught up to them. But rather than return home themselves, now that all was well, they didn't think all was well at all. Like guards they were, riding behind the coaches. But at least after a few heated words with Lachlan, they didn't cause any trouble – for now.

Their arrival didn't account for too much added tension, no more than to be expected from that lot anyway, with the perpetual scowls they reserved just for Lincoln. There was an unexpected tension, though, one serious problem Melissa and Lincoln hadn't counted on. Having tasted of the forbidden, they were both sorely taxed being without the contact they now craved. Not even an innocent touch could be stolen without having disapproving eyes cast upon them.

It got to where they couldn't bear to look at each other, for fear they'd do something to ruin this effort to have her family accept him. And it became increasingly embarrassing, because it was so obvious.

Kimberly, easily guessing the problem, since she was aware they'd had the wedding night before the marriage, was quick to distract Lachlan whenever

Lincoln's looks turned too heated in Melissa's direction or when Melissa was caught staring at him in a daze of yearning. And Lincoln wisely stayed out of their coach the last day on the road, using lack of sleep as an excuse to nap in his own coach.

He didn't sleep, of course. He plotted, earnestly, a way to get Melissa to himself for just a little while, without earning himself the boot in the process. The trip north offered no hope whatsoever. They'd been taking only two rooms in each inn they stayed the night at, one for the men – pure hell after the MacFearsons showed up – and Melissa and her mother in the other.

Having tasted of Melissa fully, not being able to kiss her now, or even touch her, was going to drive Lincoln crazy, he was sure. They wanted proof he was unbalanced? They'd surely have it if he couldn't find a way to get her alone in the coming weeks.

They reached Scotland in good time, but there was still a long stretch to the Highlands ahead of them, which required one more night spent at an inn. Unfortunately, yet another of Melissa's uncles caught up with them that morning. And although the numbers present now required an extra room to accommodate all the men, this inn didn't have any more available. Extra bedding was supplied, since most of them ended up having to sleep on the floor.

Lincoln tried to sleep, he really did, but the MacFearsons, boisterous in life, were just as boisterous in sleep, and the snores finally drove him from the room. He had the thought of finding a soft pile of hay in the stable, but he didn't get that far. Coming up the stairs as he was going down was yet another MacFearson, and unfortunately, one of the runners hadn't caught up to this one yet.

"Sae this is where ye've been hiding," Charles said in a furious undertone just before he tackled Lincoln's legs and they both went tumbling down the stairs.

Bumps and bruises notwithstanding, neither was hurt much by the fall. It didn't end there, however. Charles was enraged, hadn't had enough sleep in the last few days to be able to think clearly, and was determined to punish Lincoln for running off with Melissa after he'd been denied her. He apparently felt he could single-handedly do that. Listening to excuses wasn't on his schedule.

It became a wrestling match. There simply wasn't enough room there at the bottom of the stairs for them to maneuver back to their feet. And Charles was wisely keeping Lincoln down, quickly finding that to his advantage. Every time Lincoln drew back his arm for a punch, his elbow encountered a wall or the floor. Every time he tried to tell Charles to desist, he was rolled over again or interrupted with a snarl.

It became a matter of getting on top of the scuffle, to get a decent punch in. Lincoln finally landed a good one that surprised Charles.

That served to quiet him for a few moments, long enough for Lincoln to get out, "She's here, yes, but so are her parents and so are a good number of your brothers. I'm going to Kregora as a guest."

That should have been the end of it. Lincoln certainly thought it would be, and he started to get up. He was tackled to the ground again.

"The hell ye say. Like I'd bloody well believe that?" Charles said with an added snort, before the wrestling commenced again in earnest.

Neill hadn't been sleeping yet either and had heard the original fall down the stairs. Coming to investigate, he went back to wake the rest of his brothers before doing anything. They were gathered at the top of the stairs now, most of them sitting on the steps being highly entertained by the rolling around going on at the bottom.

Neill finally remarked, nudging the brother next to him, "Should we no' step in tae help?"

"Help who?" Malcolm replied, fingering the bruise from his black eye, which was mostly gone but still tender. "I dinna think Charlie has the right of it, but it goes against the grain tae be helping Linc."

"We could stop it at least," Jamie suggested.

"And be accused o' interfering – again?" Ian Four said, tongue in cheek.

"The innkeeper will complain," Neill pointed out.

Adam was too amused to hold back a chuckle. "Why would he? He's getting his floor nicely dusted."

"Shush, Neill, this is far too entertaining tae interrupt," Ian Three added, grinning himself. "They'll wind down soon enough."

They didn't. Charles was too stubborn, and he wasn't getting hurt enough to want to discuss the matter, which is what Lincoln continued to try to do – until he lost his own patience. He was annoyed, sporting a few more bruises than he'd gone to bed with, and although this was an excellent opportunity to get rid of some of his own frustrations, he was too tired to take advantage of it.

"Enough," he growled in Charles's ear. "You're getting nowhere with this."

"Are ye daft, mon? I'm winning!"

"If you're winning, you ass, then get up," Lincoln challenged him.

Still sprawled on the floor, Charles might be momentarily on top, but he was facing up, with Lincoln's arm wrapped around his neck. The choke hold made getting up just then out of the question. It did afford Charles a view of the top of the stairs, however, and although the only light was a candle in a wall sconce at the bottom of them, he could still make out their audience at the top.

"Och," he hissed, "why'd ye no' say *they* were here?"

Lincoln leaned his head up just enough to see around Charles's head. His own dropped back to the floor with a mental groan. "I did, you bloody idiot."

They both got quickly to their feet. Charles, aware of his blunder now, mumbled, "I'll no' apologize. Ye did run off wi' Meli and deserve a thrashing for that, if no one's got around tae it yet."

"No one has, and *you* certainly didn't," Lincoln replied while dusting off his clothes.

Charles's response was, typical for him, a snort. Lincoln ignored it to toss up the stairs, "I suppose thanks are in order, that you didn't participate in this nonsense."

Adam shrugged. "Ye made a good point recently, mon. We're no' children now wi' a disparity o' sizes tae warrant such. That our Charlie doesna acquit himself verra well is his own fault for no' learning better – or yers for acquitting yerself too well."

The left-handed compliment got no more than a nod from Lincoln, too annoyed – and now embarrassed – to appreciate it. "If you will excuse me, I'll continue on my way to the stable in hopes of finding some sleep tonight, which *had* been my intention, considering you MacFearsons don't only behave like savages, you snore like them."

"He's right," Lachlan remarked behind them, having quietly witnessed the whole thing. "Ye do."

41

The castle had been warned of their impending arrival. Rooms had been prepared, a lavish meal was already under way for the evening – a *large* meal, since the rest of the MacFearsons had beat them home, to Kregora rather than their own home. And it looked as if the brothers meant to move in for the duration, all of them, until what they considered to be a waste of time was realized and Lincoln was sent on his way back to England – without their niece.

It wasn't going to work. It would, if the MacFearsons would just go home, if Lincoln had to deal only with Lachlan. But Melissa had said it herself: If he ever got his foot back in the door, there'd be a testing. And who better to test him than his worst enemies?

But he could have withstood that, adversity thrown his way at every turn, if his willpower weren't already being taxed to the limit. Which is why he knew it wasn't going to work. His frustration was so high in not being able to even get near Melissa that it wasn't going to take much to snap his temper. And that was what they were waiting for and hoping would happen. He knew it. And even knowing it, he didn't think he could prevent it.

He'd been shown to his room, where he was to abide for the duration. It was a grand room, but, then, all of Kregora was grandly impressive. An ancient edifice on the outside, but very modern on the inside, cold stone covered with rich wainscoting, windows enlarged, glass installed, decent plumbing, comfortable furnishings.

His trunks sat at the end of the huge bed he'd be sleeping in – alone. He made no move to unpack them. He was prowling a path through the sunbeams that entered from three tall windows on one wall, realizing just how colossal his dilemma was, when a voice intruded, swung him about to one of the corners that was in partial shadow due to the sunlight concentrated in the middle of the room.

"Ye canna hide in here," Ian Six told him. "That will solve nothing."

"Where the hell did you come from? I didn't hear the door."

"Because I was already here. Ye were sae distracted, ye didna notice me."

"If you tell me we are to share this room, I just might kill you."

Ian laughed heartily. "Then glad I am tae tell ye m'room is down the hall. Kimberly has no qualms aboot piling her brothers into four rooms when we visit – has two large beds in each for just that purpose – but she'd be appalled tae stick any other guests in wi' us. Fortunately, Kregora is big enough for her no' tae be appalled often. Ye've been given m'da's room, as it happens, an honor, since it's surely the best guest room o' the lot. I had a feeling she'd put ye here, which is why I was here afore ye."

"And where will the legend be put, then, if he decides to make this the more the merrier?"

The note of unease was detected through the sarcasm. Ian answered, "He willna show up. He doesna travel far from home anymore. His legs swell up these days if he does too much walking, sae he keeps close tae home. But ye'll be meeting him this time around, I'm thinking. Sae dinna think o' him as the legend, mon. He's Meli's grandda, that's all ye're needing tae know aboot him."

Lincoln had to ask it, a question that had plagued him often all those years ago. "Why was I never allowed to meet him before?"

Ian grinned. "Because as children we were all o' us bursting proud o' 'The Legend,' and all o' us protective o' keeping the image intact. Tae meet our da was tae see that he's just a normal mon – reclusive, aye, grouchy back then, aye, but still just a normal man."

Lincoln snorted at that answer. Ian laughed at him and settled farther back in the chair in the corner. Seeing that he was making himself more comfortable rather than leaving, Lincoln scowled.

"What are you doing here, MacFearson, other than annoying me?"

"Och, touchy ye are. Could it be I'm here tae do ye a good turn?"

"Not bloody likely."

"As it happens—'

"As it happens," Lincoln cut in, "I need some space in this house that—"

"Castle," Ian corrected.

"Whatever," Lincoln continued. "Space that *doesn't* include you and your brothers. Consider this room a sanctum – mine – not to be trespassed, violated, or otherwise entered by any of the savages that share your surname."

"Ye'll be saving us both a lot o' time if ye'll just be quiet for a wee bit sae I can say m'piece."

Lincoln moved to the bed, dropped back onto it in a show of extreme exasperation. He put a hand over his eyes, counted to ten, then twenty. He needed more hands, since he had no trouble hearing Ian as he continued.

"Meli is no' just m'niece, she's also m'friend, and let me tell ye why, so ye'll understand what else I'm going tae tell ye."

"Why not restrain yourself instead and keep your opinions or whatevers to yourself?" Lincoln mumbled.

Ian ignored him as he was trying to ignore Ian – with little success. "I dinna remember if it was e'er mentioned tae ye, but m'mother died only a year or sae after I was born, afore I had any memories tae store o' her."

"It wasn't – mentioned that is," Lincoln replied uncomfortably.

Ian nodded, continued, "I bring it up tae explain why when our sister showed up right after ye left, her being older than all o' us, I sort o' took tae her like the mother I ne'er had. From then on I was more often at Kregora than at home, especially after Meli was born. Now all o' m'brothers had experience o' bairns as more and more o' them were born, but me being the youngest, I'd ne'er been close tae one afore then and was purely fascinated by Kimber's."

"Are you getting to the point soon?"

"M'point is, I've an understanding of Melissa, better'n m'brothers, because her and I became friends. And as happens wi' some friends, I can sense her feelings, sometimes e'en afore she's aware o' them."

"So?"

"Sae I know ye formed some sort o' bond wi' her that first day ye met her. It wasna love yet, but it was . . . something. After just a single meeting she knew she wanted tae wed ye. Ye knew it as well, came tae ask for permission tae court her the verra next day. I watched and I listened. She could talk o' nothing else but ye on the way tae London. Whate'er the link was, it was too strong tae go away, e'en when ye took too long tae make another appearance, and she began tae think ye ne'er would."

Lincoln had sat up and was now frowning at Ian. "You aren't telling me anything I don't know."

"Nae, what I'm telling ye is I know it as well. And what I am assuring ye of is I want tae see ye marry her just as much as ye do. For whatever reason, ye both knew from the start that ye were meant for each other – instinct, if ye will. I allowed *who* ye are tae cloud that simple fact for a while. I'm telling ye, mon, I'm on her side, and thus on yers. Sae's m'sister. I'm telling ye, ye're no' alone here, just ye against them all. So dinna give up hope, and dinna let them get tae ye."

"You realize that under the circumstances I'm forced to doubt you?"

Ian sighed. "Aye, I figured ye would. Just keep it in mind if ye start thinking ye canna get through this. Ye can. And for what it's worth, no' all o' m'brothers are against ye. Aye, I know ye'll be doubting that as well. There's some hoping ye'll fail and fall apart again, but there's some hoping ye'll prove them wrong, too."

Lincoln restrained an instinctive snort. He wasn't sure what Ian was up to with his attempt at encouragement, possibly hoping he'd let down his guard. Not a chance. He did feel somewhat bolstered, however, and although he wouldn't thank Ian for that, it *was* just what he'd needed. He might be able to get through at least a few days more.

42

"Was that wise, d'ye think, putting him down there wi' all o' them?" Lachlan whispered aside to his wife that night at dinner.

"It wasn't *my* doing," Kimberly whispered back, her tone highly annoyed over the subject. "If you didn't notice, my brothers made sure they entered the dining room first and began systematically filling the seats from this end down, giving Lincoln nowhere else to sit other than as far from us as possible – and surrounded by them. I wish you'd talk to them. They're taking this thing too seriously and won't listen to me about leaving him alone."

"No' a chance, darlin'," he replied. "I dinna want them leaving him alone – though a mon *should* be allowed tae eat in peace."

"One exception?" she said. "Bah, you're as bad as they are!"

"Nay, they're doing for me what I'd feel uncomfortable doing m'self."

"Playing musical chairs?"

He snorted at her dry rejoinder, though it had been rather amusing to watch her brothers snatch chairs out of Lincoln's hands not once but twice, before Lincoln realized what they were doing and with dignity moved to the end of the table.

"He needs tae be provoked, Kimber, and ye know it," Lachlan replied. "We need tae see him lose his temper and see what happens when he does. How else am I tae be rid o' this unease his past behavior has left me wi'?"

"You could just trust your daughter's instincts like I do," she hissed back at him. "*She* isn't worried about his so-called temper."

"Because she's yet tae see it," he pointed out. "The lad's been showing remarkable restraint in that respect, I'll allow – at least so far. E'en when Charles attacked him last night at that inn, Lincoln showed only exasperation o'er it, no' any real anger."

"An excellent example—"

"But in no way conclusive."

She gave him a sour look. "How long are you going to make him suffer?"

"Och, dinna make it sound like we're torturing him," he complained.

"How long?" she repeated.

He sighed. "As long as it takes. And dinna be angry wi' me, darlin'. Though ye keep overlooking it, I'm wanting ye tae be right. But on the other hand, consider if ye're wrong, if he explodes and starts tearing into anything and everything around him, how would ye feel? Would ye then still trust our lass to his hands?"

Her scowl didn't ease. "We're never going to see eye to eye on this."

"Then stop trying. Let me find peace in m'own assurance. We dinna *know* him, Kimber," he told her. "Meli doesna really know him either. Her feelings are based on just that – feelings, no' facts. I'm giving him this chance tae prove himself, but he'll be proving nothing if he's left alone, wi' nothing tae react tae."

"Must I remind you that you didn't *know* him when you gave him permission to court her in the first place?"

"Dinna be silly, now," he scolded. "I wouldna know any o' the young men she met in London either, but we sent her off tae find one tae her liking. Megan would've closed the door on any that were no' suitable. But Lincoln I at least met first, and I judged him on the surface as I would any mon. He presented himself well, and his feelings were obviously earnest. That was enough – without any known facts tae discredit him. But other facts *are* known now and canna be ignored, as much as ye'd like them tae be."

"Don't think it doesn't bother me, what he did as a child. But, like Meli, I'm inclined to think that was an isolated occurrence that won't ever be repeated, and whatever caused it, he's outgrown."

"Then what are ye fretting about? He's being given a chance tae prove that tae the rest o' us who are no' as sure as ye."

"I'm fretting because siccing my brothers on him

– and don't think I don't know that's what you've done – is not a nice thing to do."

He gave her a wide grin. "They're *yer* brothers, Kimber. And I didna tell them tae provoke him. I just didna tell them *no'* tae."

"Which is the same as giving them permission."

He shrugged. "If ye mun see it that way, fine. I choose tae see it as an acceptable means tae an end. Or did ye want our 'getting tae know him' tae go on indefinitely, wi' no' conclusions drawn?"

"Point taken," she mumbled.

He leaned over and kissed her cheek. "Ye give in so gracefully, darlin'."

"Oh, shut up."

At the opposite end of the table, Lincoln was too tense to appreciate the wide array of food being laid before him. It looked delicious. He had no stomach to taste any of it. His concentration was divided between trying to keep his eyes off Melissa, who was sitting near her parents so far away, and wondering when her uncles were going to let on what they were up to.

They'd said not a word to him so far. But their antics when he entered the room were a near guarantee that they intended to. Twenty seats exactly, and they'd left him only one to sit in. There could have been more. The length of the room would accommodate a much longer table, and many chairs lined up against the walls on both sides of it indicated it could be extended if needed, or another table or two brought in.

When one of the brothers finally addressed him,

it was actually a relief, and amazingly mild, when he'd been expecting some cuts to the quick.

"Ye're in for a treat, Linc," Johnny said. He was sitting three seats down, so most of those at their end of the table could hear him. "Kimber's cook is French and doesna drown a good piece o' meat in water, which is all ye English know how tae do wi' food."

"It's an acquired taste," Lincoln replied.

"Is it, now? Simple is more like it. But then a lack o' intelligence would opt for simple."

Lincoln sat back, even smiled. "Are you trying to insult me by insulting the English? Or have you forgotten where I was born?"

"As if that matters, when ye took tae them like a fish tae water." Charles snorted. "Ye e'en sound like them. Shows who you favor."

"No, it shows how adept the English are at ridiculing an accent other than their own – English children anyway. But then that can be said for children anywhere."

They tried to find something offending in his calm reply but couldn't quite manage it, so Ian Four continued on the same subject. "How long did it take for ye to buckle under to that ridicule?"

"Two years, fourteen fights, and three suspensions from school later. That actually wouldn't have done it, but I couldn't very well fight the teachers. Even toned down, they still refused to try to understand my speech and quickly lost tolerance for the disruption to their classes that the other children were causing with their ridicule. After enough complaints, my uncle was forced to hire a tutor to teach me English all over again."

"Did ye win any o' those fights?" Neill asked with some genuine curiosity.

"Probably about half," Lincoln replied. "I wasn't really keeping track."

"That when ye learned tae fight dirty?" Malcolm was heard from.

It was asked without sneering, so Lincoln answered in kind, "No, I was finished with school before I sought out a few different means of protecting myself. Didn't even think of it when I was still young. And besides, my later years in school were rather enjoyable, so there was no need."

"Then why?"

Lincoln shrugged. "I was drawn into a rather . . . disorderly crowd in my early twenties. Considering some of the disreputable places we could end up in on a lark, it seemed a wise course of action."

A couple of them nodded, actually agreeing with him. He realized, about the same time they did, that they were having a somewhat normal conversation, certainly not what they'd intended, he was sure. Ian Five corrected that.

"Takes skill tae fight fair. 'Course, if ye havena a chance o' honing skill due tae clumsiness or pure stupidity, then, aye, resorting tae trickery would be yer only option."

"Sit down, Linc," Callum said when he stood up abruptly "If ye canna take a few insults, then ye dinna really want Meli."

"The one's got nothing to do with the other, you

ass. After I wed her – and I *am* going to wed her – I won't put up with this nonsense any further."

"If ye can manage tae wed her, ye willna hae tae," Adam remarked. "Ye'd be a member o' the family, and we take care o' our own."

"Spare me that dubious distinction, if you don't mind," Lincoln said. "And I'm leaving because I have no appetite, and rather than offend any of you, I'm going to my room to laugh myself silly over your pathetic attempts to insult me. Have a good evening, gentlemen."

43

Melissa went to bed seriously disgruntled with her father. She was beginning to feel like a prisoner, even though she knew what he was doing and why. He hadn't actually placed a guard at her door to make sure she stayed in her own bed throughout the night, but he might as well have.

He'd been lingering in the hall outside her room when she retired. Unable to get right to sleep, she'd decided to raid the kitchen an hour later and had found him still out in the hall, talking with one of their kin. She'd closed her door before he saw her.

She did finally sleep, despite her annoyance, but it was a fitful sleep, filled with wild dreams and even a nightmare that woke her abruptly in the wee hours. Nothing new, that particular nightmare. She'd had it many times before in one form or another, about the lake and the blasted dragon that owned it. She usually woke just before she was eaten. This time she woke just before Lincoln was eaten.

She hadn't dreamed about the lake since she'd

met him, so it was the first time he'd been in one of her nightmares. That wasn't odd, though. Over the years many of her friends and relatives had made appearances in her lake nightmares and been swallowed up by the dragon – she didn't always wake before the beast won. But in this nightmare Lincoln had been trying to save her. A heroic effort, though pointless – the dragon always won.

She shrugged off the dream as she usually did. These dreams never kept her awake afterward, at least not since she'd been a child. They weren't premonitions, weren't harmful other than to her peace of mind. They were too common to bother her anymore, except with an annoyance that she was still having them, even though she was grown now.

But finding herself awake in the middle of the night, her curiosity moved her to open her door. Sure enough, a clansman was sitting on the short wall bench out there, reading a book by candlelight. She had a mind to leave her room to see what he'd do, whether he'd warn her to get back in, or go fetch her father instead. It was so obvious what he was doing there, when he had no business being there at all.

Ironically, she hadn't thought about trying to see Lincoln alone at night, until this made it so clear her father thought she would try to. She'd instead been plotting how to see him alone during the day and had already set in motion a plan that should give them a few hours together come morning.

Ian Six was going to take her riding and invite Lincoln to join them. As long as they were chaperoned, her parents couldn't object. And he'd promised to give them some time to talk in private, though, he'd stressed, talking was all they were to be doing.

Talking was all she'd had in mind. It was what was needed right now, since they hadn't managed any conversation on the trip north, at least nothing personal. No one expected them not to speak to each other at all, but they couldn't very well say what was on their minds with dozens of ears tuning in on each word that passed between them.

She was worried that Lincoln would get fed up and return to London – without her – that he hadn't realized what a monumental task it was going to be to win over her family. She hadn't realized it either, had really thought they'd soon give Lincoln the benefit of the doubt.

The journey home should have been pleasant. With them all crammed into close quarters, it had been an excellent opportunity for her parents to learn more about Lincoln and thus relieve their worries. But then her uncles showed up, and because of his animosity with them, he didn't say much after that. And last night at dinner it became clear that they simply weren't going to leave him alone.

She'd been too busy herself, trying not to stare at him during the meal, to realize he was being provoked unmercifully at the other end of the table. It had appeared they were only having normal conversation down there. She did notice he wasn't eating yet when everyone else was. And then he left without eating at all.

His anger was obvious, if quiet and well contained. Hers was obvious as well, at the fact that he'd been driven off, and she wasn't going to be quiet about it.

But her father beat her to saying anything, gave her uncles a severe tongue-lashing as soon as Lincoln departed the room. Lachlan was fond of food and figured every man shared that fondness, so he wouldn't tolerate any guest of his being disturbed at mealtime. Any other time of the day, though, was apparently fair game.

Melissa hurried to the stable, her excitement building with each step. She didn't expect anything to happen today of a sexual nature. That wasn't what had her heart pounding. She did expect to be held by Lincoln at some point today, and to gather encouragement again so they could return to Kregora, both assured that everything would be fine in the end.

They needed that – at least she needed that – since postponing their marriage had been her idea, one she was praying she wouldn't regret. But a little time alone and they'd be able to withstand anything, she was sure.

Ian Six was already in the stable readying their horses. He was alone, with only the two horses.

"He's no' here yet?" she asked. He didn't look at her, seemed to be purposely avoiding it. "Well?"

"He's no' coming."

"What! Why?"

He stopped what he was doing, sat down on an overturned bucket, and still wouldn't look her in the eye. "It's m'fault."

She groaned. "What'd you do?"

"It's what I didna do," he explained. "I was hoping he'd trust me, so I didna actually say ye'd be joining us. But I told him he'd enjoy the ride when I invited him. I stressed he'd *really* enjoy the ride. It was a hint broad enough to knock him off his feet."

She put her hands on her hips. "Bah, why would he trust you or your brothers tae do him a good turn, when you've all been sae down on him?"

He finally looked at her. "Because I'd already assured him I was on his side."

"Are you, then?"

"Aye," he said somewhat sheepishly. "I know I was wary tae start and hoping ye'd find yerself someone else. But I've seen enough tae agree wi' ye. He's no' likely tae lose control as he did as a child. Besides, there's no getting around the fact that ye love him, and love isna something we can direct wi' will. It mun take the bad wi' the good. There's no choices in that, I'm thinking."

She leaned down, kissed his cheek. "Thank you. But I gather he didna believe your assurances?"

Ian sighed. "Nae. O' course, he may just hae

other plans for this morning – or no' trust himself tae having ye alone for a bit. D'ye want tae cancel the ride, then?"

"Nae, I want him joining us," she said, then added in a determined tone, "I'll see tae it."

44

Melissa marched into the castle, stopped at the bottom of the stairs and started shouting up them, "Lincoln Ross Burnett! Are you standing me up, then? You're late! The horses are saddled and waiting!"

The rooms immediately emptied around the hall, everyone wanting to find out what she was shouting about – servants, clansmen, and closer relatives alike. Three of her uncles and her father filed out of the breakfast room. Her uncles were frowning. Her father merely looked curious.

"And where is it ye're going, that ye're shouting about?" Lachlan asked.

"Riding," she told him. "Ian Six invited us. He figured we were due for a wee bit o' time away from prying eyes and ears."

"Is that wise?" Malcolm asked.

"And what has wiseness tae do wi' it?" Melissa countered. "I've no' talked tae the mon privately since he brought me back tae London."

"Which is as it should be," Charles humphed.

"We could've been wed at this verra moment,

Uncle Charles. Give us some credit for wanting tae do this right so everyone can be happy for us – or at least at ease. We're no' running off. We're just going for a ride, wi' Ian along."

"Ian doesna make a good chaperon. He's too fond o' ye, will let ye do as ye like."

Melissa rolled her eyes. "Are you trying tae put wicked ideas into m'head, Uncle Charles?"

He blushed, mumbled a bit under his breath, too. Lachlan chuckled. He was relaxed about an innocent outing and had no objections. She had figured that being open about it would ease his mind.

Lincoln hadn't appeared yet, though, which had Melissa remarking aloud to no one in particular, "D'you think he heard me?"

"Everyone else did. How could he no' hear ye as well?" Lachlan replied.

"Unless you stuck him in the dungeon. He *is* upstairs, aye? I didna miss—?"

She didn't have to finish. Lincoln – or someone – could be heard coming down the hall upstairs, not quite running, but close to it.

It was him, and he stopped at the top of the stairs for a moment, a distinct hesitation upon seeing the small crowd gathered below. As soon as his eyes settled on Melissa, though, he hurried down to join them.

Melissa grinned. "Well, then, you're no' standing me up? We're still going for that ride?"

"Absolutely."

She beamed at him for playing along without

303

asking her what she was talking about. But she quickly took his hand and dragged him toward the front door. She sent a wave back toward her father and uncles.

"We'll be back in an hour or two – or three," she promised. "Or at least afore lunch."

"I know ye will, darlin'," Lachlan said significantly. "Ye wouldna want me tae worry."

"Och," she grumbled as soon as they were outside. "He would have tae put it that way."

"What are you up to?" Lincoln asked.

"The ride Ian suggested, o' course – and wondering why you didna want tae join us?"

"'Us'? He didn't mention any 'us.'"

"He hinted I'd be coming."

"The hell he did."

"He didna tell you that you'd enjoy it?"

"Well . . . blast him, why didn't he just be specific and tell me outright, instead of leaving me to guess what he had in mind?"

"Because he wants you tae trust him. You can, you know. He wants tae see this turn out in our favor. And it was his idea to offer himself for chaperon on this ride, so we could have some time tae ourselves."

Lincoln sighed. "I appreciate that, more than I can say, but I doubt I'll be able to trust any MacFearson – ever, even him."

"You will."

"When they're still trying their damnedest to keep me from what I want most in the world?"

She stopped, turned to face him, assured him, "If

I didna think we have a chance tae change their minds about us, I'd be suggesting we leave here right now."

"God, I wish I could be as certain as you, Melissa. Then this might not be driving me crazy."

"Och, that's the one thing we canna have happening," she chided. "We're here tae prove them wrong about you, no' prove them right."

He raised a brow at her. "Are you teasing me?"

"Are you actually in doubt?"

He snorted, took her hand again, and continued along the path. Ian had all three mounts ready and waiting just outside the stable.

His only question was "No objection from your da?"

"Nay, why would he? This is a normal outing. As long as we dinna try tae hide anything from him, he's no' reason tae restrict normal activities."

Ian nodded, mounted up. "Let's be off, then."

The plan had been to ride about the lake, since it offered such pretty views, but with her nightmare still so fresh in her mind, she suggested they ride to the coast instead. It wasn't that far. An hour there, an hour back, they'd still be home before lunch.

Ian rode behind them so he wouldn't have to crane his neck constantly. He meant to allow them space to talk privately, but he still took his role seriously, so they weren't to be out of his sight.

They had a bit of sun, but it didn't last long. The weather was still nice in that it wasn't raining, and they were in no hurry to get anywhere, really. They rode side by side at a slow clip, easy enough to talk, though they weren't talking yet, but rather spending most of the time just glancing at each other now that no one was around to curtail that pleasant activity. Most subjects they needed to discuss weren't going to be as pleasant.

Melissa expected some complaints. It couldn't be easy, what Lincoln was having to deal with. She broached that after they reached the coast. They stopped on a high bluff overlooking the ocean and a good deal of the coastline. Ian dismounted to see if there was an easy way down to the shore from there, or if they'd need to ride farther west first.

"How are you holding up?" she asked Lincoln. "No' feeling like killing anyone yet?"

"How should I know? I went crazy two days ago."

"Bah, you're teasing me now."

"If I were teasing, the answer would have been yes."

She sighed, dismounted as well, and walked to the edge of the bluff. A gust of wind shot up to disturb her skirt, enough that she needed to hold it down. Her hair was a lost cause, a riot of tangles after the ride.

She stared out at the gray water and the darker gray clouds beyond. "I'm sorry."

"Shush, it's not your fault you come from savage stock," she heard behind her.

She swung around with a gasp but this time found him grinning at her – and standing right next to her. The wind was playing havoc with his hair as well, black strands whipping about his face. She'd forgotten just how windy the coast could be – and chilly.

He put his hands on her shoulders, started to pull her closer. Ian's voice moved them apart again.

"There's a path o'er here," Ian shouted as he headed back toward them. "I thought I remembered one from years ago when I came this way."

"Why were you here afore?" she asked.

"It was long ago. Charlie, Neill, and I made a day o' it, followed the coast for a good five hours once. We found a few sea caves. At least we called them caves, though they were no more'n crevices worn away by eons o' the Lady Ocean dancing around her cliffs."

"Getting poetic in your old age, Ian?" she teased.

"Bah, nay, it just sounded better'n calling them holes in the cliff wall. Leave the horses here. The path is a wee bit too narrow for them."

"Is there a point to going down to the shore?" Lincoln asked.

"Aside from its being interesting? No, it'll just give me something to do while ye two get reacquainted."

"By all means, then."

There was only a small strip of rocky shore between the cliffs. It was picturesque, something of a cove, with the ocean butting up against the cliff and blocking them from going farther in either direction without swimming. Which made it very private. And Melissa and Lincoln were both wishing that Ian weren't with them by the time they reached the bottom and saw just how private the area was.

"Your caves are down here, Ian?"

"One is. That big boulder is hiding it."

She went to look. Sure enough, there was a low overhang of dirt and rock with a few tufts of grass and a dark pocket behind it. It would require almost crawling to get inside.

"Think anything is in there?"

"Other than sea urchins and spiders?"

She chuckled. "The kind o' thing for young lads tae explore. I'll settle for this brisk air and— Och, where did that come from?"

The rain rolled in off the ocean so quickly that none of them had noticed it coming. There was no question about exploring the crevice now. They all hurried into it. It really was no more than a low recess eroded in the cliff wall though, with barely enough room for two to sit huddled in it, let alone three. And Ian, being the last to enter, got thoroughly drenched before he squeezed inside. It was dry inside though, the walls a mixture of dirt and rock, and not so dark once they were in it, with the light from outside filtering in. And no spiders – at least none willing to investigate the intruders.

A few minutes later the rain started to ease off, more a drizzle now, and, with Lincoln sitting so close to her, Melissa began thinking of other things. She stared at Ian, pointedly enough that he finally got the message.

"Och, lass, have a heart," he complained. "It's bloody well dropping buckets oot there."

"*You* have a heart," she countered. "And the rain is stopping. Give me five minutes alone wi' him. You're already wet. What can we do in five minutes?"

"Ye're going tae owe me," he grumbled as he pulled his wet coat closer about him.

"I already owe ye." She grinned at him. "I'll name m'firstborn after you."

"Faith, spare us that," he said as he began to crawl back outside.

He was no sooner out of sight than Lincoln was drawing her closer to him. "I should have wed you first, then brought you home and wed you again for their benefit. This would be much easier to get through if you were already mine," he whispered by her ear.

"But I am already yours. D'you think I gave m'self tae you wi'oot knowing in m'heart it would be forever?"

He groaned. "I want to make love to you so bad I can barely stand it."

"I want that too, but he'll be back in a few minutes," she replied wistfully.

"Then let me taste you while I can."

His arms tightened around her. The kiss was ravishing, with pent up desire too long denied. He was crushing her. She didn't care. She was gripping his hair too tightly without realizing it. He didn't feel it. God, she loved kissing him. She couldn't smell him – the scent of damp earth in their small space was too strong – but she could taste him, feel him – and she wanted so much more . . .

"Get out!"

It was Lincoln shouting. She was so surprised she couldn't react for a moment. She hadn't heard it, the sound of rubble falling inside the hole around them. Though she did now, he had heard it immediately, and there was a sense of urgency about him, and violence, as he shoved her out to safety.

No sooner was she on her feet outside the crevice than he was hugging her so hard she couldn't breathe. "You're all right? Tell me you're all right!"

"I'm fine, Linc, really," she assured him. "It was just a few rocks falling."

He stepped back, put a hand over his eyes, tried to compose himself. He was still visibly shaken, though his voice was at least calm now.

"I know. I'm sorry for overreacting. But my father died like that. With dirt and rock crushing him. He only survived a few days, just long enough for them to dig him out and get him home. This brought it all back."

"Hush, you dinna have tae apologize."

"I wonder if my past will ever stop haunting me."

"It will," she said, and now she was hugging him as hard as she could. "You willna have time for past reflections when you marry me. Only laughter and sunshine are packed in my trousseau."

He leaned back to see her face, smiled at her. "You promise, Meli?"

"Aye, I do."

Ian came running over to them then. "What happened?"

"It's no' safe in there," Melissa said. "The walls started tae crumble."

"Then let's head home and hope we don't catch our death in this weather."

That was easier said than done. Startled by the first onslaught of rain, their horses had run away.

45

They were found late that afternoon about halfway home, crossing an open heath. The riders came from the coast behind them, had missed them on the first pass through the area – possibly when they took cover in the charred ruins of an abandoned croft after the downpour had started up again in earnest.

Twenty-three riders. It was like an army bearing down on them – or a murderous gang. The foul weather certainly didn't help tempers, and Lachlan had lost his own several hours ago because of his worry.

"There'll be no more outings until this matter is settled one way or another" was the first thing he said to Melissa. "Ye're trying tae make this a normal situation, but it's far from that. No more."

Melissa merely sighed. "You're no' e'en going tae ask what happened? Or d'you think that we were having fun, walking home in the rain?"

"Ye lost yer horses," Adam answered her. "We already knew that."

"Yers and Ian's horse returned tae the stable,

which was when we set oot tae find ye," Ian Four added.

"Lincoln's stallion isna familiar enough wi' his new surroundings, though. He's probably causing havoc somewhere and will hae tae be tracked down," Johnny said, and then volunteered, "I'll take a few o' m'brothers and see if we canna find him afore dark sets in."

"Ye should've returned home at the first sign o' rain," Lachlan admonished.

Lincoln couldn't believe they were actually nit-picking over trifles, while Melissa was standing there shivering. "She's caught cold," he said curtly. "Do your scolding in a warm place."

It didn't help that he was, in effect, criticizing Lachlan. The MacGregor reached down and pulled Melissa into his lap, then rode off without another word. It would have been too much to hope that one of them might have offered him a mount so he could have carried her home.

Lincoln wouldn't be the least bit surprised if he'd be left to walk the rest of the way himself. He was, in fact, surprised when Ian One offered him a hand to ride behind him and they set out to follow Lachlan.

"You're getting soft in your old age, MacFearson," Lincoln remarked when Ian One's horse slowed down a bit a few minutes later.

A chuckle. "D'ye think so? Then let me tell ye how I see this now, from my perspective. When Dougi confessed that he more or less started the thing back then, it changed m'view somewhat."

313

"The hell it did. You're still against my marrying Melissa."

"Aye, but there's only one reason now. Afore that confession there were a whole lot more – yer betrayal o' Dougi and a host o' other meanspirited things. And had ye no' gone crazy, m'brothers and I would be owing you some serious apologies."

"I take it you don't feel you're to blame for my 'going crazy'?"

"Faith, are *ye* blaming us for that?"

"Considering I don't agree I was crazy, no. What I blame you for was never asking what really happened and assuming that my actions were the result of 'going crazy.' I was in a volatile state of mind, faced with losing my best friend for good if I couldn't straighten that mess out with him. You and your brothers weren't even going to let me try. That's what I blame you for, Ian."

"Well, there's no changing that, and no changing that ye werena behaving normal. And wi'oot some other reason tae blame for it—"

"I've already given you reasons."

"Aye, desperation, pain, rage – a nasty mix that, but still no' enough tae account for a complete lack o' reason and self-preservation. D'*ye* want tae see Melissa, whom ye claim tae love, endangered by such?"

"So now I'm risking her life by loving her? Do you realize how farfetched that reasoning is, Ian, when nothing like what happened then has ever happened again? Nineteen years gone by, and not one thing to even remotely suggest that I might be harboring some kernel of craziness deep inside me that could be unleashed at any time."

"But it did happen," Ian reminded him. "And what happens once can—"

"Spare me," Lincoln interrupted in disgust. "Better yet, let me give you a different summation. The lot of you are too guilty over your own actions back then to give in now and admit that you were wrong."

Ian sighed. "If ye mun see it that way, so be it. We just want our niece tae be happy *and* safe in her choice o' husband. We dinna want tae spend the rest of our days worrying aboot her in yer care. And nothing has happened tae prove yer point o' view."

"No, the proof you're waiting for is to have *your* point of view confirmed. But that isn't going to happen. Provoke me until you run out of ways to, and it still won't happen, because I'm *not* crazy. But I swear, if anything *could* drive someone crazy, it's you MacFearsons."

Ian actually laughed. "D'ye think so, lad? Maybe that can be added tae the legend."

Lincoln snorted and said no more. And the rain started again. He and Ian were both sneezing by the time the walls of Kregora came into view.

Up ahead Lachlan's worry should have eased, but it grew steadily worse. Melissa wasn't trying to wheedle an apology out of him for assuming the worst. She wasn't saying anything. And his daughter being this quiet wasn't normal.

He'd wrapped her in his thick coat, which was a bit dryer than hers, though not much. They'd run into the heavier rain when they'd reached the coast as well, before turning back inland in their search.

"How bad is the cold ye've caught, darlin'?" he leaned over her shoulder to ask.

"Just a wee one, though maybe a bit o' fever, too," she said.

He could barely hear her. "Yer mother will take care o' it, as soon as we get ye home."

"I know," she replied with a sigh. "But who will take care o' Lincoln if he gets sick, too? He has no one here tae care about him but me."

"I will," Lachlan said grudgingly.

"Promise, Da?"

It wasn't lost on him that even in sickness her concern wasn't for herself but for the man she loved. Faith, he wished he could trust that man and give her what she wanted, his blessing. He'd never had to deny her anything before. Of course, she'd never before asked for something that might endanger her either.

46

More than half of the MacFearson brothers caught cold that day. By the next afternoon half of Kregora was sneezing as well. It wasn't a serious contagion, though it hit some worse than others. Typical aches and pains, a few fevers, general grouchiness. But as soon as someone started to feel better, someone else would sneeze in his or her direction and start the cycle all over again.

Melissa's fever had been much worse than she'd let on, which prompted Kimberly to insist she spend a few days or more in bed. Kimberly then caught the cold from her and ended up in her own bed, at Lachlan's insistence, which left it to him to make sure they both took their tonics on time and stayed put – no easy task where his wife was concerned.

He remained healthy himself. And fortunately, Lincoln's cold was mild, without any fever, and was gone in a few days, so Lachlan didn't have to play nursemaid to him as well, as he'd promised Melissa he'd do.

That was why they ended up sharing dinner alone two days later. No one else felt well enough to come down for it. Lincoln almost didn't enter the room, though, when he realized that it would just be the two of them.

Lachlan noticed his hesitation and said, "Dinna worry about it. We can discuss whatever ye'd like or no' talk a'tall. I am too fond o' m'belly tae bother it wi' disagreeable blathering at a meal."

Lincoln nodded, took the chair next to him. "Without one of your brothers-in-law dissecting my every word, trying to pull out an insult they can make use of, some simple talk would be most welcome."

Lachlan chuckled. "Ye know I liked ye when I met ye. I still like ye. My objections o'er m'lass have nothing tae do with that."

"I know. How is Melissa?"

Lachlan would have laughed again, since he got asked that question every time he saw the lad, but he was familiar with that kind of concern, which was nothing to make light of. And wasn't Melissa asking him the same thing each time he saw her? The both of them could think of nothing but each other.

"Her fever is lingering, or she'd be up by now. It's almost gone, though, so she'll likely be oot o' bed by tomorrow, in the afternoon at least."

"If not, may I see her?"

"Aye, if you agree tae do so from her doorway," Lachlan replied, then assured Lincoln, "Which has nothing tae do with anything other than I'm trying tae keep this thing from passing back and forth anymore'n necessary.

"Understood."

"Good. Now, tell me something about yerself that I dinna know yet."

Lincoln gave that some thought, then finally grinned. "I love fishing. So did my uncle, for that matter, so much that he had a fish pond built on his property just for that. He introduced me to it soon after I moved to England."

"Och, aye, a fine sport that. As it happens, I enjoy it m'self."

"How could you not, with such a magnificent lake for a backyard?"

"True."

"I find it one of the most relaxing endeavors."

"Ye are due some o' that, I'm thinking," Lachlan said. "I've a fine set o' poles. Ye're welcome tae borrow one while ye're here."

"Thank you, I'll definitely take you up on that," Lincoln replied. "But I'm sure that isn't the kind of knowledge you were fishing for."

Lachlan burst out laughing over the double entendre. "I'm so transparent, then?"

"When it comes to your daughter, yes. And there is something about me you may find somewhat interesting."

"Aye?"

"You wondered why I speak like an Englishman," Lincoln began.

"Ye're already explained that, that yer teachers pounded the burr out o' ye."

"That isn't really an accurate explanation, merely a brief one."

"And the long version?"

"One doesn't forget the language one learns from birth, and I spent the first ten years of my life not far from here. It's still in me, and as strong as ever."

"I'm no' sure I understand."

"What was drilled into me was discipline. My uncle found an excellent tutor. By treating English as a new language, rather than the same language with different accents, I was able to speak as those around me did. My uncle was pleased, my tutor was pleased, my teachers were pleased. I wasn't, but that was not relevant."

"Commendable, but I'm thinking ye havena come tae the point yet."

Lincoln chuckled. "I guess I'm rather transparent as well. But because I still prefer what I was born to, every word I utter is a conscious choice."

"No distracted mistakes?"

"None."

"Impossible."

"No, actually, just difficult, but possible because of the discipline I developed."

Lachlan began to frown. "Ye're about tae tell me that this discipline ye learned has carried o'er tae other aspects o' yer life, aye? Like yer temper?"

"Indeed."

"Bah, no mon can control his emotions all o' the time," Lachlan insisted.

"I'm no' saying I dinna get angry," Lincoln

countered. "Though I've probably felt that emotion more'n the last month since the MacFearsons reentered m'life, than I hae in the last ten years. I'm saying if I do get angry, ye're no' likely tae know aboot it."

Lachlan gave a hoot of laughter over the burr he was hearing, but it wound down quickly when he recalled what Lincoln was hinting at. "Sae ye canna be provoked? There's no way tae re-create the past tae see if it repeats itself? Is that what ye're saying?"

"The past had many variables that I'm not willing to submit myself to again, thank you very much. More specifically, the pain. My anger has never again reached that point either. Desperation, though, is getting close."

Lachlan smiled tolerantly. "I can see that ye believe fully what ye're saying. But I'm a mon who believes everyone has a breaking point. Ye reached yers early, when you were still a child, and have since mastered yer emotions, so it ne'er happens again. On the one hand, I find that greatly reassuring. On the other, it makes m'decision e'en harder."

Lincoln sighed. "There really is no way to prove that I'm as sane as you."

Lachlan sighed as well. "I'm beginning tae see that. But dinna give up hope, lad. I need tae reassess m'thinking."

47

Melissa was extremely frustrated with herself, and her body in particular, for not recovering from her simple cold as quickly as she usually did. It had been many years since she'd had such a high fever, and, typical of fevers, it was worse at night.

Unfortunately, that meant it affected her dreams, and every night while the fever had lasted, she'd had her nightmares about the lake behind the castle. A few of them were truly terrifying, waking her up in a drenching sweat.

Worse, everyone else had already recovered, but she was still being told to stay in bed four days later. But enough was enough. She'd keep her distance from everyone, so as not to pass on the last lingering effects of the cold, but she was *not* staying in bed anymore.

She probably would have had more patience if her family would just admit that they were wrong about Lincoln. She wouldn't have minded being restricted to her room if she could have been planning her wedding while she was there, instead of still wondering if she would be having the one she'd always dreamed about.

Elopement was still a possibility. It was just very disappointing even to have to consider it. She'd had more faith in her family. She never would have suggested to Lincoln that they return if she hadn't.

She should sit down and have a heart-to-heart with her father. No, actually, she should talk to her mother first. Kimberly would know whether or not Lachlan was getting close to a decision.

But before that, Melissa needed to know what had been going on while she'd been stuck in her sickbed, and how Lincoln was holding up. She had worried the whole time she was confined to her room that without her presence to bolster him, and so much animosity on all fronts coming his way, he'd start thinking of giving up.

She went to find him now, but most of those she asked hadn't seen him that morning. Finally one did know and told her that he'd gone fishing.

"Where?" she asked.

"Where else?"

She chewed on her lip. It was a good lake for fishing that they had. There was no dragon living in it, of course. And it never bothered her when her clansmen took their little boats out on it. It bothered her when her father did, but he knew about her dreams and took pains to keep it from her when he felt like fishing.

It was a good day for fishing, too. The sun was shining nicely. The weather was mild for the end of summer, even if she was still slightly chilled herself due to the last small bit of fever she couldn't seem to shake.

She hoped Lincoln was just fishing from the shore of the lake. There were several really good spots for that, as well as at the end of the short pier that all the fishing boats were tied to.

Malcolm and Charles had wandered down to the lake when they'd heard that Lincoln had gone fishing. Ian Six had come along to keep the peace – if that were possible. He knew that his brothers were looking to cause trouble, Charles in particular. Of course, Charles was a natural instigator anyway. He didn't need Lincoln around to prove what an ass he could be, Charlie managed that all on his own.

But in Lincoln's case Charles actually carried around with him a list of insults that he consulted often – when he thought no one was looking – scratching off each one that didn't get a reaction out of Lincoln. He seemed absolutely determined to be the hero of the family, the one to finally push Lincoln over the edge to reveal his unstable nature – if he had one.

They arrived too late, though. Lincoln was already out in the center of the lake in one of the little fishing boats. But they stuck around for a bit in case he decided to come back in early, wandering farther from the pier until they came to a nice patch of shade to relax in. The angle of the sun across the water had been too bright at the pier, making it nearly impossible to see through the glare to the center of the lake. But the grassy spot they found in the shade gave them a clear view.

"I wonder who was foolish enough tae tell her he'd gone fishing?" Ian said.

"Tell who?" Charles asked.

"Meli. She's coming down the path tae the pier," Ian answered, staring in that direction.

"Why foolish?" Malcolm asked curiously as he glanced that way as well.

"Ye dinna know?" Ian replied in surprise.

"Would I be asking now, if I did?"

"Because she's got a real fear o' that lake," Ian explained. "Why d'ye think she's ne'er gone in it since that one time as a child when she almost drowned."

"She wouldna remember that," Charles scoffed. "She was barely oot o' swaddling when that happened. And she's no' afraid tae go swimming. She's often taken our cousins tae the pond near home."

"I said she's afraid o' the lake, ye dafty, no' of swimming," Ian replied. "She confessed tae me once that she thinks there's a really big . . . fish in it, big enough tae swallow someone whole."

"Fish?" Charles frowned.

"Fish?" Malcolm chuckled.

Ian scowled at them both. "Verra well, a bloody big dragon, tae be more precise."

Charles started rolling in the grass laughing, but Malcolm said seriously, "Ye're no' joking, are ye?"

"Nae."

"Sounds like a childish thing she should've outgrown," Malcolm said.

"Aye, and she knows better. It's just something she canna shake, a deep fear she's got no control o', so she simply stays away from the lake."

"Then what's she doing standing on the pier waving at that bastard?" Charles asked.

"Tae get his attention maybe?" Malcolm said, tongue in cheek.

She'd done that. Lincoln was waving back at her. But she obviously couldn't see that. She was shouting at him now and still waving, though he probably couldn't hear her any more than they could. He must have realized she couldn't see him, though, because he stood up in the small boat to assure her that he was aware of her presence.

"Takes an Englishmon tae be that dumb," Charles remarked dryly as they watched Lincoln's boat begin to rock unsteadily in the water.

"Or a man sae much in love he'd rather put his woman at ease than care for his own safety."

"What rubbish," Charles scoffed yet again. "When did ye become his champion, eh?"

"I'm no' his champion, but I dinna think he's crazy, which is the only objection left tae his marrying the lass. And e'en if he was, he's sane enough ninety-nine percent o' the time, or at least all the times we've witnessed since she set her cap for him, for her feelings tae tip the scale in the matter. She loves him—"

"Bah, she only thinks she does. She'll find

someone else soon enough, once Lachlan stops dillydallying and gives him the boot."

"Did anyone e'er mention what an ass ye are, Charlie?" Ian shot back.

Charles was quick to take a swing at Ian, but Ian was quick as well in moving out of the way. Charles decided not to pursue the insult and angrily jerked his coat back down. His scowl promised later retribution, though.

"Ye've a special closeness wi' Meli the rest of us dinna share," Charles pointed out stiffly. "How can ye e'en think of allowing Linc tae hae her?"

"There's a better question for that," Ian countered.

"Let me guess—"

"Spare us," Ian cut in. "Yer mind canna support guessing."

Charles dove at Ian this time. They rolled in the grass several feet before Malcolm was able to separate them. They were both angrily jerking down their coats this time.

Malcolm tsked, brought them back to the subject. "What's the better question?"

"Charles is incapable o' understanding—"

"I'm the one asking now, no' Charlie," Malcolm cut in this time.

"Verra well. He asked how I could allow Linc tae have her. The better question is, How can I think o' denying her what her heart insists she have?"

"Ye canna prove tae me that she loves him that much," Charles said, his tone still full of animosity. "Women are too fickle."

327

"Are ye saying Kimberly is fickle in what she feels for Lachlan?"

"Kimber's an exception," Charles mumbled.

"Kimber raised Meli."

"I hate tae break up this fascinating diatribe o' nonsense," Malcolm interrupted yet again. "But what's Meli screaming aboot?"

The two younger brothers scanned the lake and pier again. Lincoln, as they'd figured would happen, had fallen into the water, his boat, though still upright, bobbing beside him. Melissa, on the edge of the pier, was screaming her heart out. Though they still couldn't hear what she was saying from their distance, it was a safe guess that she was calling for help.

"She thinks he's drowning," Ian said.

"We can hope."

"That isna funny, Charles. And we'd better go calm her down. I dinna think she can see that he's fine and trying tae get back in the boat. The sun glare on the lake is too strong o'er there where she's standing. All she might be able tae see is an empty boat."

"He'll be back in the boat afore we have a chance tae reach her," Malcolm said.

"Still, it will ease her mind if she sees us coming tae help."

"She's no' going tae be looking this way tae see it. She's jumped in."

"I'll be damned," Ian said, sitting back down in disbelief. "She's swimming oot tae save him herself. She's terrified o' that lake, yet she loves him enough

328

tae enter it for him. Are ye paying attention, Charlie? Ye wanted proof, and now ye have it."

Charles didn't remark on that, said instead, "She just sank."

Ian shot back to his feet, but he couldn't see Meli in the water anymore either. "She's swimming underneath," he said in a panic, trying to convince himself. "She mun be."

"Nae, she sank, I tell you, like something pulled her under."

Ian didn't hear the last. He was already sprinting down the shore toward the pier, following Malcolm, who had started ahead of him. But neither of them had a chance of getting there in time. They were both too far away.

48

Kregora was silent. No laughter, none of the usual banter among the servants. All speech had reverted to whispers. No one wanted to disturb the mournful quiet.

Lachlan sat in a corner of his daughter's room, his head in his hands. His cheeks were damp. Every few moments another tear would roll down to keep them that way. He'd never felt so helpless in his life. He'd been unable to help his daughter. And he'd been unable to help his wife, who was breaking his heart in her efforts to bring Melissa back to them.

Kimberly was kneeling by Melissa's bed, talking to her as if she could hear her. Melissa's eyes were open, but there was nothing behind them. They were vacant, unseeing.

Kimberly gave up for the moment, trying to reach Melissa, and came over to cry in Lachlan's lap. Finally, something he could do for her. But her sobs were ripping him apart. He couldn't bear it, her being in this much emotional pain.

"Her mind is gone. Her eyes are open, but she doesn't hear me!"

"The doctor said she can recover." He'd also said she might not, but he'd told only Lachlan that part.

"It was too much fear. She's run away from it and won't come back. It was all her nightmares combined! Blast that lake. We should have drained it."

"Nae, we should have put her back in it when she first got frightened of it, instead of being soft and just keeping her away from it."

Lincoln had saved her. He'd been the only one close enough to do so, able to swim to her and find her under the water before her uncles had reached them to help. He'd pulled her to shore. They'd thought she was dead. She hadn't been breathing. But then the water had spilled out of her lungs. Her eyes had opened at the same time, and they hadn't closed since. But she wasn't really there, wasn't seeing anything. It was as if she were still unconscious.

The doctor mentioned shock, but he had no real experience with it to suggest how to get rid of it. He had only a few names of other doctors who might know more, though he didn't seem very hopeful in that regard. He'd just told them to keep her warm, keep her comfortable, that there was nothing else they could do. But she wasn't really awake to be cared for, to eat. If she didn't come out of it, she could waste away . . .

They didn't hear the knock on the door. Lincoln finally just opened it, stood there undecided whether to try to gain the attention of Melissa's parents. He probably looked as distraught as they did. He'd been told what the doctor had to say. He was numb. It was too much to comprehend, that Melissa might not recover – and unacceptable. Nor had he understood what the problem was, or why she'd retreated into herself, why they were so frightened for her.

Her uncles, waiting outside her room with him, explained about her fear of the lake and why she never went in it. A lake monster. Something children would think of, but for her it was a thought she'd never let go of. For her it was real. If she entered the lake, she'd surely die. That she'd done so for him had them amazed, and a few of them were reassessing their opinions of him.

As the hours passed in their vigil and he seemed to be ignoring them, her uncles thought he couldn't hear them as they were whispering among themselves. But he'd caught drifts of what they were discussing – him, as usual.

"She really does love him."

"She's always been a sensible lass. She mun see something in him that we dinna see."

"She didna love him tae begin wi', but there was something aboot that first meeting that had them both knowing they wanted tae marry. She was sure o' it. He came the verra next day to request permission tae court her. It wasna love yet, it wasna just attraction. What does that tell ye, then? They knew – be it fate or some unexplained bond – they knew they were destined for each other."

"As if he hadna been sent tae England, they'd hae met and courted normal?"

"Aye, exactly. The bond was meant tae be. It was just late in catching up tae them."

Lincoln didn't hold much hope that they'd remember any of those words after Melissa was recovered. And she would recover. If he had any doubt of that, he'd probably be out of his mind already.

"Can I see her?" he asked Lachlan. "Please."

The older man nodded but made no move to leave. After a moment more, Lincoln added, "Alone?"

It was nearly a full minute before Lachlan nodded again. He stood up, carefully set his wife on her feet, and, with an arm around her, led her out of the room. She was too distraught to notice. The door even closed behind them. Lincoln hadn't expected quite that much privacy.

Melissa had no color. It wasn't the low lighting in the room. She really had no color at all on her face, was as deathly pale as . . .

Her wet clothes had been changed and a plain white nightgown put on her, long-sleeved, high-necked, but it appeared to be comfortable, the material very soft. Her hair was dry now, most of it spread out on the pillow under her, though one dark auburn lock curled across the blue cover, which was drawn up nearly to her neck.

She was so beautiful, even in her paleness. That her eyes were open was disconcerting. It had led him to believe she was fine, merely shaken up, when he'd carried her back to the castle. But they were vacant, unseeing . . . lifeless.

He sat on the edge of her bed. One of her arms was outside the cover. He took her hand, brought her palm to his cheek, placed it there, held it there. It was cold, her fingers stiff. If he couldn't see the very slight movement of her chest as she breathed shallowly, he'd think she was dead. It sent a cold chill through his body.

"Melissa?" No reaction. "I'm going to assume that you can hear me, so I will tell you some things you will find of interest. Your dragon is dead."

Still no reaction. He'd honestly thought that would do it, had been counting on it. It was the reason her mind had retreated. Perhaps a little more elaboration.

"I killed him myself – didn't trust anyone else to do it right. It wasn't easy, but I sent him to the bottom of the lake, where he'll rot and never bother you again. Did you hear that, Meli? You're safe now. Did you really think I'd let a mere dragon hurt you?"

Still no movement, not even a blink. She might not be hiding from the dragon, as most of them assumed. The dragon was something she'd apparently lived with for a very long time. She might simply not have a good enough reason to return. He could give her at least one.

"Meli, it's time to come back to us so we can marry. Your parents won't object anymore." That wasn't positive enough. "I have their blessing now. We can be wed just as soon as you're ready."

Her finger twitched by his temple. His heart leaped with excitement but just as quickly plummeted. Her eyes were still staring at the ceiling, empty. A muscle reaction that hadn't been voluntary. It was killing him, but he controlled his disappointment.

He brought her palm lower to kiss the center of it. Her hand had warmed considerably next to his skin.

"Really?"

His eyes flew to hers. Her voice had been weak, scratchy, but she was looking at him. She'd come back. He didn't know whether to laugh or cry, felt like doing both, shouted with joy instead.

"Yes!"

The door flew open behind him. Half her family fell into the room. They'd had their ears stuck to the door eavesdropping, and they hadn't counted on Lachlan's opening it immediately at Lincoln's shout.

While Kimberly rushed over and collapsed on Melissa in tears of relief, Lachlan pulled Lincoln aside to ask, "How did ye do it?"

"I lied to her," Lincoln said in a tone completely lacking any apology for doing so. "I told her we had your blessings to marry."

Lachlan took a moment to digest that before he burst out laughing. " 'Twas no lie, lad. I needed nothing more tae convince me than her entering that lake – for ye. I canna deny that kind o' love any longer. Come what may, m'daughter needs ye tae be complete."

Lincoln was grateful to hear that at last, but it simply paled in comparison to his relief that Melissa was back among them, her mind intact. He hadn't been willing to admit that she might not recover, had refused to even consider it, yet the possibility had been there nonetheless.

He squeezed in between those gathered around Melissa's bed now, in time to hear Adam ask, "What's wrong with yer voice, lass?"

"I mun have screamed tae much calling for help. 'Tis a wee bit sore, is all. I could use some water, though."

"I think ye've had enough water for one day," Johnny said meaningfully. "How aboot a nice bracing shot o' whiskey instead, eh?"

"Your ears are due for a boxing, Johnny," Kimberly told her brother. "Go tell cook some honeyed tea is needed. That will soothe the scratchiness."

He left reluctantly but found a servant just outside to relay the order to, and he was back in a moment announcing, "The *non*bracing stuff is on the way."

"Sae what happened?" Adam was asking. "Ye're a good swimmer. Why did ye sink in the water?"

Melissa blushed. It brought back any remaining color she'd still been missing, and then some.

"I felt something brush against my leg. It was probably just my skirt, but that's not what my mind was telling me. It brought all m'worst nightmares tae life, made them real. I'm guessing I fainted."

"The water is no' a good place tae faint, blast it!" Ian Six complained.

He'd probably aged a few years in his fear, running to reach Melissa and knowing he'd never make it in time. And then for her not to recover immediately . . .

"I suppose not." She grinned at him.

"Ye think 'tis funny, then?"

She reached for his hand to squeeze it. "I'm just sae relieved tae know the dragon doesna exist – or wasna paying attention tae notice us – that I'd be finding anything funny right now, aye."

"Ye still think he's down there?" Ian Four chided her incredulously.

"I know there's no dragon. Logically, maturely, I know it. But the child in me refused tae e'er believe that. But nae, I was joking. I know he's gone now. M'Linc put him tae rest once and for all."

Lachlan hadn't been one of the ones with his ear against the door, so he asked, "And how did he do that?"

"He said he killed him."

"Ye believe that?"

"Aye." Lachlan was frowning at her doubtfully. She smiled at him. "It's all in what you want tae believe, Da. I will forever now have an image o' the dragon spiraling downward in the water, dead, tae rest in peace on the bottom o' the lake. E'en though I *know* he was ne'er there, the child in me is now sure o' that, too."

49

It was very odd, to be among the MacFearsons and not have most of them scowling at him. It was even odder not to have even one of them scowling at him. Lincoln was finding the situation both unique and disconcerting, particularly since the issues they'd held against him hadn't been resolved. Were they really going to let Melissa's feelings take precedence over their fears, as seemed to be the case?

A lot of the MacFearsons had returned to their own homes, now that Lachlan's blessing had been announced to them all. But a good half of them were lingering at Kregora and probably would continue to do so until after the wedding. Because they still didn't trust him? Or because they didn't have wives or lovers to return to, and the atmosphere was livelier and more entertaining at Kregora?

Lincoln made no remark about their change toward him, but it was as if he were already accepted into their family, just as they'd said would happen if he married their niece. They weren't married yet, but with the MacGregor's blessing it was as good as done in their eyes. Thus he was now one of them. Bah, the devil should be so lucky.

His own grudges wouldn't be as easily forgotten. At least, he had himself convinced of that. He was the one who'd taken the severe beatings back then, not them. He was the one who'd lost his best friend, not them. They had merely gotten rid of a nuisance, as they saw him. He'd lost his friend, his home – his mother.

No, he was sure he could never forgive or forget any of that. Then he wasn't so sure – after Dougall approached him a few days later.

It was the first time he found himself completely alone with his old childhood friend. He'd been having a chat with Lachlan in the parlor prior to retiring for the night. Lachlan had apprised him of some of the plans Melissa and her mother were making for the wedding, before he went off to bed himself.

Melissa had been ordered to stay in bed all of yesterday. Though she had come downstairs today, that little bit of exertion had quickly tired her. She was still in a weakened state from her near brush with death.

Lachlan had sent her straight back to her bedroom when he noticed, to her great chagrin. So Lincoln wasn't getting much chance to talk to her himself. The one time he'd been allowed into her room on the day of her near drowning was an exception her parents weren't going to repeat – not until after they were married anyway.

Lincoln was finishing up a warmed brandy

before he retired himself. His cold had returned briefly yesterday, after his dunking in the lake. Now it was gone again. The brandy before bed was merely to make sure he went right to sleep so he got enough rest to keep it gone.

Dougall showed up in the parlor moments after Lachlan left it, as if he'd been waiting around for just that to happen. He stopped there at the door, though, possibly having second thoughts about approaching. Lincoln could almost see his resolve bolster through, just before he continued toward the fireplace where Lincoln was standing. Whatever was on his mind, he was quite determined about it.

"I'm wondering if we can be friends again." Dougall blurted it out, without any preamble.

"No."

Dougall turned away, obviously disappointed. But then he turned back to ask, "I'm wondering if ye'll change your mind someday?"

"No."

Dougall sighed, turned away again. Lincoln wondered aloud, "Do you always believe everything you hear?"

Dougall turned back once more, grinning widely now. "Ye were teasing me?"

"Of course not."

"Och, ye're as bad as ye e'er were. I ne'er knew when tae believe ye or not."

"Yes you did," Lincoln replied. "You're just out of practice."

"I wanted tae congratulate ye. There's no lass

341

finer than our Meli. Ye were luckier than ye know, the day she fell in love wi' you."

"I came to that conclusion myself long ago." Lincoln smiled. "Did you marry?"

"Nae, only a few o' m'brothers have. For m'self, I canna find a lass who'll put up wi' m'family – or me, for that matter – for more'n a few days," Dougall added with a grin. "I've a son, though."

Lincoln's brows shot up. "Taking after your father, then, are you?"

"No' really. I'm no' e'en positive he's mine, though I like tae think sae. He looks like me."

"What's his mother have to say about it?" Lincoln asked him.

"She denies it."

"But you doubt her? Why?"

"Because she hates m'guts. And she was already wed when we – er—"

Just a single brow rose this time. "Seducing married women, Dougi?"

"Nae, I didna know she was already wed," Dougall insisted, blushing slightly. "I make a habit o' finding oot such things aforehand, when I'm interested in a lass. But she was the one started it. And that's no' bragging," Dougall assured him with a chuckle. "She's the only lass who e'er *did* give me the come-hither look. I dinna hae the striking looks most o' m'brothers were blessed wi', after all. I took more after m'mother than the MacFearson."

Dougall did turn out rather plain-looking compared to the rest of the savages. But if he wasn't compared, he was a fine-looking man on his own. However, in this area of the Highlands, he would be compared. It was inevitable, simply because there were so many MacFearsons to compare him to, and in that case he came up lacking.

"It was at a party the MacGregor was having," Dougall continued. "He throws some grand ones, he does, a few times each year. And she lives here," he added in a whisper, as if he thought she might be listening at the door. "Everyone was drunk tae their gills that night."

Dougall went on to explain in full detail his one night of sin with a married woman. It was as if he'd gone nineteen years without having someone to confide in, which just might be the case. His brothers protected him fiercely, but he'd never really been close to any one of them.

They spent half the night catching up just the way normal old friends do. The difference was, their friendship had been severed rather violently. But Lincoln now had so much happiness in his life to look forward to that he just might be able to ignore the pains from his past.

50

It could be a serious inconvenience to be an only child. In Melissa's case her slightest little ills got exaggerated all out of proportion by her parents, who had no other children to coddle and worry over. It wasn't the first time in her life that she'd been made to convalesce much longer than necessary. She hoped it would be the last, hoped that Lincoln hadn't been taking notes on how to care for her from her parents.

She'd been told, more than once, that she simply made a very disagreeable patient. That probably was all it was, her high annoyance over such coddling. There was certainly nothing else in her life now for her to be annoyed about, when everything that had been wrong had just corrected itself – or would be corrected, as soon as her wedding took place.

She could begrudge the fact that she'd nearly had to die for her father to "see the light," as it were. She didn't, though. She was too thrilled to have her family accept Lincoln to nitpick over why they did.

She just wished their minds could have been put at ease completely.

They'd given in instead, gracefully but reluctantly. Yet she had a feeling they'd always be watching Lincoln more closely than was necessary. And eventually he'd probably notice and come to resent it.

Her grouchiness, which she blamed on being confined too long, was actually a combination of several things that she wasn't quite experienced enough to realize. Her wedding date had been set for four weeks down the road, too long away when she wanted to be sharing Lincoln's bed already. Each time she found Lincoln alone, she'd no sooner take a few steps toward him than someone else would show up. There were just too many people living at Kregora. Frustration at every turn.

And her father was still reaching for her brow every time he saw her. She was now swatting his hand away before he could, but that only caused him to send Kimberly to her to make sure her fever was still gone. And you simply didn't swat away your mother's concerned hand.

Melissa received the letter that morning. It gave her a legitimate excuse to seek Lincoln out. Not that she needed any excuses now. But they still weren't allowed any real privacy together. She didn't have an official chaperon, but if they weren't always in sight of someone, her father would be wanting to know why. They could talk privately though, just as long as they didn't try to go off alone to do it.

She located him in the stable. His stallion had been found and returned a few days ago, but was a bit unmanageable after running wild. The lads who worked in the stable were too hesitant to approach the horse when he was apparently snapping at anyone who got near, which left it to Lincoln to groom him until he settled down.

She stood there for a few minutes watching Lincoln before he noticed her. Ian Three was down at the end of the stable seeing to his own horse. He nodded at her when she entered but made no move to approach. He was going to ignore them – or seem to. At any rate, he was far enough away not to hear any conversation they had.

She still didn't let Lincoln know she was there yet, was enjoying too much just watching him. He had his day coat removed, his sleeves rolled up to his elbows. Sweat beaded on his brow, appeared on several spots of his white lawn shirt. He was due for getting his hair cut. It was beginning to curl about his shoulders.

He'd never seemed so . . . Scottish to her. Her father never hesitated to put his back into a task and get his hands dirty right alongside his clansmen. English lords just didn't do such things.

"You've done this afore?" she finally remarked. "I'd think a lord o' your consequence would leave such things tae grooms."

His brown eyes lit up with pleasure on seeing her. His firm lips formed a supple smile as he straightened up from his task. He ran one bare forearm over his brow to clear the sweat. Without benefit of the cloth from his shirtsleeve, he merely smeared it.

"I favor stallions, have had this one for many years," he told her. "He has several grooms at home accustomed to him and his occasional antics, but when they aren't around, yes, the duty falls to me. And, no, I don't mind. It's rather relaxing, actually."

She stepped up onto the lowest post of the stall he was working in, rested her elbows on the top post. "And why d'you favor stallions?"

He shrugged and continued brushing the animal. "I'm not exactly sure. Probably because I enjoy the test of wills and asserting who owns whom."

"Is he sure who's the owner?"

Lincoln grinned at her. "He likes to think he is. At times I'm sure he only tolerates me. Now, what brings you to the stable?"

"Och, I almost forgot. I've had a note from your Aunt Henriette, telling me that your mother has returned home tae the Highlands. I canna imagine why she would send it tae me rather than tae you."

The change about him was immediate and overly obvious. The warm light went out of his eyes. His mouth became a hard slash, his expression stiff, closed off. And his tone, when he answered, was positively frigid.

"Possibly because she knows I could not care less," he suggested.

Melissa choose to ignore the change in him – for

the moment – and remarked casually, "Hmmm, well, I suppose she's assuming we are as good as married already, and sae I would find the news o' interest."

"Why?"

"In case I want tae visit her."

"You don't."

She put her hands on her hips in an annoyed manner, no easy task with her feet balanced on a post. "Dinna be telling me what m'wants are."

He raised a brow. "Are we about to have our first married disagreement – prior to getting married?"

Instead of answering, she went straight for the heart of the matter. "Were you thinking this would ne'er come up, when she's going tae be m'mother-in-law? You wanted tae put that old bitterness tae rest," she reminded him. "Said that's why you came back tae Scotland."

"It didn't work. Seeing her only made it worse. And it doesn't matter now that I have you."

"It matters tae me."

"Why?"

"Because she's going tae be a member o' m'family," she said, stating the obvious.

"In her case you can overlook that."

"Overlook one o' the grandmothers o' m'bairns? I dinna think sae."

He looked chagrined and intrigued at the same time. "You're already planning on babies?"

"Certainly."

"Er, how many did you have in mind?"

She laughed at him, guessing the train of his

thoughts. "No' sixteen, that's for sure. Three or four will do nicely. And dinna be changing the subject. Your mother will be included in all our family gatherings. If I dinna invite her, m'own mother will. These are times o' fun and laughter. Are they always tae be painful tae you, wi' her included?"

His tone turned stiff again. "Obviously, some things can't be helped. I'll survive."

"Did you e'er give her a chance tae say she's sorry?" she asked.

"She had ample opportunity recently."

"Did she? If you were as stiff and unbending as you are now, I dinna think so."

He sighed. "What are you expecting me to do? Forgive her for abandoning me? She gave me away, Melissa. She literally gave me to her brother to raise."

"Does she know how you feel about that?"

"She knows I despise her."

"But that's the problem, Linc. You dinna despise her a'tall. You love her as much as you e'er did. That's why it hurts sae much. And that's the pain that needs tae be put tae rest."

51

Melissa wouldn't let up badgering Lincoln until he agreed to go see his mother. It took several hours before he gave in. It also took her agreeing to go with him. That, however, required a chaperon.

Jamie volunteered to ride over with them. So did Neill, who was with him. They left right after lunch. But although Melissa was going along, she didn't know what she could do to help. This thing was between mother and son. Yet there had to be a way to patch those old wounds of his.

Melissa wasn't sure what she was hoping for. By all accounts Lincoln had good reason to be bitter. But a simple "I'm sorry," could work wonders. That was assuming his mother *was* sorry, which was assuming a lot. If she wasn't, then this trip to try to end their breach would accomplish nothing. But Eleanor Ross hadn't seemed like an uncaring woman. The few occasions Melissa had met her, she'd seemed quiet, unassuming – and carrying a lot of pain herself.

It was the first time Melissa was seeing the home where Lincoln was born. It was an ordinary house, if very large, and it spoke of wealth in its fine details. It had probably been a happy place at one time. And it was probably just her imagination that made it seem like a place in mourning now.

They drew up on a hill before the house to wait for Jamie, who was lagging behind. Neill was suddenly looking rather nervous as he stared at the house below them.

"Jamie and I dinna hae tae actually meet yer mother, do we, Linc?" he asked.

"No, you can wait outside if you like. I doubt we'll be very long."

Melissa wasn't about to let that pass. "Why dinna you want tae meet her?"

"The last time I did, she was a raving mad-woman, screaming like a banshee. No offense, Linc, but those o' us who saw her like that thought surely it mun run in the family, that she was as crazy as ye."

Lincoln was staring at him now, incredulously. Melissa got angry that they were only hearing about this now, when they were almost there. "What the devil are you talking about? When was this?"

"Was after Linc got beat up the second time, I think. She pushed her way into our house, immediately started screaming at our da. He didna know what tae make o' her, didna know what had been going on wi' Linc. But ye know how he is, slow tae react. And that he just sat there staring at her only made her wilder. She accused him o' being the worst father under creation, that all he knew how tae raise was savages."

351

Melissa's eyes flew to Lincoln. But his expression had closed off. Nor was he going to question Neill about his revelation. But she recalled distinctly that one of his complaints had been that his mother had never done anything to stop what had been going on. Apparently, though, she'd tried, if ineffectively.

Her grandfather wouldn't take well to being yelled at in his own house. He never took well to criticism about his own sons. She wondered why they'd never heard about this before now.

"What did Grandda do?"

"He did as she asked."

"Really?"

"Aye, it was probably the tears," Neill said. "She started crying afore she ran home. But he told us all tae stay away from Linc."

"But you didna do that."

"Meli, none o' us e'er sought out Linc tae cause him harm. Every time it was him coming tae us. And after Da threatened tae break oot the strap, we took pains tae avoid him. Yet we'd already decided tae avoid him. His mother coming o'er changed nothing. What still happened after that was all o' Linc's doing. He just wouldna leave it alone."

"Enough of this," Lincoln said in a cold tone. "It's been hashed and rehashed. Let's get this over with."

He rode down the hill without waiting for them to follow him. Melissa sighed, said to Neill and Jamie, who'd finally caught up, "Dinna mind him. All this time he thought that if his mother would just have confronted your da, the whole thing would have settled down. He didna know she tried tae do just that."

"Faith, but she accomplished nothing in that trying," Neill replied.

"Exactly."

They followed Lincoln down to the house, Melissa feeling some distinct dread now. If Lincoln had been wrong about his mother's efforts on his behalf, what else might he be wrong about? Had she forced him to come here to find out that all this time he'd been blaming the wrong person?

Lincoln was already waiting in the parlor. Neill stayed outside. Jamie escorted Melissa in and lingered in the hall but left as soon as Eleanor showed up.

Lincoln was pacing in front of the fireplace. Nervous? Or just impatient?

"It's going tae be all right," Melissa tried to re-assure him, even though she didn't believe that now.

He didn't answer, and then Eleanor came into the room. Her expression was guarded, as if she already knew what they were there for.

Still, she offered a smile for Melissa's benefit – if that slight twisting of her lips could be called a smile. "This is a pleasant surprise. Have you two set a date yet?"

"Aye," Melissa replied. "Within the month. You'll come, I hope?"

"Certainly – if Lincoln doesn't mind."

There it was, laid bare before them, the problem.

Eleanor hadn't meant to open that subject, though, and she paled a bit over her blunder. Lincoln was amazed himself that she'd done so. He simply stared at her.

Eleanor sat down. "That wasn't what I meant to say."

Lincoln wasn't going to let it pass. "What then? If you can find the time? If you have nothing else to do, you might come? Or have you just not had enough time to think of an excuse to decline?"

"What are you accusing me of?"

"A lack of interest? After all, it's only your son's wedding – a son you lost interest in years ago."

He turned away, didn't see how stricken Eleanor was. But he was hurt as well, having barely got those words out. Melissa couldn't bear it. She was afraid that this was going to end up much worse than it had already been, and it was her fault for bringing him here for this confrontation.

She was about to suggest they leave when Eleanor said in a soft, hurt voice, "I never stopped loving you, Lincoln. If you thought so, you were wrong."

He swung back around and snarled, "What the hell else was I to think? You didn't take me away, you *gave* me away! You cut me off from my home and you!"

"I had no choice."

"You could have come with me."

"No, I couldn't."

"Why?"

"I – I can't tell you."

"Why?"

"It's a promise I made."

"Rubbish. Christ, I should have known I'd get no answers from you."

He started for the door. Eleanor cried out, "Wait! Sit down. It's time you heard all of this."

He stopped. He didn't sit down. He stood there in the doorway, filled with such rage and pain Eleanor had to look away from him to be able to continue.

"When the MacFearsons brought you home to me, beaten and senseless, and told me what had happened, they said that would be the end of it. I had no reason not to believe them. I sent for the doctor. You had broken bones, several bad cuts, too many bruises to count. Your left ear had taken such a hard blow you wouldn't be hearing from it for a while."

"You aren't telling me anything I don't know, other than that the MacFearsons brought me home after that first beating. I never knew how I got home."

"You don't remember that you wouldn't listen to me? I ordered you to stay away from the MacFearsons, but you kept sneaking out to find them again. Even locking you in your room didn't work. You were beyond my control."

"So because you couldn't control me, you got rid of me?" he said.

"No! You were killing yourself. Each time you came home, you were hurt worse. And I couldn't get it to end, on either side. I know now it was the fever that made you behave so strangely, but at the time—"

"What fever?"

"You developed an infection, more than one, actually. Your ear was the worst. By the third day you had a raging fever. The doctor tried several different medications, but nothing was working to reduce it. You were in too much pain, and it wouldn't let you rest so you could mend. What he gave you for the pain didn't work either, not completely, just made you think you were well enough to go out. It distorted your judgement. And half the time you were delirious."

Melissa stared at Eleanor wide-eyed. A fever. Such a simple thing, and no one had guessed.

"Like he was crazy?" she said.

"I dislike that word," Eleanor said with a frown.

"I dinna like it either, but he was accused o' being crazy back then. Was it the fever, then, that made him behave so abnormal?"

"That and too many medications that weren't working and shouldn't have been given to him at the same time. I nearly shot that doctor, when I realized he was treating Lincoln with newfangled medications that had yet to be proven effective, like he was using him to experiment on. That the fever finally put Lincoln into a coma was a blessing. It terrified me at the time, but it let him mend naturally."

"Sae you didna force sleeping drafts on him, tae keep him in bed nearly a month?"

"Good heavens, no. That was tried at first and

didn't work. The pain countered it, and I refused to let the doctor use bigger doses."

"How long did he remain unconscious?"

"Just over three weeks. During that time I was in communication with my brother Richard. He agreed to take Lincoln for a year or two."

"Is that what you call the time I spent there?"

Lincoln's voice was calmer, if still bitter. He should be relieved, though, to finally have it confirmed that he hadn't gone crazy back then, that something as common as a high fever had been the culprit. She was certainly relieved. This was going to put her family's worry to rest.

"That's all it was to have been, your stay in England," Eleanor answered him. "But then Richard found out he couldn't have any more children and wanted to make you his heir. He convinced me that it would be better for you to remain there. He didn't do it deliberately, and he was very subtle. I don't think he even realized how selfish his motives were. He cared for you greatly, he wanted what was best for you, and he felt that he could raise you better than I could. He was right in that respect. We were too isolated here, and without your father— You needed a man in your life to guide you."

"But why did you send me away to begin with? Because I disobeyed you when I had that fever?"

"Lincoln, do you really have no memory of how you were before that?" Eleanor asked him. "You had been running wild since your father's accident. You were breaking rules long before that fever."

"How would you know?" he replied scathingly. "You were forever locked in your room, unavailable to me."

"I know I had completely lost control of you," she told him. "That fever only pointed out how much. But I also *know* it was my fault, that I didn't have enough time to devote to you. I know I have no right to ask you for forgiveness. I really did think it was the best thing for you at the time, to live with your uncle, even though I would have preferred you to remain here with me. I ignored my own wishes to do what was in your best interest."

"But it wasn't in my best interest. When my father died, you might as well have died, too, for all the attention you gave me after that."

Tears started falling from Eleanor's eyes. "I had to make a choice, Lincoln, one of the hardest things I've ever done. I had to choose between you and your father."

"So you could mourn him without any distractions?" he said derisively.

"So I could take care of him."

Lincoln became very still. "What the devil does that mean?"

"He made me promise I'd never tell you, or anyone, and I didn't while he was alive, but . . . he didn't die back then, Lincoln. He died only two years ago."

52

Lincoln was sitting down. He was in shock. Melissa was dazed herself. Never would she have dreamed that such deep, dark secrets would be revealed here. She was almost afraid to hear more – afraid for Lincoln. His world had just been turned upside down. His father had been alive all these years? To have that knowledge kept from him must be devastating to him. And he did look that – utterly devastated.

"Why?" was all he asked eventually, but he asked it twice, "For God's sake, why?"

Eleanor was crying in earnest now. "The accident destroyed his body and most of his mind. He'd been literally crushed. He was paralyzed from the neck down, would never walk again. He couldn't even lift a hand to feed himself."

"All the more reason for his *entire* family to be there for support."

"That's not how he saw it, Lincoln. It was his decision. When he realized the extent of his injuries, he wanted to die, begged me to kill him. I couldn't do it. I loved him too much, was too selfish to lose him completely. He accepted that, but in return he made me promise I'd announce his death to everyone, even have a funeral for him. And there was no time to talk him out of it."

"What do you mean?"

"The injuries to his head took away his identity," she explained. "He had brief periods when his mind returned, when he could talk, when his memories were intact. It was during one of those times that he insisted you be told he died. But the rest of the time – most of the time – his memories weren't there, were simply . . . gone."

"Amnesia?" Melissa asked.

"It was nothing like that."

"Then he didna create a new identity for himself?" Melissa said.

"No, I wished so often that he could have, but when he wasn't himself, he wasn't cognizant of anything, really. It was like he was in a perpetual daze. He could open his eyes. He could chew his food if it was put in his mouth. But he didn't know who I was, he didn't know who he was. The doctor claimed he had no active thoughts when he was in that state. He didn't talk. It was as if he didn't know how."

"I still don't understand why he would want to be dead to the world," Lincoln said.

"Not the world. He didn't care if anyone else knew about his crippled state. It was you he didn't want to know, and the only way to keep it from you was to let everyone think he'd died."

"But *why*?"

"He couldn't bear for you to see him like that. He was a proud man. He wanted you to remember him as he'd been, not as he'd become."

"So he denied himself to me, completely – forever?" Lincoln said, his tone anguished.

"Try to understand, Lincoln. He made that decision soon after the accident, when he was in a lot of pain. And he'd also just realized the extent of the damage to his mind, that there were going to be periods when he wasn't himself. His reasoning was that he wouldn't have been there for you either way. And he was mostly right. The times he was himself could be so brief, if I wasn't in the room with him when they occurred, I would have missed them."

Lincoln paled a bit when he realized. "That's why you were always locked in your room? He was in there?"

"Yes. Only two other people knew he was still alive, his doctor and his valet, who was so devoted to him he remained to help me care for him."

"But so many years . . . you kept him from me for more than half my life."

"I tried many times to get him to change his mind. But over the years his condition only worsened. The times he was lucid became even briefer. So he remained firm in his decision, never faltered from it. You were never to see him like that or even *know* he was like that. In the end he simply wasted away. If he hadn't been such a strong man to begin with, he never would have lasted as long as he did."

"Why didn't you tell me this two years ago, when he really died?"

"Because the promise I made was to be forever," Eleanor replied. "I wouldn't have broken it now except . . . it was a promise I never should have made. I never agreed with it, but I had to respect his wishes."

"Is *this* why you sent me away?" he demanded. "So I wouldn't find out?"

"You were getting too curious about my locked door. I caught you several times lingering in the hall outside it. But that was only a minor part of the reason. It was mostly your lack of discipline, how wild you'd become. The fault was mine, because I couldn't spend more time with you. But you were lacking a man's guidance, which was why I thought Richard could help, at least for a few years, and why I'd already been discussing the matter with him prior to that trouble you had with the MacFearsons. That only confirmed to me that you really did need a man in your life."

"You could have found more time for me," Lincoln said.

"But that's the decision I made," Eleanor replied sadly. "You or your father. When he was himself, I had to be there, I was all he had."

"You were all I had!"

"I know." Eleanor began crying again. "Don't you think I've regretted it? That's another reason I sent you to Richard. He had time for you. He wanted you. You became like a son to him. Still, I tried to get you back after a few years, even if it meant disrupting the progress you'd made there. I was selfish in that. I missed you so much. But you didn't want to come home by then."

"Didn't I? But to what? More of never seeing you? More of you ignoring me?"

"Lincoln, it couldn't be any other way. Don't you understand? Your father had only a few minutes a day, or a week, sometimes it went as long as a month that he was himself. A few times it could last up to an hour, but mostly he had time only to say a few things, and then he'd be gone again. If I wasn't there, in constant attendance, I would have missed most of those times. I loved him so much. My heart broke every time he was lucid and we could talk, knowing it wouldn't last long, that he'd soon be mindless again. Yet it was all I had left of him. As it is, I did come to England to see you, knowing I wouldn't be there when he 'awoke' from his mindless state. I came as often as I could. But you were rarely around to visit with, and when you were, it was obvious you didn't want to talk to me. And I was helpless, unable to explain to you really why I'd done what I'd done, but unable to reach you without explaining. It was almost as painful to see you as it was never to see you. Can you understand? And forgive me?"

He said nothing. Several moments passed, and

still he said nothing. Finally he spoke, "Forgive you for loving my father to the exclusion of all else, certainly. Forgive you for not telling me all this when it mattered – I'm not so sure. But then I doubt I'll be able to forgive myself either."

53

Lincoln had walked out. His tone had been cold, but only to mask the pain under it. Yet what he'd said . . . Melissa had a distinct premonition of dread. He was blaming himself now, for what, she wasn't sure. But she'd been afraid that might happen. And none of what she'd hoped would be accomplished by this meeting had come about. They'd resolved nothing, were no closer than they had been. He'd instead found out things that would have been better left unknown.

She couldn't even imagine how hurt he must be right now, to know his father had wanted to be dead to him. Nor could she begin to fathom what it must have been like to be Donald Ross, to live the rest of your life counted in minutes, not years, because that's really all he'd had, minutes here and there when he was actually cognizant of who he was and who was around him. And Eleanor, to have lived with that all these years, to want to be there for her husband so much that she gave up any semblance of a normal life of her own – and gave up her only child. How utterly horrible.

Eleanor was to be pitied. The end of Donald's life as he'd known it was an accident, but Eleanor had had choices. Right or wrong, her choices had affected others, and she'd had to live with the consequences. Lincoln had all that to contemplate, what his mother had done and why. . . .

"I'm sorry," Melissa said, such an inadequate word, really, under the circumstances.

"Please, don't apologize," Eleanor replied, her tone weary. "I knew he'd never forgive me if he heard it all, which is why I didn't try to tell him sooner. There was hope when I first gave him up that I'd get him back, but as the years passed, I knew I wouldn't. He had too much resentment over it, saw it as my abandoning him."

"You didna assure him that wasna sae?"

"Of course I did, but he didn't believe me. He was so enraged it was almost impossible to talk to him back then. And the anger never really left him."

"Anger is sometimes the only defense against hurt," Melissa remarked.

"I thought of that," Eleanor admitted. "But I couldn't seem to get past that to reach him, the few times he allowed me to see him."

"Perhaps because he wanted tae hurt you as much as you'd hurt him?"

Eleanor smiled sadly. "Well, that's human nature, isn't it?"

"Human nature that most often comes wi' a severe kick in the face," Melissa replied. "You canna hurt someone you love without it hurting you e'en more. Linc just got that kick in the face, I'm

366

thinking. He'll be needing time tae digest what you've told him."

Eleanor came over, squeezed her hand gently. "I appreciate what you're trying to say, but it's too late for Lincoln and me. I lost my son when I sent him to my brother. Those years are gone, can never be relived. He was right. I abandoned him. The reasons don't matter."

"But they do."

Eleanor shook her head. "Lincoln won't see it that way. It was a mistake, I know that now. I think even Donald regretted it toward the end, that he'd denied himself ever seeing his son again. I should have corrected things when I could have, but I didn't. I abided by Donald's wishes, because I couldn't bear for him to spend what little time he had to be himself being upset. So I never argued with him, when arguing with him was needed – at least where Lincoln was concerned."

Melissa realized that Eleanor had given up back then – and was doing so again now. She couldn't grasp that reasoning herself. But then, family was paramount to her, and Lincoln would be, was already in her mind, part of her family now – and so was Eleanor, for that matter.

So she didn't spare any feelings when she told the older woman, "It's ne'er too late. Dinna make yet another mistake, thinking it is."

Melissa went home with a heavy heart. She was afraid she was going to have to say the same thing to Lincoln, but with him it wouldn't be so easy. His foundation had toppled. He would have to readjust his thinking completely. Where he'd placed blame before, where would it fall now? On himself, from the sound of it. But Eleanor was ultimately to blame. She could have told Lincoln the truth, when it still would have mattered. She could have pushed her way back into his life, instead of letting him close her off because he believed she didn't want him.

He wasn't at Kregora when she returned with her uncles. She hadn't really thought he would be, assumed he needed some time to himself just now. His absence gave her time to tell her parents what they'd learned.

"A fever?" Lachlan said. "Faith, that's wonderful . . . er, no' that he had it, but that—"

"We know what you meant. Keep that foot out of your mouth," Kimberly admonished him dryly.

He grinned, winked at his wife, hugged his daughter. "I knew he wasna crazy."

"Rubbish," Kimberly mumbled.

"And there's no reason tae hold off the wedding sae long," he added. "As soon as the guests can get here will be soon enough."

"Sae *you* set the date so far ahead, Da?" Melissa scowled at him.

"Dinna be annoyed wi' me, lass, I just wanted a wee bit more time tae get used tae him, is all."

Her uncles had a different reaction to hearing the story. When they realized that they'd caused grief to a lad seriously ill – ill with fever as a result of their beating him, a beating that should never have occurred to begin with – and on top of that, they were probably responsible for his "running wild," which had caused his mother to send him away . . . well, the fight that ensued included all nine of them that were present.

At least they took it outside, its being well ingrained in them all that they *not* come to blows in their sister's house – if they could help it. And Lachlan didn't lift a finger to try to break it up, just stood there with his arms crossed and watched them have at each other, flinching every so often as he witnessed a particularly grueling punch.

Kimberly wasn't inclined to intervene either, though when the fight didn't look as if it would be breaking up before someone got seriously hurt, she did finally order her servants to toss buckets of water on them. There were five new black eyes at the dinner table that night.

Lincoln wasn't there for the meal, though. He still hadn't returned. With Melissa starting to worry over how long he'd been gone, Lachlan sent out his clansmen to search for him. They didn't find Lincoln, but they did find a rider who got lost trying to reach Kregora after dark. He had a letter for Melissa. It was from Lincoln.

She read it, sat down, and began to cry. "He's no' going tae marry me."

"The devil he's not," Kimberly said.

"He says I deserve better'n him."

54

It was the deepest sort of pain, to see all your dreams come tumbling down and be the one who'd pulled out the stone to topple them. Lincoln was filled with such bile it was near choking him. He rode straight to London without stopping except to change horses, other than briefly at the first inn he came to, to jot off that note to Melissa and have it delivered.

He should have spent the night there. The morning would have given him a new perspective. But he'd been afraid that being still so close to Melissa, he'd selfishly change his mind and return to her.

It was killing him to let her go like this. And it wasn't that she deserved better than him, as he'd told her. It was that *he* didn't deserve *her*. He was a man who hurt the people who loved him the most. He couldn't protect his mother from that, could only try to make it up to her, but he could protect Melissa from such a bastard as himself.

He was remembering so much more of his youth now, all the things he'd blocked away because they pointed out the real fault, which had been his. He'd wanted so much to be accepted by the MacFearson brothers that he'd actually tried to emulate them. They'd seemed without structure, could do whatever they liked, had no one to obey, but in fact they'd merely been raised differently than he had, with more leeway. That their father would have taken a strap to them if they continued to cause trouble with him proved there had been discipline and consequences for them to face after all.

So he'd become unruly, and his mother had tried to help him back to the proper path by giving him a father figure, his Uncle Richard. But instead of accepting that he'd brought it all on himself, he'd damned her for it – and continued to focus only on that as the years passed.

How could he have forgotten how foolish he'd been before that incident at the pond? The fever? Had it pushed his memories that far away? He didn't know. And it didn't matter now. The damage was done, and he'd done it himself. All the letters he'd ignored, all the times his mother had tried to see him and he'd found excuses to be absent. She had tried, so often, to bridge the gap between them, and he'd just pushed her further away, until she stopped trying.

He was practically sleeping in the saddle by the time he reached London. He'd stopped a few times along the way to rent a new mount, though only after his own was showing signs of wanting to trample him and would probably balk if he ever approached him again.

He went straight to bed and slept nearly twenty-four hours. He really should have done so sooner, because sleep really did put everything in a different perspective for him, showing clearly what a complete ass he was to have reacted as he did.

He was doing it again, pushing aside the people he loved the most. But not this time. He'd been blaming himself for something a child had done, and he'd let that child live inside him too long. He'd wanted to protect Melissa from the child, but the child was gone. He'd wanted to punish the child, but the child had been punished enough. If it wasn't too late, if Melissa wasn't fed up with him, he was going to get her back.

It was the dinner hour when he came downstairs. Only his aunt was present for it.

"Where's Edi?" he asked casually as he joined her at the table, aware that he was taking her by surprise.

"She's spending the weekend with her fiancé and his family, to discuss their wedding plans – and what the deuce are you doing back here? Have you settled everything with Melissa's family, then?"

"Probably made things worse with them, actually," he replied.

"Oh, no."

"At least her uncles will have cause to celebrate," he added dryly.

Because Henriette knew of their objections, she surmised correctly, if incredulously, "Don't tell me you've withdrawn your suit?"

He didn't answer that yet, asked instead, "Did

you know that my father was alive all these years, that he died only two years ago?"

Henriette gasped. "Good God, Lincoln, who told you such nonsense?"

"My mother – and obviously you didn't know. Uncle Richard probably didn't know either, for that matter. She wouldn't have wanted to risk the chance that he might take pity on me and tell me."

She stared at him hard. "You aren't joking?"

"No."

He went on to tell Henriette the whole of it, up to and including his last and biggest blunder, that he'd ended his pursuit of Melissa.

"So it's true then," she said when he was done. "You really *are* crazy."

He knew what she was referring to. He even smiled. "No, just a complete ass. It was my first gut reaction, one I should have ignored but didn't. The thought was to protect her – from me."

"And punish yourself."

"That, too."

She tsked at him. "You're lucky that girl loves you. I'm sure she'll understand – if you don't take too long to rectify the situation."

"I intend to leave for Scotland in the morning. But I'm not sure she'll want me back. She's already been through so much with me, butting heads with her family over me, even her parents. And she was there to hear it all. She must be thinking there will always be problems of one sort or the other that will surface because of my past."

"Will there be?"

He shook his head firmly, said, "No, but it won't be easy to assure her of that, particularly when I just behaved like such a bloody ass."

"Everyone's allowed to be an ass a few times in their lifetime."

He snorted at that philosophy. "Not everyone hurts those they love in the process though. Were I Melissa, I'd be saying good riddance."

"Were I her, I probably would, too." Henriette replied with a chuckle. "Fortunately for you, your Melissa is a very special lady. But you already knew that. It's why you loved her from the start. And you do still love her, don't you, m'boy?"

"With all my heart."

"Then put away your doubts. Love always wins out, don't you know."

"I believe only women carry that view, Aunt," he replied dryly.

"Nonsense. Well, maybe . . . oh, never mind. Let's just say I have enough faith for the both of us. Now, about the rest, I'm sorry about your father. I simply had no idea—"

"No one did."

"I'm just amazed that Eleanor never let on, not a single clue. Her letters were frequent, but always only about you. She wanted to know everything you were doing, how your schooling was coming along, what your interests were, who your friends were – absolutely everything. If my letters to her weren't at least three pages long in reply, she'd think something was wrong. I imagine she read them to your father. He would have been starved for information about you as well."

"Would he?"

"Now, don't do that," she said, because his tone had turned skeptical. "I would imagine his decision wasn't just prideful, wasn't just because he wanted you to have only good memories of him. That might have been part of it, but consider this – and he would have realized it as well – that for you to have any time with him at all when he was himself, you would have had to live in that sickroom with him, just as Eleanor did. Otherwise you might never have found a chance to speak with him. He wouldn't have wanted that for you, didn't want it for her either, but there was no help for that. And had you known, you would have curtailed your activities, would have tried to be there more often. Such a sad situation either way. But he had Eleanor. She loved him enough to be there always. You don't still resent that, do you?"

"No, I'm glad he had her."

He just wished they both could have had her, as it should have been.

55

Lincoln rode back to Scotland at a normal pace. Perhaps not exactly normal, since he was still in a tearing hurry But at least when the sun set he found an inn where he could spend the night in this time.

He came upon the MacFearsons the second day on the road. He was surprised. He'd really thought they'd be collectively saying good riddance to him and never venture across the border again. But then, he didn't think they were heading south because of him, even though they stopped when they saw him and lined up across the road, a solid wall. They were good at making walls.

"Lost?" he asked as he drew up in front of them.

"Coming to fetch ye back to the altar," Johnny said.

Lincoln raised a brow. "You mean I'm actually saving you the trouble?"

"Ye're going back to Meli?"

"Certainly – if she'll still have me. Does your task mean she will?"

"We canna answer that," Ian One said.

"We left her crying her heart out," Charles said.

"She was done crying, Charlie," Malcolm corrected in a chiding tone.

"It was Kimberly who ordered us tae drag ye back," Ian Four explained. "She was in a fine snit."

Lincoln flinched. Melissa's mother *would* be sorely displeased with him for running off, since she was aware that he'd compromised her daughter. And why hadn't he recalled that before he went off to brood?

"I will endeavor to make it up to your womenfolk," Lincoln said.

"Aye, we hae no doubt ye will."

Another surprise – confidence in him? He began to frown. They were being far too amiable.

"Has something happened that I'm unaware of?" he asked.

"We hae some apologizing tae do."

Ian One had said it, but there were too many nods of agreement from the rest of them. And he finally noticed that more than a few of them were quite battered.

"If you had to fight over it, don't bother," he said.

"Nae, the fight was needed. There was too much guilt, ye ken, when we heard it had been a fever that had made ye seem crazy back then."

"So you tried to beat the guilt out of each other?"

"Something like that." Jamie grinned.

"Did it work?" Lincoln asked curiously.

"No' really, but then we dinna need much excuse for a good fight," Jamie replied.

Adam interjected, "I speak for all o' us, Linc, in

saying we're sorry for the grief we caused ye. It ne'er should hae got sae oot o' hand, but when it did, we should hae used some common sense of our own, in realizing something wasna quite right wi' ye."

"I was wrong myself in blaming you for my being sent away, when that had nothing to do with you, as it happens," Lincoln allowed, then suggested, "Why don't we do each other a favor and put it to rest? Water under the bridge and all that."

"Let's get ye home, then, afore Kimberly pulls oot too many hairs," Ian One said.

Home? How nice that sounded. Yes, Scotland was going to be his home again – he hoped.

But as they opened "the wall" for him to pass through, Charles was heard to say, "Ye were too easy on us, Linc. I would've made us grovel a bit more."

"Shut up, Charlie," they almost all said unanimously, Lincoln included.

They arrived at Kregora late the next afternoon. They'd been seen coming, yet Melissa wasn't in the hall when Lincoln entered it. And then she was, standing in the doorway to the parlor, breathtakingly beautiful with her joyous smile that told him so much, told him she was still his.

He held out his arms to her. She flew into them. Her uncles tactfully turned their backs. Her father didn't.

Coming down the stairs to witness their reunion, he said, "Ye run off on m'daughter again and I'll bloody well tear ye apart."

He didn't sound like he was joking, yet Lincoln wasn't concerned. He was rather pleased actually. Such a statement meant he'd been accepted into the family.

"That won't be necessary, sir."

"Good. Now, where's that kirkman?"

Lincoln laughed, but he was to find that Lachlan wasn't joking about that either. It was fine with Melissa's family now for them to marry that day, right then and there for that matter. Lincoln still had some amends to make, however, with his wife-to-be.

He pulled her aside to do just that, into her father's empty study. He immediately got down onto his knees. She immediately tried to tug him back up. He couldn't be budged. "I'm so sorry, Meli. Can you forgive me for—"

"Stop it, get up," she interrupted.

But he persisted, "Can you forgive me for—"

"Aye, aye, now, get up," she admonished.

He didn't. "You don't make it easy to apologize."

"I'm glad you noticed. When you're really needing tae apologize, I'll make you do sae, dinna doubt it. But what you did, I understand, Linc. I know you needed some time tae digest all you learned. And I ne'er doubted you'd be back."

"Liar," he said with a tender smile, and instead of getting up, he pulled her down to her knees.

The door was closed. He was amazed her family was allowing this, though he was sure they wouldn't allow it for long. But he wasn't going to waste a moment of their privacy. He kissed her, gently, but with a wealth of passion, telling her just how much she meant to him.

"I love you so much, Meli. As soon as I got to London, I knew what a jackass I'd been, that in turning you away I was just trying to punish myself for all the mistakes I'd made. And in doing so, I was making the biggest mistake of all."

"Shh, I told you I understand. So does your mother. She came here that day, thought you'd be here. She's realized her own mistakes, too, and isna going tae repeat them." And then she grinned. "You'll find her changed, and maybe a wee bit pushy, if you give her any more cold shoulders."

"I won't say she should have got pushy a long time ago."

"Good, I'm glad tae be hearing you willna say it," she replied, tongue in cheek.

He chuckled, drew her closer, began kissing her again, her mouth, her neck, lower. He quickly got carried away. Because she was so acquiescent, it was easy to do so. She'd never deny him anything. She wanted him as much as he wanted her. It was balm and bane, knowing that, and would be until they were married in fact, not just in their hearts. But before he got too frustrated, aware that the door could open on them at any moment, he took his mouth from her and just held her close until their breathing quieted.

"Soon, Meli, just another day or two. I can be patient, now that I have no doubt you will be mine."

"And what makes you think *I* can be patient?"

she replied, then clasped his cheeks and began kissing him again.

Lachlan's cough interrupted them. Lincoln started laughing this time. "I believe that answers your question."

56

They were married two days later. Lincoln didn't mind waiting this time – he was even the one to suggest it – since he wanted the wedding to be as perfect as Melissa had hoped for, and that required giving the guests time to get there. He had in fact sent a note to the Duke and Duchess of Wrothston before he left London, suggesting they go to Kregora soonest if they wanted to attend their goddaughter's wedding. A presumption on his part, but then, like her father, Lincoln had had no intention of waiting until the end of the month to marry – if Melissa would still have him.

Megan and Devlin St James arrived the day after he did. Their son, Justin, was with them. It was Lincoln's Aunt Henriette who held up the wedding. Though she'd left London only an hour after he did, she'd had to detour south to pick up his cousin.

Ian MacFearson senior showed up for the wedding. What a treat, to finally meet the legend after all these years and find that he was just an ordinary man – if a little gruff around the edges.

Big, barrel-chested, his hair completely gray, but still robust, he had a booming voice that couldn't be ignored. And a seriously large family. The few wives but many children of his sons were all present. Lincoln had to wonder what he'd got himself into, until he looked at Melissa and knew exactly what he'd got himself into – heaven.

His mother was there also. There had been one awkward moment when they faced each other for the first time after her revelations. So much had held them apart for too many years, yet it took no more than her putting her arms around him for the gap to close.

"Welcome home, Lincoln," he heard her say against his chest.

His heart wrenched. Moisture gathered in his eyes. No words were needed. All the years of pain and bitterness flowed away with that simple embrace.

But with everyone present and accounted for, the kirkman was fetched and their vows were spoken before all. It was a humbling moment for Lincoln, the culmination of his dreams, the righting of a life gone wrong. Fate had stepped in to give him all he could ask for. He now had a purpose in life – making his wife happy.

They sealed their vows with a kiss. Considering how long they'd been denied each other, it wasn't all that surprising that the kiss became rather passionate – and didn't stop. Nor was there any indication that it *would* stop. Lachlan coughed. Kimberly coughed. The kirkman coughed. Soon most of the MacFearsons were coughing and clearing their throats as well, but the newly married couple was oblivious to them all.

It was Melissa who finally pushed herself away from her husband and, with a chuckle, said to her family, "You've all caught colds again, aye?"

A round of general laughter followed. Lincoln didn't blush, but he didn't join in the laughter either. In fact, if Melissa hadn't been immediately whisked away and passed around by her family for their congratulations, he would have dragged her off to bed and wouldn't have felt the least qualm about telling the assemblage that they'd join the celebrations later.

He was saved a great deal of ribbing from the MacFearsons by restraining himself. Not that he cared just then. He'd much rather have his wife to himself. But the well-wishing and celebrating their joy were part of her dream. He couldn't deny her that. And he was able to satisfy himself with the knowledge that he would have her to himself later. His pursuit was finally at an end.

Thirty minutes later Melissa dragged him off. God was good to him.

THE END